SANCTUARY

J. KENT GREGORY

authorHOUSE®

AuthorHouse™
1663 Liberty Drive
Bloomington, IN 47403
www.authorhouse.com
Phone: 833-262-8899

Published by AuthorHouse 10/28/2022

ISBN: 978-1-6655-7440-2 (sc)
ISBN: 978-1-6655-7442-6 (hc)
ISBN: 978-1-6655-7441-9 (e)

Library of Congress Control Number: 2022919801

CONTENTS

PREFACE

As this book project neared completion, I was often asked, "How long have you been working on your stories?" But as I reflected on how long it had been since I first began writing the story "Sanctuary," the short story that lends its title to the book, I was somewhat surprised to realize that I had been working on what would become this book for almost half my life.

As I recall, I began writing the short story that became "Sanctuary" when I was twenty-seven (or so) on my grandmother's old black typewriter that was sitting on the table in the log bunkhouse on the property of my aunt's and uncle's cabin. It sat in the woods, on the shore of Pig Lake of the Whitefish chain, in northern Minnesota. This place was special to me—a place of peace and escape and beauty—a sanctuary itself. I had vacationed there every summer from the mid-1970s through the 1980s and occasionally came back through the 1990s when I could get away from my graduate studies in the Twin Cities. For several years in the 2010s, I would come back to this place to hunt with my cousins and sometimes with my son and brother.

This first story was finished by the time I began my itinerant career as a visiting professor, and I carried it with me everywhere I went until settling in New Orleans. It was lost in the destruction of Hurricane Katrina. I thought about that story and its loss a good deal over the next few years until I finally sat down to rewrite it as best as I could remember. So there I was, trying to rewrite what I had originally written in my late twenties, but of course through the lens, if you will, of someone who was now in his mid forties. How's that for meta text?

"Sanctuary" was to some extent inspired by Hemingway's "Big Two-Hearted River," and a kernel of it took shape around a piece of advice that a friend had once given to me. Some of the other stories grew out of this original, and many of them contain nods to Hemingway, Rick Bass, Barry Holstun Lopez, and, of course, Norman Maclean. Many of the stories remain open at the end, without an explicitly written conclusion. This is intentional. Though I certainly do have my thoughts on and understanding of the symbols and themes in my works, I encourage readers to bring themselves - their own understandings, and interpretations - to these works. That is why the stories are left open, so that the readers have the freedom to imagine or consider for themselves what the endings or resolutions might be.

Finally, I want to thank all those who encouraged or offered support (sometimes unknowingly) to me along the way: Greg Hicks; Logan Nothstine; Matt Hamel; the Thomases (Aunt Noel, Uncle Terry, Joe, and Lou), for the Cabin and the Lake and the typewriter; my parents; and, certainly, to my family (Kenton, Livia, Mary Catherine, and my wife, Stephanie), but especially to my wife, Stephanie, for her love and support and for proofreading my first two stories, "Sanctuary" and "Scouting with My Daddy," and to Mary Catherine for encouraging me to get published and for the author photo.

J. Kent Gregory

A PLACE APART

Silent and golden, those are the qualities fixed in my memory. And that it was wide and flat for a cleft in these knob hills. A small brook, not even a pace wide, curved and wandered through the glen. As I approached, I heard the deep-throated calling of a solitary bullfrog who became silent when I entered. There were no bird calls, and the rushing false-wind sounds of the nearby highway were gone. They did not enter here.

Everything was golden: the leaves on the soft, grassless earth, and the trees—the oaks and poplars and a solitary beech. Though they were still mostly bare in the cold, early spring, when I looked up, I could see that their branches still held onto golden leaves here and there. I could not see the sky. This surprised me because on the floor, the trees were spaced out and not at all thick, mostly sitting on the edges and at the feet of the knoblike ridges that descended to, or maybe grew up from, the floor. These hills seemed to me more boundaries than a part of this place, the present, physical delineation between this place and the outside.

It brought to mind the ancient belief in divinities residing in and protecting certain places in the natural landscape, like groves, springs, and caves. This place was like that. But it was not quite such a place, a *locus divinus*, inviting an offering and an altar. That would have been an intrusion, even if the logistics would have permitted it, a breaking of that which was whole, unblemished.

And it was more than just a place. It was a moment in which the place that I had walked into existed, was stretched and suspended, held, as if in its own time. My younger mind used to want to think of it as a temple of sorts to give it a known definition, but in my older age, I know that it was not a temple. It was an "other", a memory of a perfect moment among the trees, the earth and water, the light and the colors. And the silence.

I have not returned, in part because the river that formed an outer boundary of the forest runs deeper and steadier now so that I cannot cross it. I do return to this glen in my mind, however, this place of still, golden silence.

There was no path or trail through this place, and the one I had been following had ended suddenly at the lip of a slope that descended into this golden place. I followed the little brook to where I thought the bullfrog sat silently, still needing a point, a destination to give direction and purpose to my steps. Even though the brook was a small, clear trickle in the cleft between its banks, with red-gold chert sherds here and there on the bottom and twigs holding their leaves waving in the current, perceptible only because of their movement, I could not find him in the clear shallows. The water was cool and smooth over the hairs on the back of my hand and wrist.

A log from a long-fallen tree lay on the leaves under the branches of the beech, and I sat there for a long time, though how long, I do not know. My restless nature quieted. The warmth was a light blanket. The smells of the trees and earth were rich and heady. The feeling was as if in a dream, a place shut off from consciousness and other concerns.

After some time, I felt as though it was time to leave, and as I set my boot onto the slope at the boundary out of the glen, the bullfrog sang again. *Stay*, he seemed to sing to me.

J. KENT GREGORY

SCOUTING WITH
MY DADDY

The morning was cold, and the sun wasn't up yet, but the stars shone brighter than I can remember them ever being. My daddy was in the front seat, driving us to country where he would be hunting turkeys and I was there to help him scout before the season started.

It was still in the early part of spring, and though it would warm up later in the day, we needed to wear warm clothes and I got to wear the same camouflage jacket that he had. I was proud and excited that Daddy was taking me with him. I wasn't even six yet but had been to the sporting clay range with him several times. I always sat in a high scorer's chair, and he let me push the button that launched the targets. When I was little, he always saved the last shell for me, helped me load it, and held the gun while cradling me in his arms. It was a while before I shot at an actual target, spending most of my time just shooting into the air over the field.

It has been decades, but I remember this first time he took me into the field with him like it was yesterday. Although turkey season wouldn't open for a few weeks yet, he had promised to take me out with him to go scouting for gobblers.

At first, I didn't know what he meant by *gobblers*, but I knew they were turkeys and that he was going to hunt them and that we needed to get up really early to look for them. At the time, I didn't really understand why we had to get up so early, but if Daddy said we had to, then that was good enough for me.

We crossed the Ohio River into Indiana and left the highway to go winding along country roads that seemed to run along a ridge with forests and fields sloping away on either side. He didn't talk much when he drove, whether he was going hunting or not. I suspect he was tired like I was; neither of us was ever much of a morning person. That may be why we both really appreciated the quiet beauty of a morning—since we rarely saw it. As we drove along that ridge road, to this day, I swear I saw a bear running from the field that bordered the road into the woods. It was still dark out, but his body was a big, bulky shadow that disappeared into the deeper shadows of the woods.

From my car seat in the back, I whispered, "Daddy, I just saw a bear run into the woods!" I must have caught him by surprise, because the car noticeably slowed down and then he said, "Wow, that is something else! Don't worry about it, though. There aren't any bears where we are going."

Not too long after that, we turned off onto another road, and he let me know that we were getting close. I nibbled the last few bits of my pancake that he had given me to eat along the way. The road descended into a valley. On the south side of it were vast fields of early season wheat, their tips catching the shining light of the silver moon.

Daddy said with excitement, "Hey, buddy, look ahead and to your left and you'll see the woods we'll be scouting." I tried looking left around his head in the seat in front of me and was able to see a hairy darkness to which the wheat fields seemed to flow like waves on an ocean. That darkness of undergrowth and early season tree limbs, just beginning to put out their foliage, looked to me like a jungle.

J. KENT GREGORY

He slowed down and turned left off the road and onto some grass, and then drove a few yards down into the trees. He turned the lights and the car off but got out and left his car door open so the lights stayed on inside. As he bent over to unbuckle me from my seat, his breath was steaming in the cold. He lifted me out onto the grass and knelt beside me while he checked my jacket and zipped it up. I could see the very pale gray beginnings of dawn upon the horizon over his shoulder.

"OK, my buddy, are you ready to go?" he whispered.

"Yes," I whispered back.

"Great! Here's your flashlight. I've got mine, but we'll only turn them on if we need to. We don't want the turkeys to know that we're here." He paused, then said, "I'm really glad you're here with me," and then he hugged me. My heart felt so big that he had wanted to bring me along, and I wanted him to be proud of me. I hugged him back.

We closed the door to the car and walked off holding hands, down a little hill with the woods on a little cliff to our right. I could hear the wind-chimey sound of a stream trickling over rocks ahead of us. After a few yards, he whispered, "OK, let's turn on our flashlights so we can see as we cross the little creek here." We turned them on, and he stepped onto a flat rock and lifted me across. He followed, and then we turned off our lights.

We stood for a second at the opening of a little dell, lit by the moonlight, to let our eyes adjust and then waded through the grass, holding hands again. My excitement was building even though I didn't know quite what to expect. But we were about to enter the woods and begin scouting for the gobblers. We crossed the dell with the grass glowing silver from the moonlight on the frost.

About thirty yards into the dell, we turned right and paused to look up the path that had been cut through the trees and undergrowth to lead to the top of the cliff. He turned to me and, in a soft voice, said, "OK, buddy, this hill is steep, but at the top it is flat, and that is where we will set up. I'll walk slow."

I whispered back, "OK, Daddy."

The grass on the path up the hill was low, not nearly as high as the grass in the dell that had brushed my legs up to my knees. Our flashlights were off, but I could still see the path, which seemed to glow in the dark, early morning air. Just as we were about to crest the top of the hill, there was a loud crashing in the trees and the brush off to our right, as if something had been startled to its feet and was smashing, blundering through the woods to get away from us. I could tell it was big from the sounds it made, but I couldn't see anything because the woods were still pitch black. Not even the bright moonlight was shining down to them. I distinctly remember thinking, *Bear!* just like the one I thought I saw on the road, so I froze solid in my spot, as did Daddy. I squeezed his gloved hand tightly.

We stood like that until the sounds faded in the growing distance as whatever it was bulled away from us. He leaned down, and I could tell he was smiling and laughing. With a certain excited giddiness, he said, "Do you know what that was? That was probably the hugest buck I have ever gotten close to. Oh my God, yes. He must have been bedded down right over there in the woods. We must have spooked him. Oh my gosh. Did you hear the *clomp, clomp* of his hooves?" I said that yes, I had, but to be honest, I just heard the crashing through branches and crunching of the leaves on the ground as the animal took off away from us.

When we reached the top of the hill, the ground opened up, just as Daddy had said it would. There was hardly any undergrowth, and most of the sky was arched over by tree limbs with their early-season buds on them. As I looked up into the sky, I could still see the stars but also a new slight grayness to the cloudless sky. We sat down at the base of a massive beech tree that was practically in the center of the clearing. He sat down cross-legged, Indian style, with his back to the beech, and I sat in his lap, leaning back onto his chest. He pulled out his slate friction call and began calling the turkeys. The woods were still silent when his calls leapt out into the stillness. He kept at it with a series of soft calls and then yelps, explaining to me what he was going to do before each call.

It was then that I heard my first gobbler. Although it was unlike anything I had imagined, the deep-throated, thundering chortle was unmistakable. I felt it inside my chest and perked up in his lap. He looked down at me and smiled. "You heard that?" he asked.

I knew then that it was a big turkey and that he was behind us through the woods—in my imagination, prowling the edge of the field near the woods. Daddy kept at his calling, telling me he was going to try to bring it closer. We heard it again, and then another one from back the way we came. He leaned down to my ear and whispered, "That one sounds like he's sitting right on top of our car!" I laughed quietly and hoped they would come closer and that I would get to see them.

As the sky above lost its blackness and the stars faded away to be replaced by a gentle blue with rose around the horizon's edges, the woods gradually came alive. First were the birds chirping and then singing in the trees, and then flitting from branch to branch. Squirrels followed, coming down the tree trunks to search through the dried leaves. Daddy had often told me about the beauty and wonder of the woods coming alive and that it was only hunters who knew and could appreciate it. I then knew what he meant; today it reminds me of an orchestra tuning up before a concert.

It gradually got lighter, but the gobblers never got any closer, so after a while, he said, "Well buddy, we haven't heard them in a bit, so let's go exploring." Now that I am older and have hunted with my daddy for years, I have come to learn that whenever he uses the word *exploring*, he is bored and suspects that the spot is dead. As a child, he was great to hunt with because he was a good hunter, but most importantly, he had an attention span that was not much beyond that of a five-year-old. To this day, the thought of sitting in a deer stand, though he has been known to do it, is more than a little disturbing to him. "I prefer to spot and stalk," he states proudly.

We got up and began walking up the wooded ridge through a fairly dense undergrowth toward the upper field beyond the tree line. We went maybe twenty yards before I felt like I couldn't go any farther. I was tired from the early morning, and the hill was steep. Still whispering, I said, "Daddy, I can't walk anymore, can you carry me?" He picked me up and carried me to the top of the ridge to the tree line, where we surveyed the grass blowing green, moving like ocean waves in the wind. We stepped out from the shadows of the trees and found some turkey tracks, but we did not see any turkeys. A little later, he carried me back. I didn't realize until I was older and hunting on that same parcel of land that my daddy had carried me in his arms a quarter mile up a pretty steep incline through thick shrubs—and back down again.

We stopped for a rest at the big tree where we had first set up. I don't remember much else from that point other than the air warming and the golden light of the midmorning sun streaming down through the trees onto the previous fall's leaves.

"OK, let's go home, buddy," he said.

My daddy picked me up, and I fell asleep while he carried me back to the car, only to awaken later when we pulled into our driveway back home.

SANCTUARY

Tom made the drive up from the Twin Cities early, hiked along the river to do some scouting for where he'd like to fish the next couple of days, and unloaded his car before Greg arrived.

He and Greg met at this time of year when the woods and rivers were in the now unpeopled, suspended quiet timelessness of the months between Labor Day and the beginning of the salmon and steelhead runs up the rivers that flowed into Lake Superior on the north shore above Duluth and Two Harbors. The river where they met was in the frontier beyond the reaches of the cities, on the threshold of the wilderness along the Canadian border, a country where the rivers had romantic names like the Knife, the Baptism, the French, and where there were increasingly occasional towns like Castle Danger.

The air was yet warm, but the wind held a chill that hinted of the coming fall and the winter behind it. The light was golden in this transitional period, caught on and reflected by the yellow-gold fringe beginning to appear on the birch and aspen leaves.

Tom hadn't taken his rod with him on his hike along the river, wanting to get to know the river again after a year's absence and to give himself more time to settle and put more distance between himself here in the peace of the rivers and woods and the troubles in the city, to enjoy the solitude. He came back to the campsite in the late afternoon. Greg had not arrived yet.

He cleared away the dried, brown pine needles, other twigs, and branches, arranging them in orderly piles away from the hard ground he intended for the campfire. He walked back to the river twice to gather the rounded river stones to form the edge of the fire pit. It was hot work, even in September, so he took off his moleskin shirt and tied it with the sleeves around his waist before the second trip. *These shirts sure are expensive*, he thought to himself, *but they certainly hold up*. This was the fourth season he'd had the shirt.

From his oil-cloth pack, he pulled out his father's iron Boy Scout axe, forged five decades ago in Bridgeport, Connecticut, to chop wood into usable lengths and to shave some into kindling—all of which he placed near the river-stone fire circle. It gave him pleasure to use his father's boyhood axe a half a century after his father had last used it; the unsharpened area a brown, aged patina with the BSA insignia—an American Eagle in the form of a Fleur-de-Lis over the banner with the BSA motto, "Be prepared." The edge was a bright silver mirror that told of its sharpness where Tom had brought back its edge. The axe was a heavy thing, but he considered that if he was willing to carry it along, then that was his right.

He then gathered dead wood fallen from the birch and aspen for the campfire. There were a few birch trees that had fallen in the past year. He saved the white outer bark skins for tinder and chopped one of the trunks into fire logs, the year-old dead wood giving off a musty, earthy scent with a vague sweet, clean smell that reminded him of a year ago when it was a tree that had stood on the edge of the campsite.

Next, he smoothed the ground for a sleeping area and walked into the woods with his father's axe, where he chopped and nicked off low-hanging pine-bough ends for bedding cushion. The sun was still high but was beginning its downward arc to the horizon as he took out his father's old brown oilcloth tarp, laying it over the soft pine branches, smelling as it always had since he was a boy. The mixed scents of the pine and the oilcloth brought vivid memories of his father to mind. He then strung a rope between two trees, draped an oilcloth tent over the taut rope, and realized he had forgotten to bring the stakes.

"Damn," he muttered to himself, but he reflected that he always forgot something, or somethings, and figured that if this was the worst of it, he was pretty well off. He set one of the birch logs on its end and, with his father's axe, chopped stakes off of it. He shuffled back to the tent cloth draped over the line and hammered the stakes with the flat back of the axe through the loops, first at the corners and then along the sides. He stood to view the results. The work and its finish were satisfying to him.

There was a slight warmth that remained to the early evening air, yet the cold was creeping back into the year, asserting itself as the sun sank lower. The night promised to be cooler than he had thought, so he carried another armful of logs to the woodpile he had made near the fire circle. With the tinder set over a wad of his oil-soaked, used, gun-cleaning patches, he struck sparks from his flint. Carefully, he built a wooden tipi over the dancing flames, continuing to add more sticks as the inner ones caught and blackened. Quickly, the fire was hissing and popping, asking for more wood, which he added, and thicker. He halved and quartered the logs he had placed nearby to make a stack that would last the next few days.

The work and preparations had been tiring and pleasing, an invigorating change that the woods brought. He leaned onto his pack, poured some bourbon into his tin cup, filled his pipe, and reclined back to keep his feet warm by the fire, with the bourbon and pipe warming him on the inside. He looked up to the blue, cloudless sky through the branches, the moon becoming visible. The stunning brightness of the sky recalled warmer summer days fishing down on the Gulf, casting into the surf with a mojito in his free hand.

The heady smoke of the crackling fire brought him back to the present in northern Minnesota. He was happy for the quiet and peace, the solitude of his camp. He was glad to get away from the cacophony of the cities and the current of life there that rushed and raged like a stream swollen with a sudden spring melt carrying everything, powerless, crashing and boiling along with it somewhere far away to a calm downstream. His thoughts drifted to the gently flowing stream close by, its voice chuckling and inviting beyond the trees at the edge of the campsite.

As he stood to stretch and pour himself another bourbon, Greg pulled up in his truck. Almost another hour of sunlight remained as Greg drug his canvas pack and rod case over the cracked leather passenger seat and banged the door shut. They hugged, smacking each other on their backs as if it had been true, measurable years since they had last seen each other, even though it had been less than a month since they had fished together on the Kinnickinnic in western Wisconsin.

"Good to see you, bud. Sorry I got here late. It took me some time to get away."

"Don't worry about it. Gave me some time to get the camp set up and scout out the river."

"Thanks for doing all that. How's it looking?"

"Good as always. It's all ours. Haven't seen or heard anyone."

"That's wonderful. Once I got past Castle Danger, I didn't see anyone either, except for one car heading south. I'm glad we keep getting to have it to ourselves."

"Me too. When did we become such misanthropes?" Tom said with a wry smile.

Greg laughed. "We're not misanthropes. Maybe we're just selfish," he said as he carried his pack and gear to the tent.

Tom was laughing too. "You're right. We are selfish!"

"Naw. We just like the quiet and tranquility more than anything. We probably appreciate them more than most."

"True. Well now, let me pour you a bourbon. My parents brought up a bottle of nice, old Willett."

Sighing as he sat down by the fire, Greg said, "I love your parents. They keep us in style." He pulled a cigarette from the wrapper tucked into the chest pocket of his flannel shirt and lit it. "How're things down in the Cities?"

"Over. You know. It was coming."

"I suppose it was," Greg said quietly and then took a drag on his cigarette, blowing the blue-grey smoke out into the twilight. "Just keep doing what you enjoy, and you'll find someone."

"I suppose."

More quiet took hold as they drank from their cups and the tobacco smoke drifted up into the leaves, a gentle wind gradually dispersing towards the lake.

After some time had passed in a drawn-out pause in which each enjoyed the quiet of his own thoughts, at last, Greg said, "Let's eat. I brought some venison steaks."

While Greg collapsed the burning logs below the level of the river stones and placed the grate he'd brought over the stones and above the glowing logs, Tom drew the cast-iron skillet from his pack, set it on the center of the grate, tossed a slab of bacon grease on it, and let the smokey, salted lard melt, then sizzle. Greg cut up two onions he had brought in his pack, threw them into the skillet along with some golden potatoes, and let them cook for a bit. He then set the steaks on the mingled juices and smoking fat, seared them on both sides, and then served them on their tin camp plates.

Tom had cut thick slices of bread from the loaf he had brought, which they used to mop up the juices and grease. When they were finished, they walked to the stream, where they rinsed their plates.

The sun had set, and an ethereal, silvery haze had risen in the trees alongside the river and in the boughs above their camp, its glow reflecting the light from the sky and the newly risen moon above the treetops. A monstrous beaver padded along just inside the birch grove fringe on the other bank, and a trout rose in the cool current upstream to their left, its back arcing through the surface, whale-like in suspended slowness. They looked at each other in heart-thrilled surprise.

"That was a big one," Tom said in a hushed, reverent tone.

"Yeah, let's make sure to fish for the monsters tomorrow night."

Back at the campsite, they readied their gear for the next morning, checking their fly boxes, but leaving their rods broken down and stowed until the morning. Greg had another splash of bourbon, and Tom added water to his cup. A breeze with the coolness of fall carried through the trees, touched their faces, roiled the smoke from the campfire, and continued on to swirl the mist rising from the stream. Legs crossed and leaning back against his pack, Tom tamped tobacco into the briar bowl of his pipe. Greg lit another cigarette. The grey-blue smoke, lit lurid by the fire, rose up through trees as they poured themselves another couple shots of the bourbon. The north woods were blessedly silent.

<hr>

The false dawn hadn't yet appeared when Tom stirred from his woolen blanket and walked to the stream to gather water, the starlight faintly illuminating the black water, setting it aglow along its gently moving troughs and peaks.

He stirred up the fire and then added a pinch of the tinder he had shaved the previous afternoon before Greg had arrived, and quickly had a suitable fire burning. He set the enameled coffee pot on the grate, filled it with water from the stream, and dropped loose grounds of coffee into its basin. It was boiling shortly, and Greg rose from sleep to the scent and came to the fire fully awake to sit down beside Tom. "Ahh, Henry's old-fashioned way."

"Yep, the old-fashioned way. Here's to Hank," Tom answered, pouring the coffee into the two mugs. Greg reached to drink his and Tom said, "Wait, want some milk?" as he spun the opener around the rim of the sweetened condensed milk can and dropped a dollop into his own mug.

"Yes, indeed. So much for packing light, huh?"

"I figure if I'm willing to pack it, I deserve it, right?"

"Yep. You got that right. Ahhh, this is good," sighed Greg as he took his first sip of the hot, sweet, bitter liquid.

Tom savored his first few draughts of the special coffee, and then as he came awake, the eagerness to get on the river broke through the lethargy and numb-mindedness of the recently arisen. He mixed the buckwheat batter while Greg set strips of bacon sizzling on the skillet. When the grease had built up, Tom moved the bacon to a cool side of the skillet and poured rounded ladles of the batter onto the flat surface of the black skillet that was now smoking with the bacon fat. While he tended the breakfast, Greg put together peanut butter and jelly sandwiches and Fig Newton cookies for their lunches, wrapping them in waxed brown paper.

Tom flipped the pancakes with a wedge-shaped chip from one of the logs he had split for firewood. They ate in silence, savoring the rustic pancakes and the sweetened coffee.

Tossing the dregs of his coffee into the fire, Greg rinsed their plates over the fire with water they had carried from the river. Tom exposed the embers and poured the remaining reserved river water over them, making sure they were cooled.

The sun still had not risen as they jointed their rods. Both preferred the split bamboo from the Bay of Tonkin to the newer models. They threaded their lines through the guides, then walked down to the river, working the leaders and tippets to pliable warmth through their fingers. The cool dew wet their canvas pants and the skin of their free hands, the cold wetness waking them up further.

The stream was a moving, rushing blackness in the predawn, an occasional riffle flashing the reflected blue light of the false dawn, alone and free from the ambient light of the cities. The chuckling voice of the river sang to them. Greg turned to the right to follow a path downstream to the mouth, where the river flowed into the waters of Lake Superior. Tom hiked a good bit upstream of the path from their campsite to the river, intending to work his way back downstream to the path later that afternoon. He climbed a bluff that looked down on a lowland almost-swamp where the river spread out and slowed, flowing around marshy islands no bigger than picnic tables, with grass and reeds growing straight up or hanging over the edges of their own islands, shading the water underneath with cool darkness where he knew monsters lived.

The monsters were probably still prowling the watery shadows, but Tom would leave them undisturbed, as there was no way down to or out of the almost-swamp. *The sanctuary of leviathans*, thought Tom, as his eyes adjusted to the growing silvery dawn light that lit the ripples where the big ones rose to some hatch.

He continued past the descent off the bluff where the path came down to the bank of the stream. There, the stream was narrower and was a true running river upstream of the almost-swamp's spread. Here, where he stopped, the trees came down to the riverbanks, arching overhead, making it seem as if one was fishing in a tunnel. Tom scanned the water surface for several minutes, watching the undulations and riffles, the foaming at the waves' peaks and edges, for a trout's rise. Its shiny speckled back curved up and through the surface to snatch a rising fly.

The curve of its spine and the span of time it took to complete the arc told him it was a large one. Rushing to tie on a fly, heart beating quickly, in his excitement he whispered aloud, "Is this a monster escaped from the swamp?" With the dry fly on, he cast out upstream, but the fly landed short of the wave where he was aiming. His second cast was better and passed the trough where he thought the trout must be holding. Gaining his usual rhythm, the third cast landed where he wanted, skirting the edge of the shore, and as it was passing the trough, the trout grabbed the fly hard, rising from the dark bottom. *God, it's heavy,* thought Tom as he set the hook. Beginning to sweat with his heart thumping, he thought, *It's one of the monsters.* The heavy liveliness of the fish took the hook and line, dashing to the far shore. Tom wanted it and had it. He knew. The fish raced ahead, upstream, to a still-living downed tree, and was gone. The line slacked. Tom stood straight with the slack line drifting downstream. His heart still racing, but the depression of loss setting in, he reeled in, lit a cigarette to calm himself, and stood quietly, trying not to let his thoughts wander.

He hiked upstream to a stretch of currents and riffles that he remembered well, where he saw the ephemeral remains on the surface of a trout sipping emerging flies. With an enforced calm, he tied on a small caddis dry fly, lifted his rod tip up, and his line back and then forward, letting the line, leader, tippet, and fly unfurl to fall in reverse order in the current upstream of where the fish held. The fly passed by the fish without drawing a strike. Tom cast again, dropping the fly further upstream, and mended his line more carefully this time as the tiny fly raced up and down the troughs and ridges of the gray current toward the trout. He saw the fish shift its position above the gravel bottom and then strike as the fly reached the surface above its lips. Tom felt the tug of the hit through the line and the resistance as he raised his rod straight up above his head to set the hook.

The fish jolted the line, fighting the strange pain pulling its mouth across the water. It dashed to the left to the bank and then to the deep to escape. It thrashed its head to throw the hated barb, then charged towards the pull, but it was still there. Tired and confused, the fish fled down the current to its dark home behind and below the boulder that sat near the center of the stream.

The fish had put up a spirited fight and had halted behind a boulder. Tom knew the fish was tired, so he looped the line over the rock and reeled in, taking in the slack as he approached the fish from behind. The fish—no monster, but still a very good size—thrashed as he lifted it out of the water. He removed the hook and knocked its head against the rock. He unfolded his pocketknife to open its pale underside and washed out the inside of the fish in the clear water. He then placed its cold, wet sleekness on the ferns in the cool shade of his wicker creel.

Tom moved further upstream past a boulder-strewn section to a deeper, slower-moving pool. He tied on a weighted nymph made of marabou feathers and yarn with a brass bead at its head just below the eye of the hook. The day was getting warmer, so he thought the fish would be waiting in the deeper, darker shadows. He spent the remainder of the morning here casting for monsters, but not finding any and missing on other, smaller fish. He caught two more browns, neither large. He kept one.

After placing this one on the ferns in the creel with the other fish, he retreated from the riverbank a little uphill and sat on a fallen tree in the shade of a copse of pines and cedars. He breathed in the citrusy freshness of the trees, took a few swigs from the still-cool water in his canteen, and unpacked his lunch. The day had now gotten noticeably hotter, and he thought how refreshing the water was in the shade of the trees. He dove into the peanut butter and jelly sandwiches, washing the bites down with more swigs from the canteen. He sat nibbling the Fig Newtons in the silent solitude of the evergreens, their needles a soft, fragrant cushion beneath him. Even the squirrels had gone quiet with his presence; the only sound was the soft breeze blowing down the river hollow, occasionally swirling up the hill from the river to sway the pine and cedar branches. This breeze still held the gentle warmth of late summer with only the slightest current of coolness, scarcely a hint—but yet, still there—of the cold Minnesota winter to come. He settled off the log, letting the drowsiness take him until the midday warmth eased.

He woke when the golden light of the early afternoon had just faded into a clear blue, and a breeze had blown up the river from the lake with a whisper of chill to it. The forest animals, having gotten used to his unmoving form, were going about their routines. A pair of squirrels were scampering across the branches above him, and a third was arguing with a trespassing jay.

The gurgling stream called to him. He lit a cigarette to wake himself up and took a shot of the bourbon from his copper flask. He gathered his rod and creel and began the trek back to his campsite, stopping here and there along the way to wet his line and try the water. He landed two more trout, both on dun-colored dry flies that he had tied in his basement back home in the Cities, and let them both go. When he got to the bluff, he paused on his way to look down at the almost-swamp where the monsters were rising to an insect hatch and late-summer grasshoppers blown off the shaggy islands into the water, their long grass and reeds now golden-green in the light and heat of summer's end. He briefly considered bringing a canoe next year to get to the monsters but discarded the idea, thinking that it was good to leave them alone and undisturbed.

By the time he got back to the campsite, the shadows were lengthening as the sun drifted further below the treetops. Greg was there already, sitting on a stump, with a fire dancing in the ring of river stones.

"How'd you do?" asked Greg, drawing a cigarette out of his mouth.

"Got five and kept two. Upstream was good. The water was clear, and I could see plenty of fish. The monsters are still down in the meadow swamp. I could see them rising to a hatch, maybe some grasshoppers that had fallen off the grass on those islands."

"Summer seems to be still holding on. I'd say leave those big fish alone in their sanctuary."

"Yeah, that's what I thought, too. I do enjoy looking down at them, wondering how big they are."

"Big."

"Man, they must be huge. How did you do lower down?" Tom asked as he sat down by the fire, stretching his legs.

"Pretty much the same as you. There was lots of action down among the boulders. I saw a large one, probably the same big guy from last year hanging out in the same deep pool below that square cliff-fallen boulder. I couldn't get his attention with streamers or dries, nothing, so he's still there." After a pause, in which he took another drag from his cigarette, he said, "I don't think any fish are running up from the lake yet."

"I don't suppose they would be. Too warm."

"True, but here's to hoping." Greg chuckled. "Let's get out the bourbon and start dinner."

Greg stoked the fire and got out the skillet and bread. He melted a thick slab of butter in the cast-iron skillet that he had set onto the grate. Tom did a final cleaning of the fish and chopped an onion. He dug a bottle of white wine out of his pack and then poured bourbon into each of their tin cups. When the butter was melted and beginning to boil, Tom tossed the onion pieces in, letting them brown before pouring in the wine. When the mixture was boiling, Tom put their fish in.

The fish were quickly done, and Greg slid them from the skillet onto the silvery tin plates. Tom unwrapped the loaf of bread from its brown wax-paper wrap and cut inch-thick slices from it. They each took a couple of slices, mopping up the juices from the plates as they tucked into the delicate fish. When they had finished, they took their plates and forks to the river where they scrubbed them with sand from the bank and rinsed their silvery mirrored surfaces clean in the cool running water.

Back at the campsite, while Greg stoked the fire and tossed on a couple more logs, Tom got the bourbon out again and poured nice-sized shares into each of their cups. Greg lit a cigarette, and Tom tamped tobacco into his pipe, stretching his feet out towards the fire with a birch log as a rest for his head. Greg sat on a stump, poking at the fire with a stick. The sun had just set below the horizon, its light's long-fading trailing a bright pale blue that became deeper above the western treetops where stars and planets appeared. The setting sun took the last of summer with it. A cool wind drifted through the trees. The fall of the year that had been touching upon them throughout the day was there.

"Ahh, this is good after a day on the river," sighed Greg on his stump. "Are you ready for some night fishing?"

"Let me relax a little and the dinner settle. But, yes, let's definitely go. The moon will be up and big tonight."

Sometime later, with the sun long fully set and the moon still low and large, having doused the fire, they moved silently through the moon shadows in the forest, their rods and lines ready, to the bank of the river. Greg went upstream a bit and Tom went down until, with about a hundred yards apart, they lost sight of each other, and thus began the annual ballet-like movements of the two fishermen in the moonlight. The sky was clear and cloudless. The moon was bright, and the stars shone out from a dark, deep-blue heaven. The forest glowed in the moonlight as if in a frozen predawn moment, and the gentle blue light of the moon undulated on the surface of the river, whose soft moving sounds were like music.

They drew out their lines and began casting. Both false-casted in the same rhythm with the thin filaments of their leaders and tippets flickering in the moonlight as they lifted up from the water's surface and flowed back and forth in the air in slow, unwinding loops. Greg cast a large, weighted, wet fly with black marabou feathers and long black hackle with a silver wire wound around the shank. It landed in the current on his third forward cast, across the river and upstream near the bank, but in the undercutting depths. As it drifted downstream, he let the extra bends in the line gradually tighten until it reached a straight tautness downstream to his right. He then carefully, haltingly, stripped the line back to him.

Tom cast a smaller dry fly tied with a dun-colored hackle overlain with bleached, straw-colored elk hair. The beautiful rhythm created by the long bond of friendship and unconscious familiarity made Tom's caddis fly imitation land after the same number of false casts and at the same angles as Greg's fly. Their second and third casts followed the same pattern.

Tom's fly drifted steadily downstream at the edge of the leafy tree limbs that overhung the bank and dipped here and there with the breeze into the water. Like Greg, Tom let the line gently go taut as it rode the current to his right. When the fly and line reached that moment of a tense straight line, he raised the tip of his rod to get as much line off the water as he could, letting the fly skate along the water's surface, sometimes leaping from one wave's peak across the trough to the peak of the next wave brought by the current. *Damn*, he thought as he watched his fly, *if it doesn't look like a real, living thing.*

The fish slammed into it, grabbing the fly in its mouth and tugging strongly, heavily towards the other bank under the fringe of the branches, and then moving reluctantly into the middle of the stream as Tom set the hook and exerted his own strength. The fish leapt and rolled, its mottled back and pale underside glowing in the bright silver moonlight, pulling against the unknown strength that drew it towards the pebbly bank away from the solitary sanctuary of the dark depths under the treed bank and away from the hidden hollow that was its home behind the submerged boulder.

The bamboo shaft of Tom's rod bowed in a tight arc, quivering, and then taut as the fish fought and made a lunge away from the shore. *Dear God,* Tom thought, *this fish is strong. Please don't let the line break.* His pulse quickening as the rod bent further. *Did one of the monsters from the swamp come down here?* And then as the line whipped downstream, *Please don't lose this one.* His breath was quickening as he let out a little slack from the clicking reel. He wiped his brow as the fish rested in the middle of the stream. A cool breeze blew through the leaves, rustling them and swaying their branches. The outstretched finger of a cloud drifted across the moon as Tom began the slow, flowing dance of easing the fish to the bank. He backed up almost onto the pebbled shore as the fish finally came in. Tom knelt with water lapping onto his knees as he cradled the long, heavy trout, glowing silver in the light, to unhook it.

ON THE GULF

The hot sun was on its downward arc as he cast his line out from where he stood on the white sand at the edge of the surf line, sending the hooked baitfish back into the blue waters of the Gulf. He had not been counting casts, just enjoying the beauty of the rhythm and the soothing, hot, white-gold light of the sun. A gentle wind was kicking up foam from the wave crests, while beyond the crests in the flats, reflections of the white summer sun flashed back to his eyes, making him squint even behind the dark lenses of his sunglasses. *Thank God for the wind*, Tom thought to himself as it blew to him, cooling his sweat-wet chest and face. Still, the heat of the past two days was a thawing, blanketing comfort after the unusually long, bitter-cold winter of Minnesota, where he had not seen a blade of green grass for five months.

As the bait fish held placidly under the bright flat water behind the white surf line, Tom put his rod into the tube he had set into the sand, took a sip from his mojito, and walked a few yards to another rod, wanting to have more than one line in the water now. He hooked another baitfish with flashing silvery sides, cast it into the flat water to the right of the first fish, where it landed with an unheard splash, set that rod into its tube in the white sand that burned his knee as he knelt to drive this one down further, and took another drink of his mojito. He moved to his third and final rod, hooked another silver-sided fish, this one flapping in his hand with more verve than the previous two, casting it out, just barely clearing the white foaming crest of a long-breaking wave. He drove the butt of this rod into the tube, again scorching his knees on the burning-hot white sand. He stepped back to wait for strikes, taking another sip from the mojito.

He sighed. The mojito was good and tasted perfect here on the shore of the Gulf, about the only place he drank one.

"¿Señor pescador, otro mojito?" said the smiling sun-browned boy resting behind him, under the palm frond lean-to he had built on the edge of the dune grass. The boy's younger sister, Maria, played in the sand in front of him.

"No, Pedro. Gracias, mi amigo." He needed to be careful about losing his head with the alcohol and heat. Pedro, the twelve-year-old, who did not taste what he was making, was an artist with the mojito, the rum from some local source, probably distilled by the old man, Juan, Pedro's grandfather, who lived in the hills away from the cluster of wooden open-air shacks near the beach. It was a rum better than any Tom could get back home, mixed with the soda and mint, with just a touch of lime juice. That, plus the sand, sun, and surf were calming amnesiacs inducing not just a forgetfulness, but an unconsciousness of his home in the still-cold north, in which she and her hold on him and her demands and the ending of things were no longer present in his mind, hovering just beyond on the fringes of care. He thought of Homer's Land of the Lotus Eaters and took another sip as he watched his lines.

~~~

It was Juan, the quiet, tanned old man, who had first taken him offshore fishing three years earlier on his first trip south to the Gulf, to a place where the Gulf waters met those of the Caribbean. It had been another long and unusually cold winter season, near the end of which he needed to leave the North, the grayness and biting cold having gotten to him. As he felt the madness just beginning to take hold, he grabbed two of his rods - a fly rod and a spinner – along with the brightest, most-colorful flies and lures he had, a couple of changes of clothes, some cash, and boarded a flight to Mexico, where he caught a bus full of locals to the coast.

The bus had wound around the hills hidden by a green, deep jungle and through the mountains to the coast, where he and a few others got out. He had enjoyed the ride, the sere heat of the air through the windows thawing him out and growing fresher with the increasing verdancy as they descended from the upland to the coastal plain where the sand was white, the water a cobalt blue, and the palm trees bent gently in the breezes from the Gulf. He had ended up here, a place rarely visited, if at all, by outsiders—and certainly not one like him from the far north—by pure happenstance, or perhaps fate, as it was the first stop on the coast and seemed secluded, or, more accurately, un-visited by others enough to suit him. He could see the Gulf from the crossroads in town where the bus had stopped. The salty tang of the breeze off the water mixed with the smells of cooking, meats grilling and spices and fish, a heady mélange that the Gulf breeze had mixed with and then, in a trick of the air, cleared away.

He had gone into an open-air cantina between the sand-covered road and the dunes to think about what to do next now that he was here. He hadn't thought about much in his sudden departure, only the need for the hot sun and to fish from salt water, water that wasn't still frozen. The wooden almost-hut was raised up on wooden pilings sunk into the sand, so that sitting on his chair, he could see over the dunes and the feathery grass waving in the breeze blowing in from the water. He saw the ocean and the slow-yet-sudden curl of the waves as they broke, soundless from the sighing of the air that blew through the dried dune grass into the cantina. His wooden chair creaked as he rocked back, drinking a cold beer with a gold label that the deeply sun-burnt and creased man from behind the bar had brought him, drawing it out of an old, white dented and scratched refrigerator, setting it down with a lime and a paring knife. The heat and sweat were a pleasant change from the cold of Minnesota, and the salted wind from the water cooling his sweat was welcome too.

By the time he had eaten some fish tacos and had another cold beer, the afternoon was getting late. He could see smaller fish skipping from the crest of one wave to the foamed crest of another as they tried to escape larger fish chasing them below the surface. Along the surf line and beyond in the flat water, he began to see more of these attempts to escape. It was the right time to fish.

Tom paid for the beers and tacos and bought another beer with a lime for the beach. The barman sold him an old, grayed iron bucket with baitfish. He secured his waxed canvas rod cases through the loops of his faded brown canvas knapsack, still smelling of the fires he had fought a few years back, and followed the path through the dunes to the beach. The Gulf air blew gently over the dunes, swishing through the grass that grew on top. Little crabs bustled from one clump to another. Emerging through the dunes onto the white sugar-sand beach, he shuffled through the softness underfoot closer to the surf line. He could see the roof of the cantina directly behind him. A fish leapt out from the water in front.

Tom decided that this was a good spot. He set down his duffle and then removed the first rod from its tan canvas case. He jointed it together and rummaged through the duffle for the reel that he had wrapped in a pair of socks, finding it still snug in the middle. Screwing that onto the rod near the butt, he threaded the heavy line through the guides then tied on a braided metal leader to which he attached the hook. The rod, line, and hook were ones that he used offshore fishing for salmon in Lake Superior before they began their autumn runs up the streams above Duluth. He hoped these were good enough for the Gulf fish. *Well,* Tom thought to himself, *when you leave on a sudden, you make do with what you've grabbed,* trying not to feel regret or doubt.

Unhinging the top of the bucket, he snatched out a wriggling fish, hooked it with his salmon hook, and cast it out into the surf. The still-lively fish swam in the clear water beyond the churned sandy water between the surf line on the beach and the break line in the water. As it swam near the surface, he could see flashes from its silver flanks. Easing the drag on the line, he set the butt end down into the sand, then reached for the other canvas case. He repeated the process, then walked about twenty feet to his right, where he cast this fish out too. He set the rod into the sand like the first, then walked back to the bucket. He took his blue chambray shirt out of his knapsack, covered the bucket with it, and then placed the knapsack on top of the shirt to shield the bucket and the fish from the heat of the remaining late afternoon sun.

Tom then opened the bottle of beer, tucking the cap in his pocket, and squeezed the lime wedge through the opening into the beer. The lime was juicy. It squirted a quick shot onto his cheek. He placed his thumb over the top, tilted the bottle to mix the beer with the lime, and watched the lime slowly float to the up-turned bottom. Then he turned it right-side up again and took a sip, squinting out through his sunglasses to his lines being pulled by the still-active fish. The lime-beer mixture was refreshing, and he fleetingly mused that he needed to live somewhere someday where he could grow his own lime tree. The beach was deserted. This was the place. He took another, longer drink as he watched his lines.

By the time the sun had become a red ball sitting just above the horizon, Tom had landed four fish: two redfish, a snapper, and a small shark. The shark was a delightful shock, reminding him that he was indeed on the Gulf. He released the shark, the last of his catches, reeled in the other line, leaving his gear on the beach as he walked back with the redfish through the dunes to the cantina.

The barman smiled as Tom walked up the sundried board steps into the cool shade of the cantina. He learned that the man's name was Javier and that he was the owner. Tom offered Javier one of the redfish, asking if he would cook the other one for dinner. Dried out from the wind and thirsty from the sun, Tom declined another beer, asking for water instead. He sat at the same table from earlier, looking out to the water where the sun was beginning its slide towards night. There were three others inside with him; he supposed that they were locals who had just gotten off a bus and were enjoying drinks before walking home. They sat quietly on the other side of the room near the door to the street, two with their legs stretched out on the floor in front, enjoying the soothing sounds the waves and the breeze over the dunes that brought its coolness and salty tang to them. All three smiled and waved their greetings to him as he walked in. Tom took a slow drink of the ice water that Javier brought him, feeling it cool him from the inside out. The water cleared his head from the afternoon's heat. He finished the glass and Javier brought another, announcing that the fish was almost ready. Tom thanked him and settled back to wait with his own legs stretched out. The thought of the fresh fish cooked for him reminded him that he was hungry.

An old man entered the hut carrying a small wooden crate loaded with clear bottles that clinked as he swayed through the room and set them on the bar. The three locals waved to the man, smiling and saying, "Buenos tardes, Señor Juan."

The old man waved back. "Buenos tardes, amigos."

Javier brought out the fish on a blue glazed ceramic platter, the fish on one side with a lime, and a short stack of steaming tortillas on the other. Tom thanked him and dug in. The fresh ocean fish was good, not fishy, the salt of the Gulf in the flesh mingled with the lime. Javier came back out with the remaining fish, motioned to Tom, and asked if it pleased *Señor Pescador* to share with the others. Tom smiled and nodded and accepted Javier's and the others' *gracias* with another nod of his head.

The old man walked over to his table with a small plate of Tom's fish and one of the bottles from his wooden crate. He introduced himself as Juan and spoke some words in Spanish, gesturing to one of the three chairs at Tom's table. Tom introduced himself and smiled at the chair, saying, "Por favor." Juan sat down, setting his plate and clear glass bottle on the aged, salt-wind-warped wood of the table. Javier came behind him with a bottle of water and two short glasses. Señor Juan popped the cork from the top of his bottle, saying, "Rhum" as he poured the clear liquid into each one. Tom knew rum, although it was not his drink of choice, but he lifted his glass to salute the old man.

⁓

A fish had struck the line from the middle rod that Tom had driven into the hot sand, racing first straight out from the beach and then dashing left and right in the flat trough between the waves, trying to throw the hook. Tom hurried to it, his leather-sandaled feet kicking up sand that was then caught by the breeze to blow back at Juan and Maria.

"Aiyeee, señor!" shouted Pedro. Maria dramatically tossed her hair and spit onto the beach.

"Perdóneme, amigo, amiga," Tom said, laughing. He drew the rod out of the sand and rested the butt against the waistband of his dirty white linen shorts as he tightened the drag with his left hand. The fish had already set the hook firmly in its attempt to escape the metal weight in its mouth, so Tom raised the tip of his rod almost to the vertical and reeled in the slack. The line cut out from the guide and through the foam of a breaking wave. The fish fought him, startled and angered now by the pressure pulling its mouth, and headed back to the churning shallows.

From the tension on the line and the arc to the rod, he knew it was a large one. The children ran up from behind, cheering him on as he reeled and coaxed the fish towards the shore and away from the cooler deep where it sought to escape.

Another fish struck the third rod, on his right, while Tom was still fighting his fish, and the spool sang as the line was torn out of the reel. The children were dumbstruck, perplexed as to what Señor Tom, *El Pescador*, was going to do.

"Pedro! Maria! ¡La caña! ¡La caña!" Tom hoped his Spanish was correct, but the children understood and ran wildly to the rod, snatching it out of the hole in the sand, neither one, nor Tom, wanting to lose the fish. Tom sidestepped over, keeping an eye on his line and watching the children, holding the rod in their sweaty, sandy hands, screaming in excitement and confusion, and, like him, in fear of losing the fish.

The children held the fish on the end of their line as it dashed back and forth, Tom laughing with them, feeling their excitement, and giving them gentle shouts of encouragement. He almost forgot his own line but was called back by its rapid unspooling as his fish raced away from the beach into deeper water. He decided that it was important for the children to do this on their own, to land or lose the fish and to own their excitement and joy, so he stepped a few paces away to give them room and returned to playing his own fish.

~

Before the true dawning of the sun, the sky was lit with a light yellow-gold by the sun still hidden beneath the horizon, the yellow turning to an orange and then a deep red that lit the sky and the underside of the few puffs of clouds above the horizon. Tom stood on the rough, brown wooden boards of the ageing dock, sipping a hot coffee with Juan and stretching his arms as he sought to become more awake. The coffee was thick and dark, sweetened by a large dollop of dulce de leche, its rich, sugary, caramel-like taste blending with the dark bitterness of the thick black coffee. Tom and Juan, each silently looking out towards the horizon and at the slight chop on the water from the breeze, dipped their noses now and then to savor the sweet, bitter steam coming off their coffees. The coffee was good. Tom would make his like this when he got home. The dock smelled of the deep rich scent of fresh fish and the salty sharpness of the warm morning breeze off the water.

Before loosening their moorings, they set aside their brown clay cups, and Juan stepped lightly into his boat. Tom picked up each of the four rods from the dock, making sure that the reels were tight to the rods, and the lines strung with their hooks or lures secured to the line and their rods' stays. Two of the lines had bare hooks for the bait, the other two had colorful feather-like flashing around a rubber-core body. He handed them down to Juan, who set each into a rod holder in the boat's gunwales. He then reached for the two buckets of bait fish, both filled with salt water, one that held small, silvery fish that Juan had caught that morning in the shallows of the surf with a casting net. The fish now huddled at the bottom, some darting here and there. In the other bucket rested baby squid that he and Juan had traded for from a trawler that had just come in from a night of fishing the deep. The water sloshed as Juan took the buckets one at a time and dumped them into the bait well; he dipped each bucket over the side for more water that he poured steadily into the well so the fish could swim more freely.

Tom stepped down into the boat, ducking under the blue-and-white-striped canopy, then undid the aft mooring rope, coiling its damp roughness then stowing it in the pocket below the starboard gunwale while Juan did the same with the fore mooring rope. Tom wrapped his right hand around one of the cool aluminum rods that supported the awning as Juan started the engine. They pulled away from the dock, the engine chugging as the boat peacefully moved away from the dock and slowly moved east towards the rising sun, rocking gently over the tops and down into the troughs of the dark waves coming into shore. Tom looked back to see other fishermen moving on the dock and readying their boats, some in simple rowboats with weighted nets piled in their sterns. Just before they cleared the point that sheltered the docks, its grass undulating in the breeze from the open water, the sun lifted above the horizon, a bright-red growing sliver that lit the crests of the dark waves, turning them a blushing reddish-pink.

Once beyond the point, the breeze was less strong and the air fresher, more Gulf-pure, lacking the fish smell of the docks, and unmixed with the fresh grasses and low bushes of the dunes. The breeze just held Gulf water and salt and an almost imperceptible rising heat. Juan throttled the engine up a notch while Tom lifted the lid to the bait hold and reached into the swirl of fish to lift out one of the flashing jacks whose scales were colored rose like the waves kissed by the sun that was still climbing above the horizon. He hooked the little fish and cast it, sailing in a high arc and pulling out line to fall far back into vanishing rosy whiteness of the boat's wake. It hit the water and sank just below the surface where it was hit immediately. Tom was reaching into the bait hold for another silver jack when he saw the line go taught, straighter than the pull of the boat would cause, and quiver, jerking. He lifted the rod from its seat and began reeling in. He felt the life on the other end through the tautness of the line.

Tom's pull was too strong for the fish, and he brought it quickly to the boat, wanting it to live, yet not to fatigue it beyond recovery. Once it was alongside, he lifted his rod and line, bringing the juvenile tuna on board. It had a true silver with a deep blue-green stripe down its back, the blue-green of the Gulf. He opened the lid of the bait hold, threw the tuna in, and grabbed another jack. He cast this one out into the wake where it, too, was hit right away. They were moving through a school of tuna. He yelled to Juan over his shoulder. Juan set the helm, took the other rod with a hook, and got his own little jack. They repeated these motions, flowing back and forth between the lines and the hold, moving around each other in a smooth rhythm for several repetitions. Each fish they landed was a juvenile tuna, as they had expected, until finally, Juan caught a yellow jack. He brought it in and looked to Tom with a raised eyebrow. Tom reeled in his line while Juan slid the yellow jack into the bait hold. Juan went to the helm and gunned the throttle to the east—always to the east.

The sun had now fully risen above the Gulf's horizon as the boat plowed the blue-green waves—more blue than green, the farther out they motored—to the deep fishing grounds of the seam where the Gulf and Caribbean waters met. There, they would hunt for the larger fish. The glare from the sun, yellowing more as it rose higher, made Tom glad that he was wearing the hat he had purchased a couple of years earlier on his first trip down. It had been hanging from a dark wooden peg behind the bar of the cantina. The sun's glare on the water had been almost blinding across the white sand of the beach when he stepped off the bus that first time. The cap's white canvas body was now stained from the past years' sweat and salty rust around the center-top metal grommet, and the doe-skin of the elongated duck-like bill was still dark brown, although it, too, was crusted with this trip's dried white brine and stained with brine from years past. The hat was made for big-water fishing. Juan wore the same wide-brimmed palm leaf hat that he always wore, whether working his land in the mountains or fishing, as today, far offshore.

The sun was up when the boat crossed the stark line from the light green, almost sandy, shallow near-shore water to the deep blue-green of the big water where the monsters were. The greens and blues of the water called to mind the slick wet backs of the baby tuna. The day would be hot, but Tom welcomed the heat after the winter up north. For Juan, it was part of the unconscious rhythm of his life. The sweat felt good to Tom, but he wanted to be careful that he didn't lose his head in the salty heat and sun glaring white off the water's surface. He took a drink of the water.

The old man throttled down to a slow crawl and stepped away from the stern to help Tom rig the baits. Reaching into the live-bait well, Tom found one of the juvenile tuna, hooked it through the snout, secured the hook onto the braided steel line, and weighted it to get it deep near the bottom. Dropping it off the stern, Tom watched it sail downwards to the bottom, to the monsters he hoped to find.

Juan, his old-man sweat-slick skin burnt and tanned brown by the years of sun—even the creases on his neck and in the corners of his dark-brown, squinting eyes—hooked on the amberjack, setting a lighter weight so that it would swim in the middle depths. Tom reached back into the live well and searched among the jostling, splashing bodies to find a ballyhoo to ride just under the surface. Juan held the short, stout rod while Tom hooked the ballyhoo on, the lively fish squirming and tossing in his hands, almost leaping out. Over the stern it went too. There had been a minimum of cool fish blood, as the two men worked efficiently. Less blood meant less of a chance for sharks. Sharks were not the fish they were after.

Juan returned to the helm and opened the throttle on his boat. The bait fish on their lines swam behind, each rising with the boat's pull. The boat moved at a slow rumble along the edge of the drop-off, the deeper blue water to the starboard, the lighter, almost sandy-colored shallower water along the port side. To the port also lay the shore, too far away for Tom to see anything than the dark green line of the mountains. Tom couldn't clearly make out any other fishermen, although nearer shore he saw little slivers of white that road the swells. The wind was slight, and foam was churned up on the crests. The sun, off the starboard, had risen to become a white disc in the mostly cloudless sky, while further to the west, the sky darkened to a deep, clear blue—the blue of warmth and summer. A few white wisps of clouds remained in the West.

Tom dipped his bandana over the side to wet it, then tied it around his neck so that his back didn't burn, as it tended to do. He was still pale from the wan sun of the northern winter, although a bronze tan had begun to color his arms and face over the past day. The bandana smelled clean and salty, like the ocean, and was warm, but cooler than the sun. It soothed his skin. He sat back into the fighting chair, strapping the white leather belt on. He set the butt of the ballyhoo rod into the belt's worn cup and checked the drag, loosening it so that if a sail struck it, the line wouldn't snap or, worse, pull him over the side.

The old man twisted around in his seat at the helm and laughed. "Señor Tom, with your *pañuelo*, you look a *vaquero*, a bandito, truly." He continued to chuckle.

"Pancho Villa himself." Tom laughed too, making pistols with his hands.

Juan laughed even more, his arms raised in surrender. "Put your *pistolas* down! Careful, or the monster sail will come and steal your rod." Tom turned with a smile, took tighter hold of the rod, and pulled the long, salt-stained bill down low to cut the glare flashing off the water. The boat churned across the waves and the day grew older, the sun and wind hot, becoming hotter, drying their sweat. Tom drank more water, feeling the beginning of a cramp in his arm.

The bottom-riding line twitched and there was a pull, a weight from the depths pulling on the rod. The weight of whatever fish and the drag of the boat bent the rod downward in a steep arc. Tom yelled to Juan, who throttled down and took the ballyhoo rod from Tom, while Tom lunged and slid to the rod with the bottom line.

He tested the line and could feel through the tension connecting him to the thing at the other end of the line that the hook had set. He loosened the drag, always careful not to lose a fish through silly, overeager amateur mistakes. It was tough, as he was eager. The thrill of a hooked fish always did that to him. The old man reeled the ballyhoo line in and then did the same with the juvenile tuna while Tom fought the fish on the bottom.

There was no jerking fight to the fish, but rather, a massive heaviness and a refusal to move that was the fish's fight. It became a standoff, the great fish refusing to move and Tom not yielding, either. The line was strong, but Tom knew to be careful, strong but gentle, with his rod and line.

The great fish was not bothered by the line tugging its mouth, only puzzled by this thing that pulled from above. It settled in the dark blue depths, where the filtered light of the sun barely reached. Tom could feel the fish begin to stir in the depths of its home, where the water was cooler than at the surface. In its freedom, the fish moved off into the current and Tom, with Juan at the helm, had no choice but to follow if he wanted to hold on and bring this fish up to him. Juan eased the throttle into reverse, slowly, patiently, following the sharp angle of the thrumming line connecting the rod in Tom's sweating hands. After the first shock-thrill of the hooking and knowing the barb was set, the fear was in him now, the fear of this unknown monster, several fathoms down, and of losing it, never seeing him, and never bringing him in to the boat.

Tom and Juan began a careful dance as Juan swung the boat around, its prow now pointing toward the fish in the easterly direction it was swimming, and Tom easing along the edge of the boat, slowly, gently releasing enough line from the spool to allow him to move but not enough to let the fish feel the slackening and sense a freedom from the tugging at its mouth.

With the boat's pirouette complete, Tom stood at the prow with his line still at the same angle in the water, but the fish had stopped its movement through the blue night of the deep. *Did the fish sense something? What is it thinking?* thought Tom. *Don't lose your head in the sun and heat; the fish is not thinking, only feeling.* Tom took a deep drink from the water they had kept cool in the hold. Gripping the rod with his right hand, he lifted his long-billed hat with his left and fanned his sweating face. A breeze from the Gulf had picked up for the moment, and the tufts of air that pushed against his slick, briny face by flapping his sweat-stained hat were pleasant, but an unsatisfyingly brief respite from the fight and the heat.

This fight was not like those that other fishermen, tourists, or writers spoke of, with the fish and the fisherman in an aggressive slug-fest battle: a free-for-all, with the fish running, breaching, or dancing on the water to throw the hook while the fisherman strained on the line, the rod jerking stiffly in his hands as he sought to muscle the fish into the boat.

No, this fight was a standoff, with Tom and the fish waiting for the other to make a move and decide the next stage of the contest. It was like a scene from a western movie in which two gunfighters stared each other in the eyes while standing in some dry desert with salty sweat beading on their brows below their hats, a tense waiting for the other. He admired, loved this giant fish. Tom held steady, his rod tip up, but bent down and forward, the line's angle holding straight through the surface of the water. His sweat was now running in rivulets down his brow, collecting in the corners of his eyes, stinging them. Tom tried to blink the bitter sweat away, and that helped, if only briefly. He licked his lips and could taste his own sweaty salt on them, mixed with the rawer brine from the sea air. He thought to himself that he was now fully thawed out, no doubt about it. His limbs and hands were looser than up in the cold, but a faint fatigue, a near-soreness, the hint that he had felt earlier, was lurking at the edge. The old man sat in the shade of the awning in the cockpit and watched.

The engine was idling now, the boat bobbing in the gentle waves, waiting for the next move from either fish or man. Feathered clouds floated high above them in the air, where the sun was now directly overhead, too bright to look at for too long. Tom turned his gaze to the horizon where the sky was a gentler, soothing robin's-egg blue. They were far enough out now that the land behind them, to the west, was only a faint blue-gray line, barely there, on the horizon. It was so small that imagination could have created it. Ahead and to the starboard, there was nothing, only the horizon and the waves. No birds had followed them this far and no fish or porpoise were breaking the surface. Just water and sky and the heavy unmoving mass of the fish below. The complete purity of the isolation was welcome.

This stage, and perhaps the next of the battle, would be one of Tom sensing with his hands and chest, waiting for vibrations or a tug through the line, something that would tell him of the fish's intentions - maybe a sudden slackening of the line as the fish moved toward him or upward to breach, but he was sure that this fish would not do that until the end, and the end was not yet.

The old man was mumbling something that Tom could not make out over the chuffing of the idling engine and the soft smack of the waves against the boat's hull. It sounded like, "Make your move, make your move," or was that what Tom was thinking in his head? Perhaps both. Who was it directed to? Perhaps both Tom and the fish at once. Tom was losing his head, he knew. He needed to keep his wits about him. He needed to make his move.

Tom released the drag a touch in anticipation of the fish's run, and slowly, gently took in the slack until he felt a stillness and a quivering at the end of the line. It was the fish, but was the quivering a hesitation? He let his rod settle to just below the horizontal, taking in those few feet of line to give him that much more of an advantage. The rod tip quivered as it pointed down the taught angle of the line. The boat rocked, but the line held straight, disappearing a few feet under the now gentle rising and settling of the water's surface. He caught a whiff of the burnt gasoline exhaust and struck the rod up, the stiff, thick, short length of the deep-water rod bowing with his motions and the deep immovability of the fish. He held for just a moment, and then the fish made its decision. It dove into even deeper, darker depths, almost directly downward, the line whining out of the spool. No water sprayed from the unwinding line.

The fish went down even deeper and then leveled out, having found the depth, temperature, and the current that it knew. Tom mused that fish always go back to their homes—the trout to its deep, shady trough behind a boulder or beneath the shadow of hanging branches and trees, and this sail to the dark, cooler depths of his home current. The trout would seek structures for freedom, but the sail would seek no structure, hoping to find freedom again. Both were solitary creatures, but the trout's home was a specific, physical location, and the sail's was a set of conditions, an environment. The sail was an existentialist. Where was his home?

Tom let the fish run. Juan jumped down from his captain's chair shouting, cheering his excitement now that the tension of the standoff had broken. Tom could feel the strength of the fish as it swam now in its home. Its speed was aided by the cool, deep, blue current; both the fish and the current were moving in the same direction. The spool was continuing to unwind, so Juan got back into his chair and throttled the boat forward, following the line's direction to the fish. Tom felt the slowing of the fish as he took in more line. The boat gave an excited chase, with Juan cheering from the cockpit, until it caught up, stopped the unspooling, and created the beginnings of slack. Tom reeled the slack in, winding the reel fast now, saltwater wetting the spool and his hand, leaving a white brine splotching.

The fish had tired. Tom could feel it for sure now. He had taken in all the slack and could feel it weakening through the line, as the boat slowed. Juan kept the boat at an even speed with the fish, easing the throttle to match the fish's speed as it rose, nearing the surface. Tom gave another forceful, upward tug with the rod. The fish, not surrendering yet, leapt through the surface half a football field away, clearing the water and seeming to dance on the waves. Its silver-gray scythe-like tail and head shook from side to side, violently yet beautifully in its strength, trying to shake the hook and line that held him. It's deep-blue sail, so dark and deep that it was almost purple, was spread wide, flexing along the curve of its spine. Then the fish dropped, slipping, not splashing, down through the water. Tom took in more slack, dragging, it seemed to him, the fish toward the side of the boat. The fish leapt again, but danced less this time, sinking down again and not splashing. *A strange, graceful fish*, he thought. The fish settled on the surface, spent.

Juan moved the boat gently to the fish while Tom took in the remaining slack in the line. Together, they brought the fish along the starboard side. The fish rested on its side, silver belly towards the white of the boat's hull. Tom held its bill, looking into its black-blue eye, as Juan rigged the winch and then looped the rope around the base of its tail. The fish made a quick jerk but didn't flail; it was spent. Juan and Tom worked together on the winch to lift the fish out of the water and then swung the fish over into the boat. Juan raised the wooden priest above his white-haired, sun-browned head and then swung its round end, blackened with age and use, against the blue flatness of the sail's head that ran between its eyes. The priest thudded wetly. The fish's eyes began the fade to total black nothingness. It was then that Tom knew things were ended.

The way back to land was a floating dream without time; the motor's drone lulled Tom and Juan into a calm fatigue, spent as they were from the long standoff and exertions to land the fish, and the mind-weakening strain of forced and focused concentration. Their muscles were exhausted and pleasantly sore, as if from a physical job well done—like that of felling a tree in the woods and reducing it to logs by axe and saw. There was the happiness in the job, a relief from meeting the challenge, and, as always for Tom, the black, sad regret, pushed down, of the death of something beautiful. Tom saw that in Juan's eyes too.

They churned in through the waves toward the setting sun, its light and heat in their faces as they rode through the crests and into the troughs of the waves. The tops of the hills behind the bay directly ahead were tinted orange now and deepening into a rose color with the setting sun. The docks were visible as a pale yellow-orange line to his left, and the cantina and its beach, where he had fished the foaming surf, was off to the right. The bay was separated from the interior by the ring of hills, green with the deep foliage of the trees, yet here and there, craggy rocks and deep brown earth of plowed fields could be seen.

Other fishermen had come in ahead of them and had docked their boats. Most were still unloading fish and nets, but those who had completed their tasks were sitting on benches drinking water and mopping their foreheads, sweaty from their work and the heat. Juan throttled the engine down, and Tom willed himself out of the fatigue and reverie, a dull feeling like a heavy stone shoved aside and then a swimming up to the surface to breathe. It was not unpleasant, but there was work to do.

As Juan gently slid his boat alongside the wooden dock with heavy ropes coiled around the thick, aged wooden pilings, Tom leapt off the gunwale, the boat's rope tether in his hand. His sandaled feet thudded on the dock's graying planks. He wrapped the tether

J. KENT GREGORY

around one of the pilings, resting the smaller rope on top of the thicker rope that appeared as aged as the piling itself. The old man shut the motor off, walked to the prow, tossed its tether to Tom, who had hurried along the plank to catch it before the prow swung too wide. Tom pulled the boat to the dock, bumping it gently on the ropes around the wooden piling, again tightly coiling the tether around the sundried post and its wet ropes.

The air from the dock had a hotter, drier tang than the air of the morning, a musty, sweet, briny smell from freshly caught fish being unloaded. Tom swung the hoist from the dock over the stern of Juan's boat. Juan grabbed the rope dangling from the hoist and guided it over the fish. Then he knelt over the fish, looped the rope snugly around its tail, and Tom worked the mechanism to lift it from the boat. As tired as he was, he strained to swing the fish up and back over to the dock.

Until then, Tom did not realize how spent he was. The sweat had again beaded on his forehead despite the pleasing breeze blowing ashore. He leaned his forehead on the hoist's upright metal post, trying to calm his breathing and thudding heart. The fish hung, head down, the eyes black and the body silver-blue now. The stripes had faded. A crowd of brown fishermen had gathered.

It was done, and Tom decided to go back North.

THE FORGE

The valley was filled with smoke, and its scent—that of some big campfire or barbecue—filled his truck as Tom crossed the state line. The line ran along a ridge with steep, wooded drop-offs on either side. The West Virginia side was clear, free from the smoke; Virginia was burning. He didn't expect it to be so thick, but as he descended the road through Covington and then Clifton Forge, with its crumbling red-brick smokestacks, the evening sky was shaded from the darkening blanket of smoke and drifting gray-black ash that had been thrown over the Valley, blocking the setting sun that changed from orange to red to nothing, the further he drove down. He switched on his truck's headlamps and slowed down. The winds pulled at his truck. They were blowing north through the valley from the southwest.

The summer had been especially dry on this side of the mountains. Kentucky had been dry and hot, too, but not like the choking absence of moisture that the Valley had seen. The spotters in their towers and on their exposed rocky ridge-top campsites had seen the first fires a week earlier in the trees on the mountain slopes. Greg had called yesterday, asking him to join his crew. Tom had picked up the phone in his father's study, sitting in the leather chair behind the big desk, the black cord stretching from the corner. It was an old room in an old house, with dust permanently wafting down through the sunbeams coming through the large glass window that looked toward the foothills leading to the western slopes of the Kentucky Appalachians.

"Why don't you come back to Virginia early, a couple of weeks before classes start? We could use you on our crew," Greg had said.

"You all must be desperate if you're giving me a call. You know I've never fought a fire before," Tom replied.

"You've been in the Forest Service out West, so you know trees and mountains and know your way around outdoors. I think these fires are gonna turn out bad. We need people who won't lose their heads."

"I still think you sound desperate."

"Besides, you owe me," Greg added with a laugh.

"How long are you going to hang that over my head?" Tom groaned.

"As long as I need to."

"I'll be there."

"Bring your USFS gear. Don't forget your axe and spade. You'll need those. I don't know how many we'll have to distribute, and we might be short. This is looking to be big." There was a pause. "It'll be an adventure," Greg added with another laugh before hanging up.

Tom set the phone down and looked out the window to the green line of the horizon, thinking to himself, with a thrill inside, of the blue line beyond, and beyond that, the fires blowing north and east up the mountains lining the Valley. Greg was right: this would be an adventure, and maybe more than one, if the fires were going to be as bad as Greg thought. He'd heard it in his friend's voice. He also knew that Greg was desperate if he was asking him to come. He was glad that Greg had asked him, though. He didn't speak of it as an adventure when he sat down with his parents at dinner, just that the request was urgent from Greg.

After dinner was cleared and the dishes were washed and back in the cabinets, he went up the creaking hardwood stairs to his room. He pulled his USFS-issue canvas pack out of the closet; like most government-issued gear, this was the same type issued to the soldiers and had been for a while. His father had one just like it, only his had the plain US insignia marked in black ink on the top flap. Tom's had the US flanking a pine tree insignia in dark green ink. The pack still held the faint smell of the sage and pine from the high western plains and mountains. It had been just two weeks since he got off the train from his summer out West on the Divide, where he had worked the past three summers. He unbuckled the top of his pack, loosened the drawstring, and then dumped the contents in a scattering pile onto his bed's patchwork quilt that had been made by his mother's church sewing group. He spread the mound of gear to make sure he had what he wanted to bring with him over the mountains to the Valley.

The first item he set aside was his father's Boy Scout axe, the BSA fleur-de-lis insignia showing through the aged brown patina. The axe's silvery edge was dulled; he would need to sharpen that before he left. He had a pretty good idea that when he pulled into town, things would move fast. He uncovered the carborundum stone and set it next to the axe. His fire-starting kit had been buried at the bottom of the pack so it was lying on top of the pile. Tom thought that it was odd to carry such an item into a forest fire, but he felt unprepared without it, so he set it back in the pack at the bottom. The kit was a small leather possibles bag that held some matches and a ferrocerium rod; some used gun-cleaning patches that were no longer damp, having absorbed the gun-cleaning oil and being covered in burnt powder residue from the inside of his guns' barrels; five cotton balls soaked in petroleum jelly that he had found in the Forestry Service camp this past summer; a flint; and two candle stubs. He always carried more than one way to start a fire. He wondered if he was being obsessive as he repacked the leather bag. He placed it in an outer pocket of the canvas pack.

Tom's red bandana was wrapped around his knife in its oiled leather sheath. He drew the knife out to check its edge; it was still razor sharp. He remembered sharpening it while waiting for the train in the station in Missoula. He set it aside to wear on his belt. He also set aside his tin canteen, covered in a fading khaki-colored canvas pouch with a similarly fading canvas strap. The stopper's chain clinked dully against the silvery metal exposed at the top near the canvas cover's metal snaps. He needed to remember to fill it before he left.

Tom unrolled the gray woolen blanket, frayed near the bottom edge from sleeping with his boots on while on fire watch on the Divide. Unrolling it freed a mixed scent of wool, campfire smoke, and pine needles from his station on his peak this past summer where he could see both sides of the geologic spine that ran from the Arctic down south to Mexico. It wasn't so much a plainly visible spine, hidden as it was by the evergreen canopy of the pines and scored by erosion, rivers, and more geologic upheavals, but Tom believed he could make it out when he relaxed his eyes to view it all, the sky and trees and mountains, in their totality. The snows had come early out along the Idaho and Montana border, covering the mountains at the higher elevations and soaking the trees, bracken, and sage grass further down.

So, his crew had packed up camp and descended the pass with the mules and horses to Lolo, where markers said that Lewis and Clark had camped twice early in the previous century. The crew had spent their last night together at a saloon in town where they ate and drank the German proprietor's homebrewed beer. Two of the older veterans, one from the service and the other from the war, sat at a table playing poker, whiskeys in front of them. Tom stood with one of the younger guys from Wyoming—college-age, like himself, who was studying geology down in Boulder. They each ordered a shot of the whiskey that the veterans were drinking to toast the end of the summer; it burned going down. The next morning, he saddled up his Forestry Service horse lent to him by the ranger for the twelve miles to Missoula. Both his and the horse's cold breath smoked in the early morning air.

Coming back from his reverie as he thought of waiting for the train in the cold morning air outside the station, Tom rolled his blanket back up. He opened his dresser drawers to get two pairs of woolen socks; woolen long johns, one gray the other a faded blue; two flannel shirts; canvas work pants; and his double-tin cloth pants, oiled to be water resistant. The pants were hot, but they were thick and good to have in the woods while swinging axes and digging. The pants were ubiquitous among the western Forestry Service crews. His boots were brown leather special-order logger boots, made in Seattle. He didn't have them his first summer out West on the Forestry Service crew, but the veterans had them, and they did much better on the slopes and crags and standing on the logs. They didn't have to worry much about something dropping or falling on the steel toes of the boots. Once he knew he was going back for a second summer, he had ordered a pair after having his mother trace each of his feet on paper and writing down seven measurements from his feet and legs to midcalf. After two summers of hard work, the soles with their hobnails still held up, and they were well broken in—comfortable enough to sleep in. They had not been inexpensive, but they were well worth the price, and he was glad to have them, especially now that it looked like he was going to be in the woods fighting fires and not watching for them.

Tom also placed his clothes and books for school into a steamer trunk, figuring that fighting the fire would take him up to and maybe even past the start of the semester. The dormitory would not be open yet; he would leave the trunk at his professor's house while he was in the woods with Greg's crew.

J. KENT GREGORY

That evening after dinner, as the setting sun turned the wooded hills to the east a fiery red and the sky beyond a pale blue veiled with a rose haze, Tom sat on the back porch with his father and mother, all three sipping on glasses of bourbon. Unlike most women Tom knew, his mother drank bourbon, usually straight if it was good. She had been born and raised in New Orleans. Although she joked that Tom's dad had stolen her out of New Orleans, she seemed to be more than happy in bourbon country. He would later find out that ladies in New Orleans preferred bourbon to anything else—another piece of the string connecting New Orleans with Kentucky. The porch looked out east, and the sky would soon darken, the line of mountains becoming a darker black-blue-green line on the horizon as the stars became more visible above the mountains' crests. The cicadas chirred in rising and falling waves of humming music, interspersed by the high-pitched chirping from the tree frogs in the grove near the pond. When he was younger at a summer camp, one of Tom's cabinmates had picked up a tree frog and thrown it to smack against the trunk of another tree. Tom had broken the boy's nose. He didn't like that camp. He never went back.

They stayed on the porch into the darkness, enjoying the night sounds, as the summer heat faded into warmth but lacking humidity and wrapped them like a blanket. Water barely beaded on Tom's glass, although the bourbon had been cooled enough by the ice cubes to do so. They talked of the fires in the Valley, and his parents asked Tom what he thought.

"The newspapers describe them as bad already, and the winds will only make them worse. Greg seemed more than a little concerned. Desperate for help, I think."

"Well, your past few summers with the Forestry Service should serve you well," his father said, ringing the ice on the sides of his glass as he swirled the drink before he took another sip.

"That's true, but remember, this will be your first one. You promise to take care of yourself and Greg," his mother said.

"Mom, I promise."

The sky was full night now, with no remnants of the dying sun by the time they went inside, rinsed their glasses in the kitchen sink, and went to bed. A steady breeze blew with the cooling of the night air. Tom opened his screenless windows that were diagonal from each other across the room. He pulled the sheet and quilt back to lie down on the bed, covering himself with their clean coolness. His bed sat in the corner between the two windows, so the breeze blew across him. He fell asleep to the night-song of cicadas and tree frogs.

The next morning, Tom was up before the sun to shower and shave. He had a long drive ahead of him across country roads through and over the wooded mountains to get to the fires in the Valley. His father was cooking thick-cut bacon in his cast-iron skillet and making pancakes when he got downstairs, while his mom was busy making sandwiches for him to eat along the road. He sat at the table, watching his parents. His mom sliced through her homemade bread with a wood-handled, serrated knife, then spread one side of a few slices with peanut butter from a jar on the swinging pantry door. Then, onto the other slices, she smoothed jam made from the huckleberries he'd brought back from his last trip out West. She wrapped the sandwiches in wax paper and placed them in a crinkling brown paper bag. She then opened a jar of whole pickles, pulled one out with a fork, and cut it into lengthwise slices. She placed them onto one slice of bread with mayonnaise already spread on it, sliced white onions over the pickles, spread braunschweiger over another piece of bread, and then closed it all together to make his dinner sandwich. Then they all three sat down to eat the bacon and pancakes that his father served up, still warm from the gas stove. Tom spread huckleberry jam on his pancakes.

Half of the sun was just above the horizon of the distant hills when Tom's truck was loaded and he was ready to get started. Thankfully, partings in his family were always brief. He placed the paper bag with his sandwiches on the aging white leather passenger seat alongside a bottle of Willett that his parents wanted him to share with Greg. He hugged each of his parents in turn, climbed in, and drove east towards the fires.

Seldom had he seen cars on the mountain highways that wound along the hollows carved out by rivers and streams flowing down off the mountains. Occasionally, there had been a farm truck loaded with hay, since harvest had already begun. It had been dry here too.

Odd, he thought to himself. *I would have thought the rains had fallen in the mountains.* In his mind, he always envisioned the mountains, especially these here in the East, as lofty islands of green, with a deep persisting wetness under the trees in the hollows.

East of Charleston, he stopped for gas at a two-pump station and general store. After the tall, silent old man in oil-stained denim coveralls had filled his truck's tank, Tom pulled his truck over to the edge of the gravel by the gray log bumpers marking the edge before the grass. He got out to stretch for the final leg of his trip and to eat the second of the peanut butter and huckleberry jam sandwiches. The dryness here in the mountains disturbed him. In the past few years that he had been crossing these mountains or venturing into them to fish, he had become familiar with the perpetual overwetness of the forests, the slick mud on the slopes through the trees down to the streams, and the white crests on the waters in the streams of the lower elevations that were fed by the smaller streams descending from their cold bubbling spring-sources. Tom had walked the mountain slopes to those streams and rivers, through the sweet pungent ferns of the understory, with the dew and water from the green growth wetting his trousers, and a copperhead or mouse scurrying away as he shambled down to the flowing waters. If all of this was now dry, how truly dry was the Valley?

The peanut butter and huckleberry sandwich tasted good and made him want another. The bread had stayed mostly fresh, the jam soaking into the drying bread layers. He wanted to eat the braunschweiger sandwich, his last for the trip, but resisted the temptation, saving it for an early evening road snack or dinner if he arrived too late in Lexington. He washed the sweet western mountain berry sandwich down with the cold, bitter dregs of the morning's coffee left in his green thermos.

He crossed the crunching white gravel parking lot to the general store, where an old man sat at the zinc counter, his overalls dusty from the light brown earth and chaff of his field. He looked up from his nearly finished pale-blue plate and nodded silently to Tom, who gently bowed his head in turn. In the aisle nearest the counter, Tom found the standard lineup of loose pipe tobacco and chose a pouch of Virginia Leaf. At the counter, he asked the old man if he could fill his thermos halfway with coffee and he would kindly pay for it. The old man softly said, "No need to pay, but I thank you," unscrewing the top of Tom's thermos and pouring the pot down inside. Tom paid for his tobacco and left the change for the man, who nodded and put the money into the register. Tom nodded too, the old man's silence catching ahold of him.

As he drove east, winding among the clefts, he climbed steadily higher through the mountains, reaching the summits, then cascaded down alongside creeks and rivers born from springs and wetness that had made it to the mountains. The downward courses of the narrow highway were steep, and gravity claimed his truck from him leaving him with nothing but the steering and brakes until he reached the bottom — always higher than the previous cleft's bottom — then a steep climb began again and repeated to the final summit that marked the border to Virginia and the last descent into the Valley.

The mountains here were different than out West. The clefts here were abrupt, as if a jagged axe had been driven into the earth. Out West, the climbs were easier and more gradual, deceptive, the rising lasting the lengths of entire states, through cornfields, and over grassy, treeless plains to the sagebrush slopes. The sage was the sign that he was back in the western mountains. Even the final climbing slopes were deceptive because he was always on horseback. It was a gradual climb with a rare descent, not a rapid racing over tree-topped heights down to dark shaded hollows then up to the final height that was like a rampart looking over farmland and fenced pastures with occasional lone treed hills or ridges.

It was true night when he got to Lexington. The clouds above were thin, feathery streaks that glowed silver-blue through the ash haze lit by the light of the moon. The stars were evanescent spots of the same silver-blue light; some, the dimmer ones, were obscured by the veil of the burnt Valley risen into the sky.

He drove through town past the military school upon the ridge looking like a castle or prison hanging over the road, and then on towards the center of town, winding beneath the grassy hill below the white columned buildings and behind the chapel to his professor's house. The streets were quiet in the evening dark, the town not yet alive, the arrival of students for the fall term's classes still some weeks away. He turned off the main street a few blocks past the pizza parlor and a corner bar, both with their lights off, to pull up in front of the white wood-frame house and veranda illuminated by lamps flanking the dark-wood front door. A light was on from inside. The smell of smoke was much thicker here, as if every family was barbecuing.

Professor White, the Ancient History and Classics professor, was on the porch swing with his wife; Greg was on a rocking chair. They all stood up and shouted their hellos, walking to the top of the steps to embrace him, their heels clomping on the century-old planks and echoing through the rising and falling susurration of the cicadas. Greg came down the brick walkway to help him unload his gear and the steamer trunk. He and Greg carried the trunk into the front hallway to place it where the tall, willowy, dark-haired Mrs. White directed them.

They returned to the porch and sat down. Tom opened the bottle of Willett and re-filled their glasses, then filling his last. He poured the bourbon onto four ice cubes and then swirled the glass to cut the alcohol the way he liked with the first slight melt off the ice. Greg took his without ice. He enjoyed the fire of the bourbon on his insides.

It was good to be back in Lexington, his second home. The place was becoming more of his first home as the years of college went by. He figured that made sense considering he lived most of the year here. The West had become more of his second home, he supposed, while Kentucky, as a home, faded as he spent less time there through the year. He spent only a few weeks there, maybe four, out of a whole year. Another thought floated to the surface as he sipped at his bourbon, that Lexington as his home would soon be fading to a home from the past when he and Greg graduated. He thought to move out West, where there were the big mountains, old forests, colder streams, and vast unpeopled country.

As fireflies floated and flashed in the front yard under the tree, the porch talk moved to the fires moving north from further down the Valley. The Whites were afraid for their friends and some of their extended family who had farms and houses near the lines of the fires. Some, near the eaves of the trees or with their homes in the forests, had fled up the Valley in cars and trucks carrying furniture and clothing and pictures, coming to stay with family or at motels in town—an island in the middle of farm and pastureland, away from the treed slopes of the mountains and the dried grasses and crops of the Valley. Dr. White's brother had a tobacco and hay farm. The fires had not gotten there yet, but embers floating through the sky had. Mostly invisible during the day, he had first seen them at night as sparks floating up high in the air and then drifting down with the winds, landing on his hay bales and igniting them into bonfires. He was worried about the tobacco drying in his barn that he had harvested early because of the dry, hot summer.

Tom mostly listened, sipping his bourbon and relaxing after the drive, rocking in his chair that creaked with the floorboards of the veranda. The relaxation became an almost-sleepy, dreamy calm. The thoughtful voice of his friend, the deep sounds of his academic father, and the occasional notes from his reserved, away-from-home mother calmed him. But, as he receded into his own thoughts, he sensed the tension along the edges, a nascent fear from Greg and the Whites. The fire was getting closer, and those who had fled their homes may have lost them already. In some places, the fire was a wall of flame climbing the mountain ridges and running along the slopes, lines illuminating the mountains' old rolling features at night; in other places on the mountain slopes and in the Valley itself, the fire became spot fires born from embers blown by the wind. Tom worried at Greg's unusual excitement, not like the calm and often carefree optimism he knew. His own eagerness to get to the woods was laced with an increasing sense of fear, something akin to, he imagined, a cold knife cutting his insides.

This eastern fire burned in what remained of an ancient forest with trees so old and tall and boles so wide that, in places, it was like walking into dark, mysterious places or Druid-like temples, but whose edges had been driven in by men making houses and clearing for farms. It was also a forest that had not seen a fire in Dr. White's memory or in his knowledge of the Valley's history. This fire was not like the fires out West, where they were occasional yet regular, burning massive swathes of mountainsides where people did not live; but those who were there, the men of the Forest Service, old veterans and young men, some college boys like himself, were used to the idea of fighting them. The western fires were fought along their edges, with the fire crews shepherding and corralling them like cattle. It was a natural strategy for these crews who were, or were sons of, ranchers. The Valley fires, however, were to be fought the way the Valley knew—like a war, by grandsons and great-grandsons of veterans of the Shenandoah Valley campaign. As Tom was gathering from the talk, word was that the fire would be fought by marching right up to and into it. He grew uneasy with that realization, knowing only of the western way, and even then, his knowledge was only learned from camp stories at dinner or when playing cribbage with those who had actually fought the fires. Still, he was eager to head south to do what he had come here for.

Later, after the Whites had gone to bed and he and Greg had gone up to their room, Tom lay awake on top of the blankets. The windows to the room were open, the night air warm and mostly still, with a rare breeze blowing inside that still smelled of summer barbecues. A firefly had been blown in on one of the breezes. Tom watched its yellow-green light flash as it crawled along the bookshelf in front of Homer's *Iliad*, the gold lettering on the black spine flashing with the insect's light.

Greg turned over on his side, propping himself up on his elbow. "Are you awake?" he asked, his hushed voice reaching across to Tom.

"Yeah, it's hard to fall asleep. I'm ready to get started."

"Me too. I want to get started, to actually see the fires. I'm glad you're here. Sorry that I guilted you into it." He laughed at that last bit.

"I'm glad you gave me a call. Would've been mad if you hadn't. Been wanting to fight a fire myself after hearing about other guys doing it the past couple of summers. And you're right, I owe you."

"Ha, you did me a favor. She turned out to be a tramp."

"Yeah. Still not my proudest moment. At least we can thank her for bringing us together," Tom said, laughing too.

"You mean, trying to get us to fight each other?"

"What do you mean, trying? I remember you slugging me and then rolling around in the sawdust on the floor."

"Yeah, but I remember the barkeep thinking we were crazy as loons for lying on the floor, laughing so hard we were crying."

"I laugh every time I think about that. What makes me laugh the most was how mad she was with us for sitting at the bar afterwards, just ignoring her." Both Tom and Greg were trying to reign in the laughter, not wanting to disturb the Whites, which only made the laughing worse.

When Greg had controlled himself a bit, he said, "I thought she was going to spit nails when she stomped out." He shook himself laughing again, wiping away tears.

Tom took out his flask and raised it. "Well, here's to pretty Margaret, the Sweetbriar girl from Biloxi!" He took a shot and then tossed the flask to Greg.

"To pretty Margaret! Those Deep South girls get me all the time."

"Hah! Me too."

Both Tom and Greg fell asleep, the unspoken fear and thoughts of the fire having receded.

The next morning the air was thick with falling ash, almost like heavy gray, dusty snowflakes, and the sky was a blackening gray, with winds blowing northeastward, streaking the puffed ash cloud billows on their edges and undersides. The barbecue smell was fading, being overcome by the bitter tang of burnt-over coals.

"Like Vesuvius, I imagine," Dr. White said from the porch where they were standing, eating buckwheat pancakes folded up with peanut butter and jelly to make a coarse, rushed breakfast.

"Or Hades," replied Tom. He took a drink of his coffee.

Washing down the last bit of his pancake sandwich with the rich coffee sweetened with condensed milk, the way the Whites knew he liked it, Greg said, "We should get going to the courthouse. I can hear a buzz growing from that direction."

"You two gather your gear, and I'll help the missus back in the kitchen. We've got some food to send along with you," Dr. White said as he tossed the dregs of his coffee over the banister onto the azaleas and grass.

Greg went upstairs to retrieve his backpack from the floor beside the bed he had slept on, treading gently over the Whites' oriental carpets and hardwood floors, taking extra care in his hard-soled boots. Tom's gear was still in the back of his pickup, so he waited on the porch, looking up at the ashy sky while Greg was inside. Tom did not like this morning's burnt smell at all; there was an unnaturalness to it, an almost chemical quality, from wood burnt and then its coal ash burnt again. This fire was a hot forge fire, blown to a white heat in its center by the winds blowing up the Valley.

Greg, comically, soft-stepped downstairs and out onto the veranda. Mrs. White glided outside with two large blue-and-white calico cloths tied at their four corners into heavy, bulging bundles. Dr. White followed behind with the young men's two canteens slung over his shoulder, their faded cotton covers dark with wetness.

In her soft voice, gentle, musical, the accent from Savannah, Mrs. White said, "We made some sandwiches for you two and put in a couple cans of soup, some buckwheat pancake mix, some cookies, a little bit of smoked bacon and sausage, and some coffee. God knows how long y'all will be out there and what they'll give you to eat. I'm afraid they might rush y'all out there to the fires without thinking about supplies. We can't let that happen to you sweet young men."

Tom and Greg took their sacks, and Mrs. White hugged both in turn, kissing them each on the cheek. Tom felt his face warming and saw that Greg was blushing too, having an "aw-shucks" look about him, his eyes looking down to the veranda's floorboards.

Dr. White handed over their canteens. "Gentlemen, here's your water. It's going to be thirsty work once you set to it."

"Thank you, Professor and Mrs. White, for all this, and for letting us stay the night," Tom said, shyly rushing it out.

"Yessir and yes, ma'am. We're indebted to y'all. Hope to be back here in a few days," Greg said, turning the brim of his worn canvas hat in his hands.

"I can see that you gents are anxious to get along. You watch yourselves," said Dr. White, shaking their hands.

Mrs. White hugged them again and said, "You watch out for each other."

"Yes, ma'am."

They walked down the path to Tom's truck, where he lifted his pack out of the bed, stowing his calico bundle inside and securing his spade in its spot on the back. He double-checked that his father's axe was safe where he had strapped it on the side and then shouldered his pack. They turned to wave another goodbye to the Whites as they stepped into the street to walk to the courthouse and the growing noise.

"You boys remember to take care of each other!" Mrs. White shouted to them, waving her arm and hand above her head. She was not smiling. Tom and Greg turned to wave back, then marched off.

Tom hated how long goodbyes made him anxious. It was hard to know when and how to end them. It was good to be heading to the job to be done, to the reason why he had made the drive.

Greg slapped him on the back. "The Whites sure did set us up, all right. I figure we've got enough to last us a few days. Boy, it's heavy, but I'm glad to be carrying it."

"Yes, indeed! We're in good shape as far as food supplies go. Hell, Mrs. White even snuck in a can of sweetened condensed milk."

"Talk about living high on the hog. With that and the bourbon, we're gonna be the kings of the camp!"

"That's the truth," said Tom, the excitement of the adventure growing, but tempered by a hidden, as if buried and so lightly felt, fear of being thrown into a fight with this fire that was raging in the Valley, its angry heat coming north and closer to them with each moment. He wondered, not for the last time, whether he had bitten off more than he could chew.

They turned right around the corner of Nelson Street, going up the hill past the painted red-brick stores and café, and then turned left on Main Street into the crowd whose humming and occasional shouts they had heard on their walk from the Whites'. There was a mix of folks, mostly families coming with their sons, brothers, and husbands to see them off to fight the fire. There was a festival-like atmosphere to the gathering, except among a few faces—mostly the older men, who Tom figured were veterans of the war or people who had already lost something to the fire. The younger men were high-school and college age, their faces filled with the light of eagerness and excitement. Tom and Greg waded through the crowd, dodging bodies with a few "Pardon me-s" and "Howdy, fellas" traded back and forth, while little kids ran through the forest-like clumps of bodies and occasional men standing alone.

They climbed up the slope of the lawn above Main Street that formed the square green in front of the courthouse's white colonnade, where a long white table had been set up. Sitting on brown folding campaign chairs behind the table were uniformed

J. KENT GREGORY

men, each in some combination of khaki and green, taking down the names of the men and not-quite-men lined up in front of the table. There was a gentleman from the regular Army with stripes on his shoulder talking to another figure in army khaki, and there were two men in the green of the Forestry Service.

Tom and Greg waited in line, listening to the conversations around them. Greg introduced himself and Tom to an older man standing in line behind them.

"Glad to meet you. I'm from out near Kiger's Hill along the Buffalo."

"How are things out your way?" Greg asked.

"No fires yet, just ash falling every now and then. My pastures are drier than I've ever seen, though. I'm worried if sparks come falling."

"Whose looking after your land?"

"I left my two boys there with the missus to watch over the cattle and things. They'll do OK, and I don't expect to be gone more than a couple of days. I figured there wasn't much else I could do there to protect my land, so I thought I'd join the fight and do something other than wait and pray."

When they got up to the table, one of the Forestry Service men in a worn green shirt stood up with a smile.

"Greg!" he exclaimed, stretching his hand across the table to shake Greg's. "I'm glad to see you! Your crew is pretty much assembled, just waiting on a few others and then we'll send you off. Is this your friend from out West?"

"In the flesh!" Greg smiled at the older man. "Fresh in town as of late last night. He's eager to get started. Brought his gear with him too."

"It's sure fine to meet you. Name's Morgan," the man said, reaching to shake Tom's hand.

Tom shook his strong, calloused hand back.

"It's great to have another Forestry Service gent' with us, especially one with experience."

Tom looked at Greg. "Well, sir, I don't know about my experience. Mostly, it's been watching for fires and doing trail work, and a little bit of logging."

"You'll be good for us. You know what to look for, and your logging will come in handy. Plus, I reckon that you've been around fire-fighting veterans."

"Yes, sir, that's true. There were a couple veterans from the fires last year who had some stories to tell."

"That counts for something, and it's certainly more than what most of those you see around here have," Morgan said with a smile and a glance at the tall slender man in khaki standing nearest them.

"What's that you say, Morgan?" the man asked.

Ignoring the question, but with a wink to Greg and Tom, Morgan said, "Rob, let me introduce you to Greg and Tom. Y'all, this is Lieutenant Morris from the Army. As y'all can see, this will be a joint effort between Forestry and the Army."

The young men shook hands with Lieutenant Morris. They both had the uncomfortable impression that they were being appraised, their usefulness being weighed by the man in khaki.

"Have they been assigned a platoon?" Morris said.

"Rob, we call it a crew in Forestry. And yes, they have been assigned. Greg helped organize the main part of one, so he'll head that up, and Tom, here, with his western experience, will make a mighty-fine second." Greg smiled, and Tom turned to stare fixedly at him, mouthing *What?* at his friend, though he tried to hide that from the two older men, especially Morris.

"Are you sure that they can handle it? They seem awful green to me."

"Don't you worry about them, Rob. I picked them and their crew, so they're my responsibility, and I stand by them and my decision."

"Well ..." Morris didn't like it. Tom and Greg, could tell.

"I'm going to take them down to their truck and introduce them to their crew," Morgan said. "I'll let you handle things here."

Morgan led them around the corner onto Washington Street, where they could see a line of drab green army trucks with men and boys milling around the rear sides. He stopped at the alley of Randolph Street, just inside the red brick corner of the closed-for-today attorney's office. He took his hat off and wiped at the sweat on his forehead with his blue bandana.

"OK, boys, there are some things we need to talk about before you take charge of your crew."

"Yes, sir," they both said. Tom didn't know about Greg, but he was a little uneasy about what Morgan was going to say. Strangely, he was excited as well.

"The regular Army fellas aren't so bad. They're trying to do their best to deal with the fire emergency, but they're doing it in the only way they know how, and they don't know hardly the first thing about the mountains and trees and fighting natural fire."

"What do you mean?" Greg asked. Tom knew by his friend's tone that he was bothered and excited too.

"I'll explain. We partnered with the Army because they had the trucks and drivers and equipment we needed. We need their logistical know-how and supplies to contain and stop the fires popping up across the Valley. As is natural, they want to be in charge of those trucks and supplies, meaning they would dictate where they go and how they're used, which also means directing the fighting."

"I suppose that seems fair enough," Greg said wryly, with a hint of doubt.

"I think I know what you're getting at," Tom added. "They want to be in charge and fight this like a battle, a war, which I suppose it is, in a way."

"You're right," Morgan nodded, wiping his forehead again. "But it's not their kind of war, and their tactics are all wrong. Hell, their tactics are questionable in their wars, as some of us know well." He sighed.

"They, like ol' Rob back there, want to throw men and boys at the biggest, hottest fires and let them figure it out as best they can with whatever tools they have. I tell y'all what, I'll be damned if I'm going to let my men and boys be risked like that." He paused. "Shoot, we all know it's dangerous as hell."

Tom and Greg nodded. Tom was losing the excitement he had felt to be part of this adventure. He grasped now, with this sweaty, serious older man talking to them frankly, that this was a no-nonsense, maybe deadly business, and that he was second-in-command with responsibilities that he hadn't guessed at, and couldn't. This was not what he'd thought he was getting into two days ago in his father's study back in Kentucky.

"I'm not going to let them risk people like that," Morgan repeated. "And as much as they would like to be, they're not directing this operation. Forestry is."

Tom and Greg were silent.

"So, here's what we've got. Greg, you did a good job of putting together a good beginning of a crew with Tom here, and the two fellas who'll be going to your college. I've supplemented it with volunteers who have come in—mostly younger fellas from the farms and small towns. Other guys from Forestry have done the same with their crews. I'm sending y'all south around the James, near Buchanan, to fight the spot fires, which, thank the Lord, is all we have down there right now. This way, y'all and your crew will learn how to fight fires, and you'll learn how to run a crew. Also, hopefully everybody will learn to work as a team. Do you follow?"

"Yes, sir."

"Good. Now, my advice to you is to go introduce yourselves to your crew and then go over there"—he gestured to his side across Washington Street—"and get as many supplies as you can. Your guys should be on or milling around Truck 6. Get some of them to help you out with the supplies. Y'all take care."

"Yes, sir." They shook hands with Morgan and went across and down the street to Truck 6.

Tom and Greg introduced themselves to their crew—eleven of them besides themselves. Everybody was dressed in jeans or heavy khaki duck canvas and brown leather boots. Tom was hot and sweaty in his double-tin pants and loggers. Leaning against the side of the truck and speaking with the driver was Sam, who looked to be about Tom's and Greg's age, maybe a little older. He was there with his nephew, a red-haired, freckled fellow named Jesse, who stood next to him, partly listening in, but mostly looking about at the activity. Two clean-shaven guys in obviously new, fresh-pressed shirts, Matt and Howard, would be freshmen at the college this fall. They both shook Greg's hand, thanking him for picking them. They knew Greg from their hometown, just outside Richmond. Two others standing in the back of the truck, Phil and Mike, lived over by House Mountain and worked at the sawmill on the Maury River. They were both tow-headed blonds; Phil was short and spoke with a slow drawl, and Mike was tall and lanky and talked in a rapid series of questions about where they were from and what his job would be. Sitting on the tailgate was Kevin, who came from his family's farm on Irish Creek. Dave had come over the previous morning from Buena Vista, where his parents worked at the girls' finishing school. Tom saw that Dave was nervous, shifting from one foot to another. Sam gave him a cigarette, which calmed him down, maybe from just having something else to do. Sam winked at Greg and Tom. Another crewmate, Peter, was going to be a first-year at the military school.

"How did you end up with us, Pete, and not the Army crews?" Greg asked.

"I don't know, sir. I guess that they didn't want me?" the short, fresh-faced, crew-cut Peter answered, his tone implying more a question than a statement.

"Well, we're awful glad to have you with us, and don't you be calling me *sir*. We're not the Army here. My name's Greg."

"Yes, sir ... I mean ... Greg. Thank you!" Peter stammered, smiling as he shook Greg's hand and then Tom's.

Tom wondered if Morgan had put Peter with them because he didn't want the young guy to be thrown into the fires by the Army.

They took Peter and two tall brothers, Mark and Steve, along with them. The brothers had come down to Lexington from their family's cattle farm in the grassy rolling hills outside of Staunton. Greg did a good job of making sure that their crew was equipped. Most everyone had canteens or some sort of water flasks hanging from their shoulders, and Greg made sure that most everyone had two. He scavenged through the piles and stacks of equipment to get shovels for those who hadn't brought their own, enough Pulaskis and axes to go around, and a large saw that Tom delegated to the two brothers, who looked like they wouldn't have a problem carrying and using it. Tom knew that they were going to be felling trees.

When the five of them got back to the truck, and while Greg was distributing the gear, Tom spoke with the driver, an older, gray-bearded gentleman with a drooping mustache, a veteran of the war. He had come down from Staunton the day before with the two brothers. He introduced himself as Brocky.

"South to the James, right?" Brocky asked.

"Yes, sir, to the James, outside Buchanan. The first six of the trucks from Lexington are heading to spots down that way. The rest, I don't know where they're going. East or west, where the fires are getting thicker, I suppose, but I'm just guessing. Haven't heard anything for sure."

Part of Tom wanted to go to those thicker fires with the other trucks.

As he climbed down from the cab, a young boy, maybe sixteen or seventeen, but maybe younger, came running, clomping down the street. He stopped at the rear of the truck, panting and trying to catch his breath. He gasped out to both Greg and Tom, not knowing for sure who to speak to, "Morgan sent me to join the crew of Truck 6 and to introduce myself to Greg and Tom. My name is Henry."

"You found us," Greg said, smiling and shaking the boy's hand. "I'm Greg, and this is Tom. We're glad to have you, especially now, with you along, that we add up to fourteen and not unlucky thirteen!" Greg laughed, and there were chuckles from the rest of the fellas sitting on the benches. "Morgan has sure set us up with a good crew. Catch your breath and climb on up with the rest of us. We're about to move out."

With help from Greg, the boy, Henry, climbed up the back of the truck, and Tom caught the look and wry smile, but with real humor, that Greg flashed to him. Tom climbed up after them under the musty-smelling canvas covering the back of the truck. The last spot on the benches running the sides of the truck had been saved for Henry and Greg, so Tom remained standing to keep the canvas open and let more air in. It was already hot underneath it, with the humidity from their sweating bodies quickly building up to fill the enclosed cave-like truck bed. The responsibility of watching out for and helping Greg with these mostly young men and boys sure was something. Something that he wasn't so sure about. Oh well, he thought, here he was.

Tom took a deep breath and swung back inside, and Greg spoke to the crew. "All right fellas, Tom here confirmed that we're heading south to the James, around Buchanan, and then up to the slopes. We figure on hitting our portion of the fire right away and trying to pin it between the river and the slopes. Get ready to cut some trees and dig some trenches."

The truck's engine shortly clanged and wheezed and then throttled to life, shaking the entire chassis and sending a plume of black diesel soot up out of its stack that quickly dissipated in the swirling winds. Tom unfolded the topo map that the Forestry Service guys in the supply area had given them to study more what he should do with the crew. He knew the area to get to and what the—rather, his—job was, but he figured that the fire wouldn't be where they said it would by the time the truck got there.

The fire was, in reality, a series of fires spread throughout the Valley, not just one wall of flame blowing north over the wooded slopes of the old mountains and sweeping up over the rolling, trough-like plain between the western and eastern slopes where men had died decades before. Instead, the fire had sent its flaming, glowing embers to fly into dry valleys or to drift down onto dried leaves and copper-colored pine needles of wooded understories where new bonfires were lit, some joining with each other into larger conflagrations. The sky and upper air became darker the closer the crew got to their spot on the map, and the burning, cooking smell grew stronger, too—a bitter, dangerous scent bringing with it a current of fear. It no longer reminded Tom of a barbecue.

The truck rumbled and shook over the old bridge across the James near Buchanan. The river was dried to a wan tendril, withdrawn from its banks, leaving dead and rotting fish caught in the shallows when the water had receded too quickly to escape.

Skeletal trees and branches long submerged now lay exposed to the burning air, furnace-like now in its smell and heat as the crew in the back of the truck closed in on the fires.

The truck deposited them at the mouth of a cleft between two arms of a low mountain near the old banks of the river. Sam and his nephew, Jesse, followed by Matt and Howard, the two incoming freshmen, went down to look at the dried riverbed, curious to see what had once been hidden by the moving waters and that now lay exposed. Tom looked along the floodplains of the James, some of which were fields full of sickly-looking dried cornstalks with the desiccated cobs rustling in the wind and up to the yellowed, rolling hayfields above the corn. The fields stretched up some of the lower arms and ridges of the old mountains—hills, they seemed, compared with what he had recently left out West. The fields were dotted with hay bales rolled and ready to be hauled away.

He looked over the cleft and the mountain, just like he had learned to look for out West, spotting what he thought might be a wisp of blue-gray smoke on the southern slopes. He took off his canvas pack and opened the top flap to draw out his black binoculars. He scanned the northern slopes and ridges with them, not seeing any signs of fire. He turned to the southern slope to search for the smoke he thought he had seen. It wasn't there at first, but he knew from his time out West not to give up and to keep scanning. Young fires, no more than smolderings in the dried, fallen leaves, could be like ghosts, Tom knew, there and then vanishing, elusive and coquettish.

Tom kept scanning and then he found it, a small grayness, like a blurring haze, caught and held by the overhanging branches and leaves of the oaks. It was a flickering of yellow light on the underside of the grayness that had caught his eye. He held the binoculars as steady as he could to make sure and then saw it again. He dropped the binoculars to mark the spot on the slope. He called Greg and the crew over, all of them clomping down from the truck or up the bank from the stream bed in their heavy leather boots. Greg stood at his left side; Tom passed the binoculars to him, pointing up to the spot on the slope where he had seen the grayness flashing.

"I saw it there on the southern slope, a little over halfway up, maybe two-thirds." Tom pointed to the spot. "The smoke was held down by the leaves and branches."

Greg pulled a blue cotton bandana from his rear pocket and wiped at the sweat and dirty ash that had grimed his stubbled face. He put the binoculars up to his eyes, twisting the lenses to bring the trees into as sharp a focus as possible. "What am I looking for? How do I get there?" he asked.

"Do you see the lightning-scarred tree on the ridgeline?" Tom asked.

"Yep, I've got it."

"Ok, go straight down from that until you find a limestone outcrop."

"Ok, I've got that. Looks like a big limestone block with a V-shaped notch in its face."

"Yeah, that's the one. Now, scan down towards four o'clock, about a hundred yards, 'til you get to a stand of oaks that are a little greener than the ones around them. At least they look a little greener … maybe it's just a shadow."

"All right, I think I'm there … I'm not seeing anything yet … Oh wait, there's some grayness up in there, almost looks like a haze or a thin fog?"

"Yep, you've got it. Keep watching that haze. I think it's smoke."

"OK." There was a long pause. The crew clustered around Greg and Tom closely, but gave them some space, looking back and forth at Tom and Greg, Tom's sweating, grimy forehead creased in a straining gaze, and Greg standing motionless, his eyes hidden by the black binoculars. There was an expectation, a thrill mingled and heightened by a barely felt fear building among the crew who were anxious to get on the job, to fight a fire. Greg lowered the lenses to wipe the sweat from his forehead and eyes, his eyes stinging from the dirt and salt. He raised the binoculars up again.

"I see it now. A flickering, kind of like lightning … Yep, you're right. There's a fire up there."

The crew arranged their camping gear and food in an orderly line near the truck and opened their canvas packs to remove everything but the necessaries—fire-proof blankets, some odds-and-ends tools. The air was hot and the march would be uphill. They needed to move quickly before the fire changed. They slung their canteens across their shoulders or attached them to their army-drab canvas belts and picked up the real gear needed to fight the fire—saws, axes, Pulaskis, spades. Tom thought about the heavy, steep hiking they had ahead of them to get to the fire. He, like most of the crew, tied his helmet onto a loop on his pack. Tom mused that this adventure, as Greg had named it what seemed like an age ago but was only two days, might mature this crew of young men and boys some before the end.

After reporting to Brocky, who remained in the truck cab, what their plans were, Greg called out "All right, let's get that fire," and the crew set off in a bunched crowd, shambling towards the lower slopes. Sweat stained their shirts, first wetting and then cooling and then chafing their backs underneath the packs. The dried ground crunched underneath their boots. Tom was thankful for his loggers, especially as the slope steepened. They weren't cheap, but, boy, were they worth it, especially on the ankles.

Some griped that they couldn't smoke, which earned them some slightly annoyed responses: "Aw, shut your mouth. Ain't there enough smoke for you already?" and "Well, now, you wanna burn yourself up like them trees?" Tom and Greg laughed along with the others, each having a vague yearning to light up a cigarette or pipe, but that yearning diminished as the slope got steeper, the air hotter, and the burning smell stronger and inescapable.

As the path they took became steeper, the crew fell into single file like a mule string. They followed a game trail through the understory, well-traveled by deer whose hooves had left faint impressions on the hard earth, leaves from the trees above knocked away or become dust, and the plants eaten or trodden into the dirt. The hardened, lifeless path made the walking easier. Tom and Greg talked about how this might make fighting the fire easier, as the ground would be simpler to clear with their tools—as would back-burning—but the dry, crunching leaves and forest debris were a danger too. *The fickleness of fire*, thought Tom. He had heard that often out West from fire veterans who knew.

The plan was to climb the slope until they were just below the level where they had seen the smoke and then turn to their left until they found the fire. They had also figured that their best bet would be to corral the fire up against the limestone outcrop, where they would let it burn itself out. It was going to take the crew about an hour to get to the fire, or, at least, where they had last seen it before beginning their tool-clanking trudge up the mountain.

"Unless it crowns," Greg said out loud, sucking in the dry, hot, smoky air. He had been thinking the same thing as Tom.

"Yeah, unless it crowns." Tom exhaled, finding it hard to breathe too. "I guess we'll have to drop any trees that look like they might crown." Tom had heard stories about firefighters in the western mountains who had been surprised by or fought fires that had crowned. Most of the stories ended with men running like hell; two ended with men surrounded by an inescapable inferno.

Henry, the farm boy from the Valley who was coming up just behind them and had been listening in on their talk, panted in what Tom thought of as the 'Shenandoah lilt', "That doesn't seem right, felling trees. Seems like we'd be doing the fire's job for it."

With a gleam in his eye, Greg stopped and said, "Son …"

Greg's gonna have some fun here, thought Tom.

"Well, first, we fell a little to save a lot," Greg said.

"That still doesn't make sense," said the farm boy, taking his helmet off and scratching, mopping his soaken head, while leaning on his big Maine-wedge axe.

More breathless than he thought he'd be, Tom added, "To keep it from spreading. If the fire's in the tree, it'll leap from one tree to the next."

"Oh," Henry said.

"And second," continued Greg, "a fire's a *she* not a *him* or an *it*."

"What do you mean, a *she?*"

"Well, tell me, do you have a sweetheart?"

"Yes," said the boy, not knowing where this was heading. Tom did and enjoyed the break.

"I'm gonna guess she's your first?"

"Yes, and I don't plan on having another."

"Oh, I see," said Greg, acting wise. "So, you're gonna marry her?"

"Yes, indeed."

"Well, then." Greg paused. "Have you ever fought a fire?"

"No, but what does that have to do with having a sweetheart?"

"Well, son, you're gonna have to learn that by yourself." Greg took a swing from his canteen, the chain rattling against the metal side, and turned back to march up the slope.

Tom barked a laugh, smiled at the farm boy, and slapped him on the back. He hadn't fought a fire himself, and Greg had only been on smaller ones, nothing more than brush fires. They would all be learning. He turned, took a deep, burning breath, and followed Greg up the slope. Henry was perplexed, not knowing what they meant and wondering whether they were fooling around with him or whether to be mad that he had been called *son*. He decided he was already too tired and too hot to care, so, with a heavy sigh, thinking of what they might find ahead, he turned up the slope to follow them.

The hike up was hard, sapping Tom's energy as well as that of the rest of the crew. He was thankful that Sam was holding up well, as were the two brothers, Steve and Mark, though they were carrying their big, bowing crosscut saw. Some of the younger ones—Dave from BV, and Howard, the incoming college freshman—seemed to be lagging. Howard's friend, Matt, had an eye on him; Tom slowed Peter, nodding back to Dave. Peter understood. It was really the heat and the burning air, no moisture in it, just smoke and a taste of what Tom imagined brimstone would be like, a taste that blanketed his tongue from sucking in gulps of air. That they didn't stop for breaks didn't help either; but they were all eager to get to the fire.

Eventually, they got far enough up the slope that they figured they were roughly level with the spot where Tom had seen the smoke in the trees. The crew stopped. The game trail continued upwards, probably to the top of the ridge and over, Tom thought, letting his eyes follow the trail that meandered around trees and boulders that had broken off the mountain ages ago. These boulders were usually splotched in deep green moss and lichens, even in the late summer, the boulders' limestone holding the coolness of the old mountains and shading, protecting, the wet ground. Tom recalled a frost flower north of here, near the summit of Kiger's Hill. It was a magical thing, looking like a rose made of ice, having grown up through the moldering leaves that covered the forest floor at the base of an old rock, like the rocks here.

Strangely, and with the strangeness came a growing fear, the moss and lichens were absent or dead, their dried, almost burnt selves gone or flaking from the boulder's hot surface like ash. They were dead and gone. He noticed ferns, their leaves curled and brown at the edges, and rhododendron bushes, their green wax-like shine

J. KENT GREGORY

gone, with leaves drooping sickly or that had already fallen. He pointed the boulders and the dying plants out to Greg.

Greg took a deep breath of the smoky air, coughing out a sigh. "It's not just that they're dying, but the moisture has been sucked and dried out."

"One spark, floating down …"

"Yeah, let's get to our fire."

Tom took a drink from his canteen, shouldered his axe, and followed Greg down a smaller path to their left that ran along a little edge that ran parallel to the ridge top. The rest of the crew took up their gear too—spades, axes, and crosscut saw. With a few groans and a clanking of their metal tools, they shuffled down the path in single file. The path was level, and they were all grateful for it. It was narrow, but trodden flat, unlike the trek up, so a little extra care was needed to avoid twisting an ankle or slipping.

The crew was nearing the spot, and the eagerness and fear built up within them. In most, the fear was lessened by the heat and fatigue and a thrilling in their stomachs to meet their up-till-now invisible quarry and to get the job done. There was a curiosity too. What would the fire look like? Would it be flames licking and climbing up the rough bark of the tree trunks, orange and red ribbons burning along the forest floor, or just smolderings in dense undergrowth? Would it be a wall of fire, where trees had crowned since they began the hike up? Tom's curiosity had an edge of fear to it. He was eager to see what the fire had become over the past almost hour, a fire that he had known only as far-off smoke held under leafy tree limbs. He thought he knew what he would need to do, no matter what he saw, but he wasn't sure.

Some minutes later, with Greg in the lead and Tom just behind—followed by the farm boy, Henry, and then the winding line of the crew—through the odor of their salted, tangy sweat and the musty scent of their cotton packs, they smelled it. When they stopped, strung along the path, the crew heard it. The smell that they walked into was as if someone was burning a leaf pile raked from a yard and old stumps pulled from a field. They were motionless and silent, their tools resting quietly on their shoulders. Then they heard it. Ahead of them there was a hissing and popping, like a campfire, and a rushing sound, like a distant train or a wind through the trees, although there was little wind on this slope.

"We found the fire!" Greg said, a giddiness and eagerness in his smiling eyes. "Let's get started."

Tom turned, smiling too, glad that he had found that smoke and had figured correctly what it was down below. He cupped his hands around his mouth to yell back at the crew. "Gents, we've found our fire. Come on up!" There was excitement in his voice.

The crew trotted up to Greg, Tom, and Henry, clustering in around the three, anticipation and some fear in their eyes too.

"Ok, well, I'm sure y'all smell it too, and it's just ahead. Let's have our tools at the ready, because I don't know what exactly we'll see. I figure I'll go with y'all with the axes and saws to do any felling that needs to be done, if any at all. Tom, would you take the spades and Pulaskis to clear any brush and make us an escape route, should we need it?"

"You got it," Tom said.

"All right, fellas, let's get it."

Within forty yards, they came up to a burnt-over area with some embers still glowing orange and sending up thin, ribbon-like plumes of blue-gray smoke. Henry, Kevin, and Mike stepped off the path and began stomping the embers out, their heavy boots sending up small puffs of ash as they clomped down on the ground.

"Hey, y'all," Tom called to them, continuing to almost double-time it in his steps. "Don't mind this area. It's done. We need to get to the real fire." The three hurried back into the line marching ahead.

And then, there it was: ribbons of fire that seemed to be burning slowly, almost imperceptibly, up the slope, broadening their reach, leaving ash and embers on the burnt-over ground and burning long-fallen trees. Some of the ribbons were orange flames, translucent even, rising almost as tall as Tom; others licked at the rough bark on the bases of standing pines and oaks. It was hotter in this burning; the smoke that was held under the foliage made it hard to breathe and was painful, stinging their eyes.

They did not rest, but split into three groups. The axes and saws went with Greg up the slope to turn right, above the flames, to search for any trees that needed to be felled. Tom followed with a group that he split into two; half went with him to dig a trench and fire line above the ribbons moving upslope, and the other half halted rearwards to clear an escape path in case the fire blazed up to catch them. Henry, went with Phil, Mike, Kevin, and Dave to put out the burning fallen logs and the flames dancing around the bases of trees.

It took all afternoon and well into the evening to contain the fire and then let it burn out. The day spent fighting this fire was long, hot, and dry, without the passing respite of any hint of humidity. Fear was forgotten in the heavy repetition of digging, scraping, and sawing. Tom and Greg called regular water and food breaks, not wanting the young men to be so spent that they struggled down the mountain later. Henry was a good captain, organizing his crew and keeping them at it. He learned to make them take breaks. Tom noticed that Henry worked hard at those trees, particularly the ones whose bark was charring or burning. He wanted to save them from the fire and the saw.

As dusk settled, any remaining glowing embers and coals could easily be seen in the growing darkness, and the crew set to breaking them apart and shoveling dirt and ash over them, not wanting the job that they had done - this mountainside that they had saved - to burn again. As physically drained as the crew was, the idea of climbing the same slope again would be a victory stolen, their straining and sweating wasted. While they rested, before beginning the trek back down, powdered, gray ash floated in the air, landing on their faces and clothes, where it became black and then smeared by sweat.

As best as Tom could tell, they had put out the fire. It had been orderly and predictable. Other than a few light burns and ashy exhaustion, they were fine. From his knowledge of the western forests, he knew this was a small one; still, in his fatigue, he was happy with the job that they had done. Greg took the lead as the crew finally set off down the unneeded escape route. There were only the sounds of tired boots shuffling and tools clinking against canteens and helmets as they descended.

That evening in the dark, the stars and moon blocked by ash clouds, they made camp on the silent former floodplain by the almost dead river. While, by the light of two lanterns, Tom, Henry, and the rest of the crew separated their personal gear from the musty canvas army tents that had been given to them that morning in Lexington, Greg filled his canteen, using a silvery, dented tin funnel from one of the two jerrycans that the truck had left by the pile of their camping gear. He took a swig and thought to himself that there was a faint, maybe not even there, hint of gas. He was thirsty enough not to care. Tired too. He was glad to have gotten the job done and was proud of it, but he was tired and dirty. Ash was in his mouth. He took another drink but spit most of it out to get rid of the ash. He moved a little way off and sat down on a sandy, dusty log to use the portable radio phone in its faded green canvas case to make his report.

Tom could hear the tinny, military voice speaking to Greg as he held the large black phone against his head but could not make out the words. He and the rest of the crew took turns filling their

J. KENT GREGORY

canteens, each one parched and cautiously, miserly, not wanting to spill, poured the clear water swirling down the funnel into their canteens. They were quiet, tired from the hiking and the fire, some happy to be down off the mountain. Tom had liked it up in the burning woods. There was life there, even if much of the life was the dancing, threatening fire. Here at the river was stillness, death-like in the dryness and heat. He didn't know why, but as he caught his breath and took another drink from his canteen, he thought of a woman dancing the flamenco in a red dress.

Greg dropped the plastic phone headset down into its slot in its canvas case and walked over to the water station. Tom handed him his canteen, and Greg took a slow drink, mindful not to guzzle.

"Thanks," he nodded. "Lexington headquarters congratulated us on our work today and told us to 'hold our position' for now."

Tom laughed at the military language. That's what you got back here in the East with the Forestry Service teaming up with the Army, he supposed. They had seen some of it earlier that morning in town with Morgan. God, it had been a long day.

"Lex said to keep a lookout and to call back tomorrow morning, first thing, so let's get camp set up and have dinner. No campfire."

Well, Tom thought, *that part was pretty obvious,* but he supposed it had to be said in case someone wasn't thinking. The ground here had become so dry that the grass was the color of cut-and-bailed hay, the bushes were shriveled, and the trees had begun dropping leaves that were curled and browned like tobacco cigar wrappers—not the vibrant reds, oranges, and soft yellows they should have been two months later. He didn't like the movie-like image that developed in his mind, of being caught in the middle of a surprise blaze here in what had been a deep, blue river's overgrown green bottomland. Their noses were filled with the smoke and burning of the fire on the mountainside, but the dry rot of the riverbed crept in too, as did the burnt-over charcoal of the Valley burning hot.

No one from the crew grumbled about not having a fire, although Henry and Tom spoke yearningly yet calmly about needing a cup, at least, of thick black coffee.

"Yeah, I agree, a cup of coffee tomorrow morning sounds nice. I'll need some perking up after today," drawled Tom exhaustedly, leaning back on his pack.

"No, sir, not now. It's too hot around here, although I reckon my tired bones would appreciate the jolt," said Henry as he peeled back the tin top of his C-ration.

"I like mine the way my mom makes it," Henry continued between forks of turkey from his dark-gray tin ration can. "She scoops a heaping spoonful of the grounds into the bottom of the pot and fills the pot up with water, then sets it to almost boil. That's what I like. The pot is my grandmother's. She made it the same way."

"My mom makes hers the way they do down in New Orleans," Tom said. "She takes a bag of ground coffee and steeps it in cold water overnight. Comes out dark and rich, not bitter. It's thick and strong. Then she heats milk over the stove with a vanilla bean in it and mixes the milk and coffee together with some sugar."

"I bet that sure is good. It seems like a lot of work for a cup of coffee."

Tom chuckled. "It is, which I guess explains why I don't often fix it that way myself."

Greg had walked over to their spot after helping set up a tent and crouched down on his heels. "You two and your coffees. The best is Turkish coffee—dark-roasted beans ground to dust, and hot water poured over them. Then you add the sugar. It's basically the Mediterranean version of Henry's old-fashioned way. When you're done with your cup, you reuse the grounds, they are that strong."

"When did you have it?" Henry asked.

"I was traveling there last summer, doing some digging."

"Oh." The farm boy didn't know what else to say.

"Well, what's the plan for tonight and tomorrow?" Tom asked.

"Sit tight for now and get as much sleep as we can. Headquarters didn't say as much, but I'm pretty sure that we'll be moving early tomorrow. I gathered that the fires became worse north and west of here. Seems like more of the fires have jumped across the Valley. I guess we held the fire here, and these slopes shouldn't burn anymore, as there's nothing much burning south of us."

Tom had finished his C-ration and set the tin aside, while Greg finished his. Henry was already finished and was studying the two older ones. Tom sat up and drug his pack around to undo the leather straps securing the top. He reached in to pull out the bottle of Willett, wrapped in a khaki duck-canvas shirt.

"Well then, I suppose now's a good time to share some of this."

"I love your parents," Greg said.

They each poured a splash into their tin cups, the initial smoothness of the bourbon becoming a burning warmth as it passed down their throats and seeming to spread in their chests.

"That is good stuff," Greg sighed.

"It sure is. Almost a little too much for me after today," Tom said, looking back up the mountain, a blackness against the night sky that was filled with white pricks of stars. He held his breath as he scanned for glowing reds and oranges on the slopes and was glad that there were none.

"Henry, boy, have some of this from Kentucky," Greg called as he took the bottle from Tom.

"Are you sure?"

"Sure as sure. Have some. You earned it doing the job you did up there in the woods."

"Thanks. I was just doing what I was supposed to." Henry held out his cup then took a small sip, enough to enjoy. "I like it. Tastes a bit like caramel and a little smoke. Smooth, but not as smooth as my pa's."

"Your dad makes his own whiskey?"

"Yes, sir. He's got a setup by this spring that flows from a tiny outcrop in the woods behind our field."

"Well, well, well. That is something."

The crew gathered around after setting up tents or choosing a place to just bivouac. Most gladly accepted the shot-size pour that Tom put into their tin cups. Some passed. Jesse, the redhead, asked for more.

"Are they coming to visit you this fall?" Greg asked.

Tom was now looking across the river to the steep slopes of the western boundary of the Valley, down which he had come just yesterday evening. "What? Oh. My parents. Yeah, they said they'd come visit. I'm sure they'd be more than happy to treat us to a nice dinner."

"Maybe that one place up on the hill in Staunton, what do they call it?"

"White Star Mill?"

"That's the one. It will be nice to have some good food, not the fraternity house stuff."

Sometime later, after the bourbon the crew split up to their canvas tents or where they had laid their woolen blankets in the open air, Tom and Greg stood together, talking softly, away from the rest—in part, not to disturb the crew as they slept, or tried to, but also to be honest with each other.

"Thank God, there's still some bourbon left," Greg said quietly, almost in a whisper with his back turned to the campsite as Tom poured some into his cup.

"Yeah, thank God, but not that we're selfish." Tom smiled wryly as he poured the last into his cup.

"Well, maybe we are selfish, but you brought it, and we certainly appreciate the good stuff." Greg paused to take another sip, looked up at the mountain, and then at Tom. "So, what do you think?"

"About what in particular?"

"Nothing in particular. About today. About the crew. What's your gut telling you about things?"

"Our crew did a good job, nobody got hurt, and the guys seemed to fall into natural roles."

"Yeah, I thought Henry figured out what to do pretty quickly, and his four guys followed his lead. They didn't seem to question him."

"Yeah, I agree. But that was just practice, right?"

"I'm pretty sure it was. I didn't say it earlier, but I think that Lex is nervous. Nothing they said directly, mind you, but the guy I was talking to, a veteran from the war, seemed distracted. I could certainly hear a lot of activity in the background. Some things he said."

"Well, after what you said, I've been scanning the opposite side of the valley and up as far north as I could. You can see a good piece north of here across the river."

"See anything?"

"Yeah. I can't see any of the east slopes of the Valley, but I can see red-orange glows to the north and west."

"Huh, back the way we came. My talk with Lex is making sense now. Anything more about what you saw?" Greg seemed to sigh his words more than say them, and then he took a sip—the last sip, sadly—of the good Kentucky bourbon.

"Yeah, just spotty fires, maybe. You never know when you've got the canopy like we do here. Further up the Valley is different. There seems to be a spot where the fires become denser. That's where the real burning is. We may have helped stop things down here, but it looks to me like the fire jumped the Valley and collected in more or less one area. My bet is that's where Lex is going to send us in the morning."

"Any idea where they are?"

"No, not exactly. I can see where they might be, especially one area that looks to be a mountain slope, but that's just a guess because of the way the glow is shaped. But, yeah, no, I don't know where exactly it's located. My sense of distance is off in the night."

Tom handed the heavy binoculars to Greg, pointing across the river and up the Valley to where he had seen what he thought were fires. Greg scanned the slopes, looking for and then finding the glowing orange spots, and then farther away, a larger, stretching, bright reddish-orange, as if the fires had collected there and snaked across the eastern slopes, broadening and stretching to the heights.

"I found your spot. I think that's up to the west of Lexington. We'll find out tomorrow."

"Seems to me that this is the one. No more tests," Tom said, picking up his bourbon. His throat was dry, and the bourbon burned some on the way down. "I wish we could have had more practice."

"Well, me too, but I suspect I'd be wishing that even after a month of practice."

"True."

The next morning, before dawn, as the false dawn was ending, the truck stopped at their campsite before Greg had a chance to make his call into headquarters. Greg and Tom, along with some of the crew, were already up. The sound of the truck and its sliding on the dusty ground as it came to a stop woke the rest of them.

There was some stretching and groaning as the rest of the crew woke up, got their gear packed, and then loaded the packs and themselves into the back of the truck. Greg climbed in after talking with Brocky, who was still their driver and who had been sent back down from Lexington to fetch them. He was tired and said he had ferried supplies around to other crews 'til late yesterday after dropping them off. He said that many of the trucks had been sent this morning to bring crews up north and west of where they currently were.

The sun had not yet climbed above the ridgelines when Brocky started the engine and began roaring along the dusty road onto the highway towards the rendezvous point. More C-rations were passed out for breakfast and the guys dug in, forks and spoons dully clanging and rattling. Tom found himself really wanting some coffee. Henry, seated next to him on the metal bench in the crowded truck, looked up at him as he spooned pork and beans out of the can and into his mouth. His expression said, "This food wouldn't be so bad if we could have some coffee." Tom spit out a laugh. He understood. It wasn't what he would choose for breakfast, but he was used to it from occasional backwoods camps out West.

Their truck sped along a two-lane road, following the course of the river back to its headwaters and riding the edge of the exposed cliff faces, which, in past summers, was a calm, cool, shaded, tunnel-like drive. The trees here were dropping their leaves, dried to a brown crunchiness like harvested tobacco hanging in a barn. The river along its course had receded far from its bank sometime back in midsummer, leaving a dried mud that was becoming a dust that filled the air. The air that the truck raced through was a yellow-brown haze. This deeper part of the river still held some water since it was closer to its tributaries, the Jackson and the Cow Pasture, smaller rivers that still drained the remaining wetness that seeped out of the mountains. Tom was glad the river still lived. He thought of the fish clustered in the deepest, coolest darkness they could find. The fish like the native brook trout, in the shallow pools and riffles on the slopes near the fires, would be having a tough time.

South of Iron Gate, they crossed the railroad tracks and the river below the joining of the Jackson and the Cow Pasture, rolling swiftly through the town past the tannery, with its lingering smells of tanning leather, and then the old iron forge, a collection of brick and stone buildings from the last century. Both were silent in the still-early morning and had been for days as the men went to fight the fires either in the woods or to support the crews that had been scattering across the Valley to stop burnings before they blazed up. They had let the forge go cold so none of its flames and exploding sparks would add to the fires. Tom imagined that the men of the forge were grateful not to work in that heat.

No one was on the streets, and Tom couldn't see any lights shining from inside the buildings. All was dark, and the truck engine roared on as Brocky, unseen in the cab, rushed them onwards. He only knew to go north to Clifton Forge, nothing more. Greg had pulled the telephone out of its canvas pack, wanting an update from Lexington.

When the truck rumbled past the last building in town, Rainbow Rock appeared to their right above the eastern bank of the river, still in shadow, although the sun had risen above the peak of Wilson Mountain. The exposed rock arced along the trickling, but still-moving Jackson River, looking to Tom like a monstrous trout rising from a wave to sip a mayfly floating on the surface. Tom pointed out the exposed rock wordlessly to Henry while Greg was on the phone. Henry nodded. This would be a good river to fish in another time, Tom considered, probably full of rainbows—which would be fitting, he chuckled to himself. But maybe there would be some brookies that had slipped down the river from their mountain haunts.

Tom and Greg loved the elusive, skittish, rare brook trout. When they could slip away from classes, they would camp on the ridges of the mountains and, in the mornings, or evenings, at times, crawl to the edges of tiny, shallow, glass-like, cold streams, their faces in the fresh, damp earth, to hang their rods, stretching out through or over the rhododendrons to drop softly, gently tiny blue-gray caddis fly imitations onto the surface, hoping to tempt a hiding brookie, only to release it if caught. They had first met on one of these hidden secluded streams up in the Blue Ridge two years earlier, each surprised and, at first, annoyed by the other's interrupting presence.

Following the course of the river back upstream, the truck turned left and passed between the cloven northern reach of Waits Mountain Ridge, the cleft carved long ago by the slow axe of the Jackson's flow. The swaying truck followed the railroad and the river due west with Rainbow Rock behind them and the risen sun shining wanly through the smoky haze to the back of the truck. This was the first light that allowed Tom and the others to see how soot-covered and dirty they all were, with lines at the corners of their eyes and mouths where they had squinted and grimaced in the heat and fire, and the dirt smudged across their foreheads and under their eyes, where each had wiped away sweat.

"I suppose we could all use some coffee now," Henry said, loud enough at least for Tom and Greg to hear.

Tom laughed. Greg stood up and walked to the front of the truck, steadying himself on the exposed metal canopy bars overhead. When he made it to the front, he knocked on the roof of the truck's cab and leaned over to almost yell his directions to the driver. Brocky nodded in agreement, and Greg tapped the roof again in acknowledgment and thanks, then swayed back to his seat by Tom and Henry.

"What's the plan?" Tom yelled over the rumbling roar of the truck and its engine.

"I asked Brocky to cross the bridge coming up and stop at the Baptist Church on Main Street. That's where Lex is gathering a bunch of the crews, pulling several like us up from the southern ridges. Brocky knew to bring us to Clifton Forge, just not exactly where to stop."

The truck crossed the river on the old bridge. Tom stood to look down at the river with a mix of happiness and quiet sadness. It was flowing and deeper here, wider than he had expected, and that was good to him, but it was not what it had been in other Augusts in other years. He turned, looking ahead into the town with its old brick and stone buildings, a larger sibling to Iron Gate, two miles downriver. A few trucks were already in town; some men and boys were leaning against the trucks, talking and smoking. A few more had gathered near the red brick Main Street Baptist church.

Just as in Buchanan yesterday and in Iron Gate a few minutes ago, none of the townspeople were in sight. *Where are they?* wondered Tom. *Still inside sleeping or wanting to stay out of the way? Were the men and older boys in the crews fighting the fires? Had they evacuated?* It seemed strange to Tom, somehow upsetting, and gave him an unnatural feeling about it all, which added to the military feel, as that was all that there was—men and boys in army trucks, ordered off to fight and driven around by older men who were veterans.

Brocky pulled the truck over in a line with the others, bringing the roaring engine to a stuttering, clanking diesel stop. Tom and the rest of the crew stood up to take a look at the scene while Greg jumped out with Tom's map, pulled from the hip pocket of his heavy, dirty, and singed double-tin trousers, and walked to the church's courtyard, where a number of other dirty, soot-covered men had gathered under and around a green-canvas awning. Resting his forearms on the truck's cab, Tom thought he recognized some faces from the command crew in Lexington. That was the morning before. It seemed much longer, days at least.

A few of the crew climbed out of the truck to stretch their legs further and to talk with guys from the other crews milling about. Henry stood next to him.

"What do you think's going to happen?" he asked.

"Well, it looks to me that Lexington headquarters has moved here, which I bet means that we're near where the big fire is, or at least the fires that they want to fight."

"Where do you think that is?"

"Well, I'm pretty sure now, seeing all this activity, that the big fire is what I saw last night across the Valley along the ridges. Maybe sometime yesterday or the day before, the fire jumped across to the western side."

"How big is it?" Henry asked.

"Dunno. Pretty big probably, from what I saw last night. Seemed liked it was strung out along the slopes, and then it's been burning all night. I suppose we'll find out." He smiled. They waited for Greg to come back to the truck, trying to catch sight of him among the men moving under the green canvas.

Through the ashy haze in the morning sky, the sun, now above the mountain tops, was a stunning, beautiful, deep rosy red that lit the small town in shades of red and rich pink. And then the scent of the fire grew stronger, overlaying the diesel fumes of the trucks and the smoke from numerous cigarettes. The fire's smoky smell was first that of a barbecue and, as the wind shifted and swirled it from the western slopes into Clifton Forge, it grew to that of something left too long on a hot fire, just as it had smelled yesterday, further south, in the mountains overlooking Buchanan.

As they waited, more trucks arrived, and men and boys climbed out, filling the intersections of Main and A and further back up the side streets. There was talk of where they had been and of what they had done, many having been out on the fires for a few hot, tiring days already. Tom guessed that the crews that had been out there were the ones that mostly stayed in or leaned on their trucks. Not many of those men lit a cigarette. Tom didn't, either; he was too hot and had had enough smoke and fire.

Greg came back through the growing and moving crowd. Tom, followed by Henry and the rest of the crew, tiredly climbed down the open army-green tailgate. Brocky creaked the driver's door open and jumped out of the cab.

"The main fire is a string climbing the ridges west and north of here. What you were looking at last night, Tom," he explained. "I spoke with Morgan. He's sending us up to Hot Springs with two other crews, to get above the fire and stop it from spreading farther north and before it gets up the slopes below the northern end of Lake Moomaw. It is definitely on this side of the state line along the ridge. It's a hot one."

Greg took a breath. The crew shifted on their feet and murmured what they thought about the fire and of the job that they were asked to do.

Tom spoke up, "Well, OK. I don't expect it will be easy. When do we get started?"

Henry looked at Tom in agreement. He was anxious to get on the job too. Like Tom and Greg, Henry, newly proud of the work that he and the crew had done yesterday, was confident and thrilled at the adventure, thinking of this as the first time he would be tested in such a physical way in the outdoors. At the same time, on some deep level he recognized the feeling of danger, which laced his thoughts with the excitement of fear and gave a truer realness to the adventure.

"Mister Brocky, we need to pull on up ahead and wait for the other two trucks to file in." Greg said, "Here's where they want us to go." He put his finger on the map that Tom had given him, made supple from folding and unfolding, pointing to a ridge below the lake.

J. KENT GREGORY

Brocky nodded. "I can get y'all near there, but there'll be one heckuva hike upslope for you to get there. I'll look for an old logging road or some such, but I don't think there is one."

"Thanks. We'll take what we can get." Greg climbed up on the back of the truck to scan over the crowd and what reminded him of a truck depot, which he supposed it was, to find the other two trucks in their convoy. He sent Henry, who was standing next to him, running to one, asking them to rendezvous on the northside of town on the other side of the bridge crossing the East Branch of the Jackson, which was hardly more than a shallow creek in other times but was now just a bed of round river stones baked white by this summer's heat and sun. He asked Tom to do the same for the other truck.

As Henry and Tom hurried off, Greg asked Sam to see about gathering any kind of provisions that he could quickly lay his hands on. Sam took his nephew, Jesse, with him. Greg asked the others to fill up their canteens from the jerrycans, which were thankfully still holding water.

Other men in worn canvas stepped out from under the awning and headed back to their trucks. The lounging and milling crowd followed these men, their crew leaders, and loaded up. As the diesel trucks churned back to life, adding the initial belch of dark smoke from their stacks to the gloom in the air, there was confusion as the trucks looked for their partners, trying to merge back into the street, or trying to turn a corner, but having to back up twice before making it. Most of the trucks were heading north to the fires by the same road out as Greg and Tom.

Brocky idled the truck on the northern end of the bridge until the other two trucks drove in behind him, then he drove northwest along the road through the gap in the ridge below Fore Mountain, and then back and forth on switchbacks as McGraw Hill Road climbed and descended a ridge higher than Fore Mountain. The fires there had burned the mountain bald, and it was still smoking and sending fumes into the sky. The road ended at another one that bent northeast to Hot Springs, following a path at the bottom of two ridges. The steep, vast wooded ridges and small towns, whose existence were often just clusters of wooden and stone houses, passed behind them. The crew watched the slopes on their left, the southeastern reaches of the ridge, where they would soon be fighting. The sky was dark with haze and soot, the sun a fierce red-orange through a cloud-like murk of burned ash but in an oddly cloudless sky. The charred smell was now there alone, the mingled-in reek of the forges and tannery was behind them. And then the fires appeared, some were ribbons strung along, undulating with the folds and clefts of the ridges; others were blazes, shapeless bonfires burning upslope and leaving ash and charred, blackened pillars that had been oak and pine trees last night.

The line of trucks that their platoon was part of thinned out the further up the road their trucks rolled, each crew taking a side road up the ridge, attempting to find the spots marked for them on their maps. After a half-hour drive, their group split off from the line at Hot Springs, passing by the red brick and glass of the old resort.

"I sure hope that doesn't burn up before I can stay there," Tom shouted over the diesel engine's roar and Brocky's grinding of the gears as the truck slowed to make the turn.

"Shoot, yeah, if we ever can afford it," Greg shouted back.

"I hear there're some good streams up this way. Hope to God those fish have found a place to hide."

"They've been here since Creation. I figure they've made it through a few of these fires before."

"My pa used to fish up here. He said they're good with brook trout up high, rainbows down below. He never said much about bass. The mountain water's too cold, I think," Henry, who had taken up with the two college boys, put in.

"Do you fish?" asked Tom.

"Yes, indeed. Mostly with flies."

"When this is over and the rivers are back, you should come fishing with Greg and me."

Greg looked over at Tom, surprised by the suggestion, but then quickly considered that he had grown to like the farm boy, who had done a good, eager job on the fire yesterday, and was good and honest. He realized that he thought of the kid like a little brother. "Yeah, we should fish together when this is over and the rivers are healthy again."

Henry smiled. "I'd like that."

The road climbed up the slopes of the ridge. It was a steep climb, and the crew had to hold on to their seats or the support bars overhead to keep from sliding down the metal bench. The trees here had been untouched by the flames so far. They still held some leaves on their overarching limbs, though many of their leaves had fallen, and those that remained were crinkled brown and tan along their edges. The sky was a dark gray, charcoal clouds undulating with dull steel-colored billows fed and churned by the smoky heat of the fires. As their truck climbed, they saw, obscured and then revealed above and in gaps of the trees still standing on the lower reaches, that the smoke was a living wall, rising from and lit a deep red and almost-pink by the flames.

Brocky jerked the truck onto an old, unpaved logging road, a low tunnel through the trees on the near slopes above and below, whose lower branches scraped and thudded across the roof of the cab and the support bars over the bed. He slowed down, his lights still on, to follow the track that wound along the contours of the mountain, hoping that the road wasn't washed away or blocked. If it was, Brocky knew he would have one helluva time getting the truck back out. He sweated that, but he had to get the boys close to the location HQ had given them. A hike uphill with all their equipment would not serve, no sir, it would not. No, that might be a death sentence for them. They didn't know it, but he did.

He took off his hat and wiped sweat from his forehead that had been seeping into his eyes, stinging them, and ran his fingers through his shoulder-length gray hair, wet as if he had just gotten out of his farm's swimming hole. His moustache was wet too. He wondered if he'd be cooler without all this hair.

The truck stopped at a long-fallen tree, its roots, or what was left of them, twisting like arthritic fingers on the uphill slope to their left. Greg had the two brothers, Mark and Steve, set to work on it with their crosscut saw, sending dust and flakes of wood onto their shirts and the ground. They stepped away as their saw cut through the bottom of the trunk that was angled above the ground. The freed trunk thudded down, and the root cluster tumbled onto the dirt road. Greg sent Matt and Howard from the back to help roll the sections off the road and down the slope. The tree trunk was halted by trees and exposed rocks just below the lip of the road; the root section tumbled and rolled, crashing over the dried leaves on the forest floor and disappearing in the dark distance.

Much to Brocky's relief, the truck rolled on through the old logging road's dark tunnel until it opened up onto a road that ran to the heights above. He would be able to get the crew to the fire, and he wouldn't be trapped with the truck. It seemed that they had passed beyond the edge of the fire on the slopes above, so he would be able to get the boys to that spot on the map or pretty darn close to it. He wiped his forehead again, the sweat still stinging his eyes, and the truck churned upslope on the narrow dirt-and-gravel road.

The further up and closer to the heights the truck came, the darker the sky grew, and the scent of fire, which had vanished in the forest road's treed and moldering tunnel, was strong and inescapable. The winds were blowing northeast across the slopes, sending ash blowing across the path of the truck. When they

J. KENT GREGORY

drew even with the northeast edges of the fire, coming closer on their left, ash that was glowing along the edges, where fire still hung on, dropped from above and was swirled behind them in the truck's draft, to be cut through and swirled again by the two trucks following them. Blown into the air above the trucks, those still-glowing ashes were extinguished by the strong draft currents of the rushing trucks.

Tom noticed an increased hurry to the truck, its rattling jerking and sway increased. He wondered if Brocky was worried, eager, or anxious to get off this road at their spot and drop them off.

The truck and the two behind it halted where the gravel and beaten-down dirt ended in a turnaround before a treed slope. In the gray late-morning darkness, like a strange night, the beams from Brocky's headlights glowed in the ashy haze around them. The sky was dark; clouds of smoke hid the sun and would not let any of its rays through. Instead, red-orange light from the fires lit the undersides of the clouds, some of which were flat, but others were churned from the heat rising up from the burning, giving a lurid glow to their surfaces and edges, and coloring them like the ash that floated across the road from which they had just emerged. Tom was unsettled, as was Henry, from the look on his sweating face when he glanced at Tom.

"It sure looks like Hell itself," Henry gasped in the smoky air as they climbed down out of the truck's rear.

"I suppose it does," Tom replied, scuffing his boots on the dusty, dead ground at the turnaround.

The rest of the crews unloaded from the trucks, jumping down into the dust and ash, dragging their gear from the truck beds. There was only a muffled sound, the clanking of metal on metal—their tools on the metal truck beds made quieter in the unnatural air.

The crews gathered around their leaders and then walked off, up-slope, to the fire. Men further up-slope became vanished shades in the hazy charcoal darkness of this morning-night. The air grew hotter and was more difficult to breathe the further up the line of men marched. The increasing steepness of the slope tired them and made their legs burn with the effort. Rhododendron bushes, their edges curled into cigar shapes by the heat and lack of water, became more numerous the further up they went, growing around the bases and hiding the rocky outcrops on the upper slopes.

Greg was up ahead searching for the easiest path to the top, finding one through the bushes and a break in the gray rock that reflected a faint rose color cast down through the almost leafless trees from the red and orange clouds above. Tom turned to Henry, who was panting just behind on his left and shuffling through the dry leaves. He stumbled over a thin, dried branch. *He's tired,* Tom thought to himself. *Shoot, just like all of us. I should be better able to handle this. We're lower than out West, and the slopes should be easier.* He stopped and took a drink from his canteen, motioning for Henry to do the same.

"We're almost to the top," Tom told him. "See the rhododendron and the rocks?"

Henry nodded and took another gulp from his canteen. The water, although warm, tasted cool and clean.

"Be careful with your water. I bet we'll really be wanting it later. It's getting hotter. I can feel we're closing in on it," Tom said, gasping and breathing in gulps of smoky air. It was the smoke and heat, maybe more so than the slope, that got to him. The burnt air hurt and stung when he inhaled. He nodded again, and the two of them rejoined the line of sweating, panting young men.

The slope here, like all slopes in these mountains, was deceptive, always seeming to end at a line of trees or an exposed rock up ahead, only to stretch out further once the trees or the rocks were

J. KENT GREGORY

reached. Now that they were closer to the cloud cover, the black, hazy darkness and the shadows limned by the uncanny orange-and-rose light were disorienting, strange, and almost as if out of a nightmare.

Suddenly, the line of men ahead vanished, only to reappear beyond in the open grass of a gently rolling meadow plateau, clustering around the crew leaders, wiping sweaty grimed brows, and drinking from their canteens.

And there it was. A monster. The nightmare become real. The fire roared, no crackling or popping or hissing. No, this was an endless roar, consuming all other sounds. Standing, looking at the edge of it, Tom, Greg, Henry, and the crew felt the heat from the fire that they could see inside, furnace like, fringed by trees with flames climbing to their crowns. The fire that they saw, that they felt, living in the interior of the burning columns of trees, was an orange, yellow depth, white, shifting and spiraling up - heat colors that danced and boiled without form. This shapeless, mad thing created and sucked in its own wind, feeding itself.

A tall, straight pine, on the fringe of the superheated madness, with flames running up along its trunk, fell suddenly when the trunk exploded near its midsection because of its boiling, expanding pine tar, and toppled into the colors as if sucked inwards by the winds, grabbed by the fiery glow. Another, a lofty spreading oak, whose massive, aged trunk was untouched and impervious to the licking flames but whose leaves, crisped by the heat and drought, suddenly ignited, all at once, and then the fire moved on, leaving a naked tree charred above with its gray, grooved trunk untouched. As the fire moved closer, the crew's breath was taken, sucked away by the churning blast-furnace flames that pulled all air toward it. Tom could feel the moving air hitting and cooling the back of his sweating, grimed neck as the air rushed towards the flames. It was for this thing, this roaring monster, that, unknowingly, Greg had called Tom and Tom had come East.

The heated air seemed to singe their nose hairs, those not already burned away by yesterday's firefight. Each breath either burned the insides of their noses or burned straight down their throats. From their canteens, Greg and Tom poured water—warm as it was, but blessedly cool by comparison—onto their bandanas, soaking them, and then tied them in outlaw fashion over their noses and mouths. The rest of the crew did the same. Henry sucked part of his into his mouth, drinking in some of the moisture. It was a small amount, but gratifying.

Greg said something, his eyes crinkling at the edges. Tom couldn't make out the words over the roar of the fire and the exploding trees. He moved closer.

"What?" he yelled, leaning into Greg's ear.

"We look like we're about to rob a bank!" Greg laughed out hard.

"Yeah, we're some real banditos, for sure!" Tom replied, catching ahold of Greg's absurd giddiness, relieved not to feel fear for the moment as they looked at the madness ahead of them.

Their crew paused, eyes held locked by the fiery monster within the trees. Tom had imagined what it looked like, as he supposed the others did, but this blazing, roaring monster was not the image he had colored in his mind.

The crews from the two other trucks began moving out. One went toward the fire to dig and clear a fire line to contain the blaze from the sere meadow. The other crew filed off to the treed slope below the fire to contain any spread there. Tom thought that would be pretty safe, as it was back downslope. Greg had volunteered them for the slopes to the summit above the grassy plateau they were standing on.

Their crew trudged off through the crunching grass with Greg in the lead, keeping their distance from the fire, to get above it and onto the slopes to the summit ridge. Like the other crews, they were moving fast to get to a spot where they could begin their stand against the monster before it beat them there. Drained and loaded with equipment as they were, they simply could not move at a run, although they were eager and anxious to do so. They just could not make their legs move faster. This was good. They needed to save what physical resources they had left, which was little enough after the morning's climb and the heat and ash in the air.

They reached the other side of the meadow, where Greg stopped to make the final decision about what to do. Tom was beside him, his bandana down so he could breathe—not better, but at least he could suck in more air. Greg looked up the slope, considering the fire and the trees, deciding where to clear the fire line and what trees he was going to sacrifice for a fire break. Tom looked at Greg, then upslope, and back to the fire that was closer, its heat, carried by the wind, painful, even though they were still some distance from it. Tom looked around for Henry, who had become his, or, rather, their, constant companion. He wasn't up front with them, but in the middle, doubled over, panting. *So, he's near his end*, thought Tom, worried. He decided to keep an eye on him. Greg called a halt near a jumble of rocks and had the crew catch their breath and drink some more water.

Tom walked back to Henry. He gave the boy his spade and took Henry's heavier Pulaski. It was probably better that he had the Pulaski anyway. Henry looked up and nodded. "Thanks."

"Don't mention it. That was a tough climb. Besides, I'm more comfortable with a Pulaski; gotta be careful you don't split your forehead with the axe head when digging with the mattock—it's a special skill, that." He laughed, trying to add in some lightheartedness.

"Yeah, thanks."

"My luck to be better with a heavy tool on a day like this, huh?"

Henry chuckled. "I guess my luck's better."

Tom smiled and clapped him on the back. "Stick by me today. It's going to be getting pretty lively."

Greg called them all together. The plan he had decided on was to head up the slope at an angle to a contour line above that of the fire, then side-hill it back to the fire as close as they could get. At some point, three of them would halt to clear a line in the direction the rest of the crew would take, and then, further on, four would halt—three of whom would cut a fire line along the side-hilling path, while one would serve as a lookout. The rest would continue on as close as they could get to and above the fire, where they would clear a firebreak and then begin clearing back along the contour to meet up with the first two groups again.

"OK, let's move out, and remember to stay together until we split into the three teams. First, everyone take off their packs and leave them here on the rocks. Keep your tools and water." There was some hesitancy by a few to leave their packs behind, but Greg let them know he wasn't fooling around and they gave in, so they slid off their backpacks and whatever gear they didn't need or that Greg told them not to bring.

Tom already had his father's Boy Scout axe in its oiled leather sheath hanging from his belt. He figured he might have a need for it yet and, to him, there was a value to it. He wouldn't leave it behind to maybe get burnt. Greg looked at it and then at him and looked away. Tom pulled the possibles bag with the fire-starting kit from his backpack's pocket, where he had stowed it back in Kentucky. He knew it was odd to bring this bag, but he always had it with him when in the outdoors, so, out of habit, and maybe a little superstition, he put it into his deep rear pocket and snapped its flap shut. He wasn't carrying too much extra weight otherwise, just the axe, although no one would count that as extra.

Tom had known that today would get dicey, and now he knew that Greg saw it too. In telling them to leave their packs, Greg had just asked them to be prepared to run for it. What he didn't know was if Greg was being careful or whether he was going to risk the crew to save the mountains' grass and trees and wanted them not to burn any energy reserves carrying unneeded heavy items to the fire line. Probably a little of both. Hell, he would be doing the same. Anyways, this was the job they had come here to do. Still, the thought of facing real danger, maybe even running for his life from the furnace advancing toward them, was not necessarily frightening, but for sure, a layer of fear was there that sharpened his mind and focused his thoughts on what he would need to do. He found Henry by the rocks and grabbed him by the arm.

"You stay with me, you hear?"

"Yes, sir."

"There's no *sir* to this thing, you just stay with me. I don't care how tired you are. We may have to move fast."

"You mean to get to the fire? I can handle the slope."

"No, I mean to get out."

"Oh." Henry hadn't thought that far ahead, tired as he was, and maybe he wouldn't have, but now he saw.

"Yeah. And I want to have your coffee and fish your streams as soon as we get done on these fires here, and your dad's mountain whiskey," Tom said and smiled. He didn't want the boy to be too scared, just aware and careful. Henry smiled back and stood up.

The crew was filing off, one behind the other, at an angle up the grassy slope toward the fire to their left. The angle eased the climb somewhat, but Tom noticed it wearing at his left ankle and heel. *Heck*, he thought to himself, *these boots were made for stuff like this and tougher, so they're good.* He wouldn't say that things were exactly comfortable, but he wasn't feeling pain—not like what some of the other fellas were feeling, especially those like Henry, wearing their farm boots, especially now that they were on their second day, and this one was an upslope slog to be followed by an up-and-to-the-side-slope race.

They reached a height above the tops of the flames from the trees that had crowned in the meadow and on the lower slopes. The crew moved closer to the fire, seeming to close with it quicker than they were possibly moving as the winds from the Valley itself still blew strongly north and northwest, driving and herding the fierce, chaotic monster towards them.

The crew was in a tightly spaced file now, and Greg, leading them, angled up higher but then stopped. He changed his plan and called out to Sam and the four youngest in their crew, the two almost-college boys, Matt and Howard, Dave, and Jesse, to stop there and begin cutting, clearing a swath toward the rest of the crew as it continued on. Greg put Sam in charge of this squad. He kept Henry with Tom and the rest. *Oh boy,* thought Tom, *Greg doesn't like this at all.*

Greg then sent Peter, the military-school boy, a little higher on the slope to watch the fire and to keep a lookout for any signs that the fire was jumping ahead either above or below. If so, he was to warn the guys below to get away quickly and then to head side-hill to him and the crew to warn them. Peter was definitely not happy, but Greg turned away to move off with the remainder of the crew. Tom waited so he could speak with the young man, whose eyebrows were clenched and his mouth drawn tight, eyes staring at the back of Greg's sweat-stained military khaki shirt. He explained to the young man, who was just a couple of years younger than him, that being the lookout made him responsible for all fourteen lives of their crew. Tom let him chew on that. He knew the fella wanted to be a part of the action, but Peter now understood the responsibility that was his. If there was warning to do, this young one's job would be the hardest if the fires jumped because he would have to do some life-racing running on the mountain slope.

Tom patted him on the shoulder, like he had with Henry, and shook his hand. "Don't you be mad, and make sure you stay watchful. We are going to depend on you, and I'm pretty sure this fire will get dicey one way or the other."

Peter nodded, and Tom hurried off to catch up with Greg at the head of the column, grabbing Henry by the shoulder as he passed him and hauling him along.

They got level on the vertical with the fire and ran past it and up the meadow, looking down into what seemed to be nothing other than a boiling cauldron, but uncontained, sending smoldering ash and sparks swirling up on heat spirals to them and above their heads like will-o'-the-wisps from Hell and then blown by the wind from the southeast along the ridges of the Blue Ridge to rush through this forested meadow. The glow of the sparks and ashes burnt out, fading and vanishing to nothingness, thankfully, before floating to the ground.

Greg halted this section of the crew, and they began clearing a fire line. It was quick work, for the most part, as the grass and trees were dried out and dying or already dead. They tumbled the dead trees and bracken down the slope, some of them pausing, entranced by the somersaulting dried wood that disappeared into the flaming cauldron below and passed from existence. Tom was surprised at how easily the grass and dried bushes came away from the ground at the scraping of his Pulaski. The dirt underneath was brown-white dust, moistureless and sand-like. Their little squad moved steadily back towards the others, making a wide swath of dead dirt that they hoped would stop the fire from moving further up the slope and corral it to a halt further up the meadow.

The fire moved quickly, and its roar and heat caught up to them and came closer. The fire's fury was a cloud of sound that enveloped them. Nothing else could be heard, just the swirling, mad roar of the approaching flames. And with the sound, moving at the same speed, was the scorching heat. The air was already hot and dry; sweat soaked through their heavy canvas shirts and pants, the salty moisture beading on Tom's nose and getting absorbed by his bandana. When the fire's heat touched them, it was pain—not warmth, not stifling heat, but a pain like one you got when reaching too close to a campfire to shift burning logs or to put a new one in.

Tom briefly paused to catch his breath. He motioned Henry over. He took a drink from his canteen and mimed through the deafening noise that Henry should do the same from his. Henry shrugged, turning his uncorked canteen over as if to pour water out. It was empty, so Tom shared his.

They returned to hacking, dragging, and tossing dead, dried things, grass, and trees or things that had been trees at the beginning of the summer, moving slowly back towards the other squad that was making its way to them. The slope was steep, so their fire line had to be wide. They didn't want any flames on the downslope, licking fuel on the upslope.

The wind picked up, blowing into the flames below and moving them up the meadow and ridge. The young men moved faster, feeling the heat come closer on their backs and exposed necks. They kept their bandanas up around their noses and mouths. The roaring, too, came upon them, louder now but also just a constant, unchanging noise. There was no change in pitch or tone, no crashing of trees—just a wall of sound that enveloped them. They worked faster. Muscles ached; sweat evaporated before it could even drip.

And then the fire blew up. Their squad stopped working, looking first at each other, sensing instinctually that something was different, wrong, and saw first that the fire was racing up the slope to them, and then looking upslope, they realized that the fire had jumped above them, igniting the grass and brush and the trees. Then the trees on the slope near them crowned because the fire was so hot and the trees were almost dead dry. It had happened so quickly that Tom stood stunned by the speed in which this horrid, hellish monster had caught them. He said out loud, "Oh, shit," and then heard a yell. He looked around and saw a young man—it was Peter—running and stumbling side-hill across the slope to them.

"Oh, shit," he said again. He grabbed Henry by the collar of his heavy canvas shirt, pulling and then shoving him forward towards the running voice. "Go, now! Run!" He yelled, "Go!" to the rest of the squad, motioning for them to follow, and then pulled Henry by the shoulder. He saw that Greg had seen or heard too, and from the rear was shoving the squad after Tom. Tom ran, stumbling and sliding across the dry slope, dead grass and weeds falling away under his boots, his dead legs beginning to give up, towards Peter.

Tom pulled his bandana down, yelled loudly, and motioned with his arms and hands for Peter to turn around, but the deafening roar had again surrounded them, and the young man kept running forward, not hearing, not understanding the waving of Tom's arms—or maybe just too scared to figure out what Tom meant. But though Tom kept yelling, his voice hoarse from the strain and the heat and the soot in the air, the young man kept running toward him. *No, no, turn back*, thought Tom, *please, turn back; you've got to turn back.* Peter stumbled then got up and continued his dash toward them. The squad was bunched right behind Tom. Why couldn't he understand what Tom wanted him to do?

Then it was too late. *Oh, God*, thought Tom, *oh no*. Then, *shit*, and he stopped. The fire, fickle and unpredictable, driven by the winds, had jumped again. It was above them, burning the grass and trees that crowned as Tom watched, and it was racing along the lower slopes below. He could even see it ahead, over the shoulder of the young man who crashed into him to deliver his message.

"The fire's jumping and burning everywhere," Peter coughed out before he doubled over, gagging, heaving bile and what little water remained in him onto the dusty ground.

"Where's your squad?"

"Back there. They were running up the slope to get away."

Tom hoped they made it over the ridge into West Virginia. He regretted that he and Greg had stayed with the same squad, but then, the squad they left behind was supposed to be in a safer position. They probably were, but barely.

He looked ahead, back the way the young man had run, knowing they had to move somewhere quickly, and saw an untouched, unburnt grassy area before the fire. He knew what to do.

"Follow me," he yelled again, grabbing the young man and Henry, first dragging, then pushing them ahead, and then running between them to the grass. Looking over his shoulder, making sure that the squad was with him, he slid and stumbled, almost tripping over a rock as he side-hilled it to the grass. It was hard to breathe with the effort and the heat and the wind swirling the ash in the air. As he was running, he pulled the bandana back up over his nose and mouth. Better. The ash only swirled in his eyes now, and his breath was cooler than the wind. The squad was keeping pace behind him.

He reached the grassy spot, flinging down his Pulaski. They had no time to clear the ground. He reached around to his rear pocket with his right hand. He was aware of the squad grouped next to him on the left. He glanced around and saw the fires were getting close. *Where is it?* he thought, fumbling with the snaps to get to his possibles bag. *Goddammit, where is it?* The sky caught his eye, and it was hell. Roiling black clouds blocked the sky for as far as he could see, lit red and orange underneath at the bottoms of the rounding and swirling ash clouds, bunching in places near the summit's ridgeline. He quit looking around. *Pay attention to what you need to do*, he told himself. He took three breaths to calm himself and reached into his deep rear pocket.

He pulled out his bag and opened the drawstring closure. With the ferrocerium rod in his left hand and the steel striker in his right, he struck sparks into the straw-colored grass on the sloping ground in front of him. The first spark to hit the grass was blown out by a swirling gust that came around his knees. The second spark took, igniting the grass. He shoved more than motioned the guys to back them away from the little fire. The wind, no longer blocked by the huddled bodies of the squad, caught the little grass fire, blazed it up in an explosion of light and flame, and spread it up slope and to their right.

"Hurry, HURRY! Do the same!" Tom shouted. But no one else had anything to start a fire with. Not even in a crazed dream or nightmare did they think they would be starting a fire—anyone, that is, but Greg. Tom's urgent shout woke Greg's mind from its numbness. With an ironic smile, he unbuttoned his right front breast pocket to pull out a book of matches he carried for cigarettes. He struck one, adding it to the line of the blaze. He caught a mass of paraffin-soaked cotton balls that Tom had thrown to him. The two of them began tossing and dropping the little flaming cotton-paraffin bombs into the widening front of the grass, their inextinguishable hot, blue flames blazing the fire quicker.

The winds moved the flames fast, burning out everything as they advanced up the slope, then, with their gusts, blew out the tiny sparks that remained on the blackened ground. The winds also blazed up the fire they had tried to escape. It was behind and below them now, the heat scorching their backs, and Tom knew he had to decide on his next move. They were surrounded by fire. To their left, a wall of flames was advancing fast; everything it overtook simply vanished into and behind the burning wall. Upslope, beyond their fire, trees were crowning and shrubs were igniting. To their right, winds were blowing fires away from the crew. Tom wasn't worried about the ones to their right. He needed to decide quickly.

Then he saw it. Twenty or so yards in front and just upslope of them, their fire had overtaken three pine saplings, maybe just a couple years old. There seemed to be enough burnt space to the sides, and their fire was advancing beyond them.

"Follow me! Quickly!" Tom yelled, scrambling, almost jumping up hill. "Get these trees out of here!"

They hacked and dug with their axes and Pulaskis, almost hacking each other with their wild, desperate swings. The brothers, Matt and Mark, tossed their saw down and began pulling, twisting, and wrenching at the saplings' trunks and branches with the leather-covered hands. They got the trees out, doing a rolling throw to launch them away downslope.

"Wet your bandanas and lay face down!" Tom shouted.

"What?"

"Like this!" He showed them what he meant. He spent the last of his water on Henry's bandana, throwing him to the ground and falling next to him. Then, the heat was upon them.

The roar came over them, was still with them as the winds blew it louder. They were surrounded now, the fires making their own swirling winds, adding them to the air blowing madly up the valley. The winds raced over and around them, a roar almost like an undying engine, driving burning splinters into their clothes and exposed skin, almost lifting them up from the ground with their scorching buffets. With his eyes closed, Tom clawed his hands into the black, dusty ground still hot from his fire that had just burned over it. He smelled something like hair burning. It was either his or Henry's. The fire and the winds drew away the air, sucked it from them, and their faces, turned to the hot, ashy ground, tried to suck in the roasting soot air, only to cough it out again. The air was cooled just slightly by their wet bandanas, but soon they became useless, or worse, suffocating, as the moisture quickly evaporated.

Oh, God, when will this stop? Tom felt fear, but he was resigned and tired. Maybe just tired. He had done what he could. He hoped that the burn area they had made was enough. He hoped that the other squad had gotten away. He didn't think about the other two crews below.

Tom forced himself to keep his head down. He tensed and ached to see how close the fire was and how far advanced their fire had gotten, but he knew doing that was to risk burning his face or worse, and what good would it do to see anyway? The fire was either close, or it wasn't. The plan that had occurred to him as they stumbled double-time across the slope either would work or it wouldn't. He reached his gloved left hand over to keep Henry's head down too.

The roaring of the winds and fire were frightening. There was nothing else but the furious sound and heat. And then it seemed to lessen, though still loud, but almost imperceptibly, barely, it grew quieter. It was ahead of them, upslope. Then it seemed further upslope, and the only sound that reached them was a crackling as if from logs splitting and bursting in a campfire's heat. The fire's heat was less too, and soon it was just the heat from the winds, which now felt almost pleasant as it blew on Tom's now sweat-slick neck.

Tom turned over and sat up, facing down the slope. The winds immediately blew soot into his eyes. He stood and turned away from them to look up to the top of the mountain. The fire was gone, and everything was black, burnt to soot and dust, the winds stirring up small, swirling black dust devils. The sky was clouded black and gray but was no longer boiling now that the fire was gone.

He nudged Henry with his boot. Henry unburied his head and looked up at Tom. "Fellas, you can get up. The fire's gone," Tom said, and the rest of the crew turned over. Greg looked at him and gave him a thumbs-up, too numbed to say anything.

They had made it. The fire was gone. They were alive. The mountainside was dead.

~

Tom bent down, rod in his hand, to look more intimately at the ice rose that had risen from the fresh, wet earth, nested in the frosted green grass growing on the forest floor. This area had been burnt in the fire; the leaves were gone from the ground, and the dead trees provided no shade. It had become more of a meadow than the forest it had once been, green and open with blackened tree trunks rising into the sky like temple columns. He called Greg and Henry over.

"Hey, you two, look at this," Tom said, awed to see the delicate ice growth's beauty.

They both knelt on the grass to see what Tom pointed at, with their bamboo fly rods angled carefully backwards.

"It's beautiful," Henry said quietly. Greg said nothing, just nodding as he stared.

Then the three of them stood up with their rods again and moved quietly through the soft grass toward the cool sound of the mountain stream.

FREE AND HAPPY, WHEREVER HOME IS

Part 1—Peace

It was late June, and the midday Texas sun was glaring white. Hot air blew in through the windows and swirled around the inside of my truck as I headed west along the two-lane highway from Waco to Jefferson with Jerry Jeff Walker's *Viva Terlingua* album playing on my radio. I wasn't entirely happy about what I was doing, especially since I felt like I had been tricked and guilted into this by my girlfriend, but I tried to console myself, though not entirely succeeding, that I would get to realize the dream held by most boys—namely, that I would get to try my hand at cowboying and ranching. Also, at the end of each day, I would get to sidle up to the bar of some local drinking establishment with my fellow cowpokes from the area.

That second hope was dashed and left behind on the hot old-gray asphalt highway as I crossed the county line into Jefferson and saw the sign that, in no uncertain terms, as if directed at me, read, "Welcome to Jefferson County, A Dry County." Since I was alone, a long, full-throated, devastated scream of "F**k!" escaped from my mouth and was washed away by the dry wind rushing through my open windows.

My very conservative Christian girlfriend would not have approved. No sir, most definitely not.

I guess it was about three months previously, while in my apartment in New Orleans, that my girlfriend had called to ask if I'd like to come out to her grandparents' ranch that summer to help them out. They had both recently had serious surgeries and couldn't take care of the ranch themselves. They had tried having a younger relative help, but he had stolen money from them, a lot of money that they had stashed in an urn, and they didn't trust the migrant workers. That apparently left me, which, frankly, I thought was really scraping the bottom of the barrel.

My response was, "Sure, I'd be happy to do that someday," which, in my mind, meant never, but that my girlfriend took at face value, or maybe saw as a concession.

Two months later, about one month before my trip down the highway to this alcohol-free zone, my girlfriend called to inform me that her grandparents were looking forward to having me at the ranch on a specific date for the next two or three weeks.

So, there I was, rolling down the Texas highway in late June, with the windows rolled down on my truck to save money and a road map sitting on the passenger seat that occasionally threatened to be blown out the open windows. I wasn't happy about leaving New Orleans where I would have most of the summer off and could enjoy the food and bars like Phillip's and Saints and F&M's and, well, the list goes on. Things were also ending, and had been for some time, between me and my girlfriend.

As I rolled into Jefferson City proper and passed through the center of town, I looked for some sort of saloon, hoping that the very direct and clearly stated welcome sign was somehow wrong, but no such luck. I found my way to their house, situated no more than a couple of blocks from the center of town, under the canopies of several pecan trees. The old man said he'd lead me out to the ranch to show me around, but that the old woman would stay in town; she was suffering from some vicious intestinal bug that the old man had had the week before but from which he had since recovered. Its effects were described in enough detail that I was glad she wasn't coming with us.

I followed the old man, who drove ahead in his truck, to the ranch that lay a few miles outside of town in rolling, dry, virtually treeless pastureland. I unloaded my canvas and leather grip and my sleeping bag to bring them inside. The old man showed me around the ranch house that they had recently renovated and added onto. It was nice, and it was cool inside. He showed me my bedroom, where I could lay my bedroll, and told me to be careful to shake out my bedroll every time—*every* time—before I got into it to make sure there were no scorpions, which he pronounced as *scarpions*, and to make sure I slept off the ground.

"You don't want those scarpions to get ya. That sting will swell you up and hurt like heck. Yes, sir, I can tell you for sure."

I thanked him and kept my sleeping bag rolled up and retightened the ties.

Next, we went out to the barn where he introduced me to Dusty, an American quarter horse. I thought the name was fitting, as there sure was a heckuva lot of dust from the dried ground across everything.

"Every day, I want you to ride out with Dusty here and check on the cattle. We've got about fifty head. He doesn't get the exercise he would like anymore."

"Yes, sir. I'll do that." I wasn't entirely sure what he meant by "check on the cattle," but I supposed I had the idea.

"Also," the old man twang-drawled in his nasally voice as he pulled a rifle out of a leather scabbard that he had hung from a nail on an old wooden wall post, "I want you to carry this with you."

If I had known then what I know now, I would have appreciated more what the old man was handing me. My goodness, it was a type of drilling! It was a gun that broke at the receiver, and what made it special was that it had three barrels: a top barrel for a .22 caliber rifle bullet set on top of and between two bottom barrels that would hold .20-gauge shotgun shells. It was an old gun, whose wooden stock had a few dings and scratches that were now blackened by time and oil, but that did nothing but add to the character of this ranch gun.

"This is Jack's old gun." Jack was his long-deceased father-in-law from whom he, or, I guess more accurately, his wife, had inherited the ranch. The old man had a son-like love and respect for his father-in-law. The old man's name was Jack too.

"Thank you," I said. In my short time with him, I was already learning to speak little and slowly, like the old man. I also had to be careful to fight the urge to interrupt and respond or answer when I knew what he was going to finish saying or asking. Maybe I had been in cities too long, I don't know. I was also picking up what I thought of as the central Texas country twang-drawl.

While I was checking out the gun, which broke smoothly and had a really nice feel and balance, Jack said, "I want you to shoot whatever varmints you see."

That made me pause, because I didn't know what he meant by a varmint, but I also didn't want to come across as stupid. It seemed that this was something that any cowboy in Texas, or elsewhere, would know. Still, I didn't want to go blazing away at things that I shouldn't, so I thought it better to ask. "Yes, sir, but what do you mean by a *varmint?*"

And as God as my witness, this was what Jack answered: "Anything that ain't a cow, but especially *armadillers.*" I paused as the parameters and opportunities presented themselves. I had already been told that I could shoot whatever rattlers I saw, and that had given me some consolation and something to look forward to as I had thought about leaving New Orleans for part of the summer, and it's something that I held onto now that I was in the proudly dry Jefferson County.

On a previous visit to Jefferson with my girlfriend, Jack had showed me some pretty big rattlesnake skins that he had tanned and had hanging in his garage back in town. I figured that it would be pretty exciting, fun even, to come upon a rattler, shoot it, and make its skin into a hat band or a belt. Then, when somebody would ask, "Where'd you get that snakeskin?" I could answer, "I shot it."

I put the gun back in its leather scabbard and gave Dusty a rub on his nose. I could tell that he was a good, steady horse and that he liked to range. He and I would become good buddies over the next three weeks.

Jack took me to the other end of the barn from the horse's stall where an old light blue-ish flatbed diesel truck with a tank in its bed was parked. This was the ranch's all-purpose beater, although from the hay and dirt dust that had settled on its hood and cabin roof, it looked like it hadn't been used in a bit, maybe even back to the thieving relative's time on the property.

Jack explained that he had sown a new grass seed from A&M in the front pasture between the house and the road that was a better, more nutritious grass for the cattle. God knows the cattle needed it; this region was pretty dry and could get tough and scrubby. The pastures of Kentucky were lush in comparison. He wanted to keep this pasture, with its young grass, free from mesquite trees, and so my job would be to fill the tank with a mixture of a powerful weed killer, water, and diesel from the rusted metal gas tank outside, and then use the nozzle at the end of the hose to spray any mesquite seedlings and saplings that were popping up. For anything bigger, he showed me a chainsaw.

He climbed into the truck's driver's seat while I got in on the passenger side. On the second turn of the ignition key, the engine turned over, and Jack backed out of the barn to give me a tour of the property. The late-afternoon sun was hot, and the truck kicked up clouds of dust as we bounced and jostled over to the front pasture, where he showed me some mesquite seedlings and saplings so that I would recognize a baby mesquite. The A&M grass in the front pasture was soft and a light-green color, not the harsh, thick-bladed grass that made up the ranch's remaining sparse pasturage.

He next took me to a tank that was located in the front acreage outside the reach of the A&M grass. Now, I had learned this bit of western ranch vocabulary before, namely that a tank wasn't necessarily a manmade metal reservoir, but was most often what I would call a pond or small lake created by a spring or that happened to hold rain water between downpours. This particular tank was fairly large and at least partially manmade, maybe about an acre or more. Part of it was surrounded by trees that dotted a hill, an old berm made of soil that had been pushed up from what would become the tank's bed to deepen the depression so it could hold more water and to damn the water up.

"I've stocked it with bass and panfish, so you feel free to come out here to fish when you're not working. We need to pull some fish out of here anyway. We've got plenty of rods and gear back on the side porch."

Jack drove us slowly along a cow path that took us to the north end of the property where the fifty head or so of cattle were grazing. He stopped along the way to show me thorns from mature mesquite trees that lined part of the cow path. They were long and sharp and hard as iron, a dark brown color.

"These doggone *tharns* are the problem with the mesquites. The cows'll rub along the branches and get these things caught up in their hides and end up dropping 'em all over the ranch. They'll punch a hole right through the tires of the truck or jeep and give you a flat. You gotta keep an eye out for them while you're driving."

I promised him that I would be careful and would keep an eye out. They were pretty nasty-looking things, punching through even my thick rawhide rancher gloves that I had bought on my way out to Jefferson for the jobs I figured that I'd be doing.

We caught up to the cattle. They weren't scrawny, but they sure looked tough, a crossbreed of brahmin and longhorns. Most ignored us, but a couple came up to the truck, jostling it and looking for handouts, but we continued along down a slight slope off on my side into a sunken area where the trees looked to be greener and friendlier than the mesquites.

The cattle stayed grazing where they were in the scrubby grass along the path and beyond the limbs of the mesquites, while we bounced down the incline into a ravine. Calling it a ravine makes it out to be more than it was. It was really more of a spreading cleft with slow slopes from the level of the rolling terrain. The slopes were chalky white, like a lot of the ranch land, as if the sun and heat had dried everything out until it all was just bone-white dry. The sun reflected off the ground and exposed rocks and made me glad to have my sunglasses on. The truck also kicked up the dry, whitish limestone dust that made the air seem hotter.

At the bottom was a long, natural tank, maybe seventy-five yards long and of a width varying from a narrow point at one end, where a trickle entered, to about twenty-five yards wide near its other end, where a small chalky-white rise kept it in. The water was a dark blue, almost a black. I couldn't see below the surface. At the wider end, there were two low trees whose tops didn't reach much above the level of the rim. Their leaves were a deep, dark green underneath a thin layer of the white ground dust that had settled on them. The trees' roots reached down through the rocky soil, anchoring themselves in the tank's dark waters. Here at the bottom, near the water and under the trees, it was cooler. A small breeze was making hard-to-see little ripples out in the middle of the water. A fish leapt. A bass.

Jack turned off the ignition and climbed out of the cab. I followed. He wiped his face with his bandana. I did the same. It felt good in the shade down by the water. He called this place and the trickle that fed it Tonkaway Springs, or at least that's how I understood it. I couldn't quite tell whether the tank by itself was Tonkaway Springs. It was definitely fed by springs in its depths, added to by whatever water came in through the trickle, which was best described as a wadi, but I think Jack was referring to the general area down here as Tonkaway Springs. Since we had started the tour and I had gotten to know Jack better, I had learned to listen long and make a comment or ask a question only when there was a long pause. It also seemed better to ask only crucial questions like the above-mentioned, "What's a varmint?" But even the answer to that question left the situation, well, wide-open, if not downright vague.

Jack said that the springs were named after the Tonkawa tribe who had once lived here or nearby and that there had been a battle or massacre here on the ranch.

He also said that he and his wife and their family called the little wadi, and the next tank down, Bucky's Springs. "Bucky" was the name of the husband of Jack's and his wife's remaining daughter, my girlfriend's aunt, a pretty and effusive woman who lived by herself in a nice house in the hills looking down onto Austin. Jack spoke in reverence and awe of Bucky, whose given name was William. Before fleeing the country due to some unclear-to-me disagreement with the Feds about money and maybe taxes, Bucky had enjoyed coming here to the ranch to relax and fish. He never made it back to the States. There was an interesting story there, but I never got the chance to find out much more.

In Bucky's Springs proper, as I came to refer to this particular tank, lived a bunch of bass, but the biggest, unless he had gotten washed down to the next spring during a rain flood, was William, named after their rich, Fed-fleeing son-in-law. William, the fish, had been there a long time and had grown large but had never been caught, except that he was hooked once by the human William, the legendary "Bucky" himself. But he had snapped the line to escape back to his home in the cool dark bottom of Bucky's Springs. Before escaping himself, the human Bucky had come down here to the springs to fish again for William and, although he had caught other bass, he had never gotten William. I sometimes got lost in Jack's descriptions and stories of William and Bucky, not knowing whether the reference was to the fish, the person, or the spring. I think Jack got lost sometimes too.

We drove back up to the barn and then went inside the ranch house, where the air conditioning felt frigid but soothing on my hot, sweaty skin. I followed Jack into the living room, where he turned on a recording of "The Lion Sleeps Tonight." He was proud of the recently installed sound system, and it certainly was very nice, with speakers placed in strategic positions throughout the living area of the ranch and out onto the front and back patios. He put the song on loop.

He then opened up the bar and told me that I was free to its contents while I was there. It was fully stocked. He began telling me about his times in the Army Air Corps as a flight surgeon and about the officers' club on base. The drink of choice among the officers was the rusty nail, and he wanted to share it with me. I believed he was extending an honor to me, and I humbly accepted the one he mixed up for me. I had never had one before, and I was glad to try a new drink.

Oh my Lord, but it was awful. It was most definitely a drink that would "put hair on your chest," as my grandmother would say.

Not only did the drink burn all the way down, but the taste was sickly medicinal. Still, I was in this man's house, and he had wanted to share this drink from his younger days with me, so I continued to sip at it as we sat in the living room, listening to "The Lion Sleeps Tonight" on loop, hoping that the rusty nail would eventually grow on me. It didn't. Live and learn, I figured. The song didn't grow on me either, but again, I was in Jack's house.

We spent some time cooling off in the air-conditioned room drinking our rusty nails. My mom had always taught me that when I was at another person's, I should eat whatever he or she served me. I guess, in my mind, this included drinking. In this case, it was a tough rule to follow, so in the present circumstance, I considered it more of a guideline. "The Lion Sleeps Tonight" continued to play on its loop.

When Jack left me to go back to town, I turned off the song and poured out what remained of my rusty nail. I mixed myself a gin and tonic and came back outside to the front porch to relax in a rocking chair. By now, it was early evening, and the sun was declining behind the house. The porch was fully in shade, the heat had dropped to comfortability, and a breeze was blowing under and across the awning. The heat and listening had been tiring, so it was good to sit back and look across what was my ranch for the next few days. I was alone, and it was quiet except for the occasional lowing of the cattle out in the distance, now somewhere down in the direction of Bucky's Springs. The cold gin and tonic was refreshing. Water beaded on the glass.

As I thought about my time here at the ranch, I figured that things wouldn't be so bad at all. I would ride the range on Dusty to keep an eye on the cattle and kill mesquite trees and whatever varmints crossed my path, hopefully a rattlesnake. This day was ending really nicely. As the sun was setting and things became much less hot, I grilled myself a burger and sipped another gin and tonic. The country sky was clear and the stars were bright, and there was a soothing, natural quiet that unveiled the night sounds. A covey of quail was peeping in the grass tufts along the fence line around the yard, crickets were chirring, and coyotes were howling, one across the road and another behind the house, maybe down near Tonkaway Springs.

After the sun went down, I went upstairs and shook out my bedroll and laid myself down on the bottom twin bed. The air conditioning was pleasant, and the overhead fan kept a current of cool air blowing on me. I was quickly asleep.

The next morning, I got up early before the sun had crossed the horizon and had a breakfast of eggs and biscuits and a little coffee before heading out to the barn. I gave Dusty his feed and let him into the corral after giving him a carrot and some sugar and talking to him about how he was doing. He seemed to appreciate the conversation. Since the forecast wasn't calling for rain in the next few days, I took the truck to the fuel tank to put diesel on top of the poison I had already poured in. The sun was about to rise above the horizon, and it was already getting hot.

I drove out to the front acreage and spent the morning spraying mesquite sprouts that had popped up and the rare sapling that had grown. The cattle had moved to this good pasture and were feeding slowly in a gradual milling towards shade and water. The morning was a slow repeat of driving, stopping, getting out of the cab, unrolling the hose, and spraying the young mesquites, then getting back into the truck and moving a few yards over to the next area. I spent the whole morning in the front pasture, the sun glaring down and the heat rising. It wasn't the blanket-like humidity that had hung and floated under the live oak trees of New Orleans; it was a much-higher temperature, above a hundred degrees, without shade. The cab of the truck was hardly any shelter.

At noon, I headed back to the ranch house for lunch. The iciness of the air conditioning was refreshing and welcome. I made myself two peanut butter and jelly sandwiches and drank a lot of ice water. Before going back outside, I rolled down the sleeves of my blue chambray shirt, so old that it was thin and almost white, because the sun had already begun to burn my hair-covered arms. I tied my bandana around my stinging, taught, burned-red neck, and I exchanged my baseball cap for a wide-brimmed straw cowboy hat that hung from a peg by the door. I chuckled to myself because I looked like the clichéd cowboy, but the clichés all made sense because the sun was not a friend.

The ground was dry and pebbly, almost grassless between the ranch house and the barn. Dusty heard me coming and trotted to the corral fence. Putting on my leather work gloves and cinching them tight with the drawstrings around the wrists, I opened the gate to the corral and gave Dusty a carrot. He was easy to saddle up, not shying away or pulling any of those horse tricks like bloating out his belly to make the girth strap and surcingle loose. I checked to see if he was trying to pull a fast one on me, but he wasn't. He was a good horse.

Putting the gun in the saddle scabbard and a handful of shotgun shells and brass cartridges into the old brown leather saddle bag, I swung up, and we trotted off to find the cattle, clomping down the sun-hardened path that Jack and I had driven along yesterday. We found them past the shade of the old-grown mesquites, milling around and slowly moving towards the tanks of Tonkaway and Bucky's Springs. A few of the young ones had meandered up into the trees, and we pushed them towards their mommas. That done, we halted, Dusty standing, resting, and watching. I came to sense that Dusty had a certain amount of pride and looked at the cattle with, if not disdain, then at least resignation, in the way an old schoolteacher watches and anticipates the antics of third-graders. I leaned forward with my forearms crossed on the horn and took my hat off to wipe the sweat through my hair with my fingers, watching the lazy movements of the cattle.

Dusty and I made the circuit and then checked the range ahead of the cows. Any varmints like *armadillers* had scurried away, and there were no signs, no marks in the dust, of snakes between the cattle and the tanks. We stopped at Bucky's Springs for Dusty to get a drink. I stayed mounted, looking around and listening. The days were even more silent than the nights as the animals, the varmints, were hunkered down out of the hot sun. A fish broke the surface of the Springs. I wondered if it was William. We were far enough away from civilization that there were no car sounds or even airplane sounds from the sky. The almost-white blue sky had a few high-up, wispy feathered clouds, but no unnatural scarring of jet contrails. The quiet, the peace were pleasant. It was good to be somewhat alone, just me and the good horse.

While we rested under the low branches of the tree at the edge of Bucky's Springs, I thought of Bucky-William. I wondered what the real reason was for why he'd fled the country, a reason that wasn't really spoken and was occasionally hinted at. I had gathered that it had something to do with a lot of money—oil money, I think—and maybe taxes that he didn't think he should pay, so he had escaped down south to Mexico and then further, to South America. I imagined him relaxing on the veranda of a hacienda he had gotten with his money after having spent his day fishing or hunting, sitting back with his boots up, nursing a cool drink, and waiting for his wife to join him, thinking about fishing this tank and wondering if he would ever get back to get William. Good ol' Bucky.

I clucked at Dusty, and we climbed up out of the depression as the cattle came down on the other side of the Springs. The sun was hot, and the air smelled of baked dust and mesquite trees, the tang of my sweat, and the musty horse smell of Dusty. As we moseyed along, I noted some fallen trees and branches that I would bring the chainsaw to cut up tomorrow. They would make good fire and barbecue wood. Some of the bigger pieces looked like they would make good carpentry pieces. We wandered along the back acreage and the trickle of Tonkaway Springs to the trash pit. No snakes and not much was moving, but I did catch sight of a fox going about his business. A few buzzards were high up in the sky, only circling specks of black, and there was nothing in the pit. We rode the fence line around much of the back property, and it was in good shape. All was good and quiet, so Dusty and I rode back up to the barn, where I unsaddled him, shook out the saddle blanket, and rubbed him down with handfuls of hay, then led him into his stall, where I took off his harness and filled his feed bag.

"Good boy, Dusty. That was a good ride today. You're a good one." He nickered as I rubbed his muzzle and scratched him behind his ears.

The cool air in the ranch house was welcome, and the inside seemed dark after the brightness outside. I hung my hat on the peg, pulled my sweat-stained gloves from the back pocket of my jeans, and put them on the shelf next to my hat. I set my boots next to the door. In the kitchen, I poured myself a tall glass of ice water, trying to do my best to drink it slowly. That heat really took it out of you. Sitting down at the table, I thought about what to have for dinner. I called Jack to give him my report for the day, stretching the cord to the table so I could sit and drink my water while we had our slow conversation.

As the cold water brought me back to myself, I thought a little more clearly and decided on one of the steaks that my girlfriend's father had sent along with me. It was from one of his cattle, and he told me how he'd had it aged beyond the normal time. The butcher had called him a few times to come get his beef, but he had kept on telling the butcher to let it hang a little bit longer. These steaks were surely going to be tender and flavorful. I had thanked him; that sure was generous of him to send some steaks with me.

I took one of the steaks out of the refrigerator, set it on a plate, and covered it tightly with a paper towel strip to keep flies off, poured myself a gin and tonic, and took it all out to the front porch along with a bucket of ice and the remaining half of the lime. I had set up a little grill out in the front yard. I liked this porch better than the back patio with its big grill, what they called here a "pit," and its vine covered trellis. The back was new and fancy, but the front porch was better. The sun wasn't in my eyes, the view was deeper and wider, and it caught more of a breeze. I sipped at the cool, tangy drink, waiting for the sun to drop to the horizon so it would be cooler while I cooked the steak.

Four turkeys came down over the rise above the road and along the fence line that marked the boundary of the front acreage. They hopped over the fence and strutted along the inside, off to my right, to disappear into a copse of mesquites. Doves flew overhead from that direction, probably heading for the water of Tonkaway and Bucky's Springs. The quail, hidden in the barely green tufts of grass, were making their tiny-throated peeping. Occasionally, one would pop out to snatch a beetle or hopper and then dash back into its refuge. As I listened to and watched the quail, I saw another bird fly in from over the rise and land near where the turkeys had been. I watched it to make sure and, yep, it was a pheasant. I thought I was wrong, but no, there it was, with its blue head, white neck-ring, and long, straight tail, walking through the grass. I wondered what a pheasant was doing way down south here in the Texas heat.

The sun was close to the horizon behind me, becoming more orange and then red the lower it got, no longer the blinding white it had been higher in the sky. In front of me, the sky was becoming a deeper blue, and the shadows lengthened to cover my little grill. I finished off my gin and tonic and set it down on the mesquite stump that served as a stool, footrest, and table. Then I walked out to the grill set away from the house near the fence line that held the covey of quail, took the lid off, and stirred the residue to knock the gray-white ash off of what unconsumed charcoal remained from last night. I mounded those up, set some new briquettes on them, set two thick mesquite chunks on the pile, and then lit the briquettes from the bottom. I only needed one match; everything was dry and hot. The first flames were high, and when they died down to a low blue, I put the lid back, making sure the flue was just barely open at the top, open enough to draw in air.

I walked back to the porch, the gravel and dust grinding beneath my boots. I sat back down in my chair, reached down into my ice bucket, dropped a handful of ice into my glass, and then ran the cold, melted water through my hair. It was pleasant.

While the coals slow-burned, getting ready for the steak, I thought about my girlfriend's father. A quiet, calm, understated man, he had raised four daughters alone after his first wife passed away young and suddenly. As best as I could tell, it was shortly afterward that he had embraced a version of evangelical Christianity. While I didn't agree with some of his beliefs, I figured that, if that's what he needed to get through the death of his wife and raising daughters, then good for him. He did all the cooking, which was mostly done on his pit at the end of the driveway, for his family, and he had taught me some tips. His current wife, a pretty, airy blonde, nagged him about how long it took for him to cook. That seemed unfair because he cooked on his pit well, doing it his way. He was a solid man.

I took another sip of my drink and looked out across the front acreage. The quiet, the absence of human sounds, with only the sounds of the quail, the distant barking of a coyote, and the breeze through the porch—a breeze that had risen with the slight drop in temperature—were soothing, relaxing. The solitude was calming and satisfying. It was good here.

The coals were bound to be done, so I took the steak over to my grill, took the top off, seared both sides to get nice blackened grill marks on the meat and to hold in the juices, put the top back on, and closed the flue until it was just barely open. I wanted a slow, low temperature cook for this steak, and I wanted the smoke from the mesquite chunks. I leaned against the fence by the grill, sipping at my drink, moisture beading on the clear glass as the ice melted. I surveyed the land around me in a slow circle. The evening sounds were still there, but not much was moving. There were buzzards off to my left, circling high up on the winds. The land was dry, but there was a quiet beauty to it. As an older man now, I have found that every place I lived in had its own beauty.

I opened the lid again, flipped the steak, and put the lid back on. I liked it here. I decided, or maybe realized is a better word, that it was better than spending the summer running around New Orleans.

I took the lid off again and forked the steak onto my plate, put the lid back on with the flue closed, and walked back to the porch, where I put the plate on the mesquite stump and scooted it in front of my chair. I tossed the dregs of my drink into the yard and refilled the glass with ice and melt-water from my bucket. The juices were pinkish, almost red, and were spreading across the bottom of the plate. I cut into the steak, and the center was the almost-red of the plate juices. I cut a piece from the center. It was tender, and it felt like it melted in my mouth. There was a richness, a thickness to the flavor that lingered. I sat back, savoring it, and took a drink of my ice water. In my mind, I offered thanks to my girlfriend's father for sending it with me.

I took my plate and silverware inside and washed them off before coming back outside with a cigar and a cutter. It was a true Romeo y Julieta from Cuba, one of a handful given to me by a girl I had squired around town the year before. She had, at that time, recently returned from a diplomatic trip to Cuba; I suppose it was more likely a boondoggle than a true diplomatic trip. She worked for some Texas Representative.

I snipped the cap and lit the other end, drawing in slowly to light it. The smoke was rich and held a hint of spice. It reminded me of my grandparents' house. True Cuban cigars, grown and rolled in Cuba, were everything they were cracked up to be. Slowly smoking my cigar with my legs stretched out and my feet resting on the mesquite stump, I sat out on the porch into the night, letting my thoughts flow languidly across Texas, New Orleans, to my move up north at the end of the summer, and back to the ranch.

When the cigar was finished, I went inside and showered, shook out my bedroll, climbed in under the sheets, cool against my skin, and was immediately asleep.

<hr />

The next day and the ones following were pretty much the same. I woke up, had my breakfast, and went out to the barn, where I fed Dusty and made sure his water was full before heading out to poison the mesquite shoots. After lunch that day, Dusty and I rode out to check on the cattle, who had moved to the lower back section of the acreage, below and past the trash pit. Not much else was out. No snakes or varmints. Just some birds—quail peeping, doves speeding from dusty, rocky areas to the Springs, and buzzards floating high up and far away.

Before dinner as the sun was getting close to the horizon, Dusty and I returned to the ranch house to get a fishing pole and bait. As we ambled close to the big front tank, I saw an armadillo trotting along the berm. Taking the drilling from the saddle scabbard, I loaded a .22 round into the rifle chamber and drew a bead on him and panned ahead. Taking deep breaths, I then lowered the rifle and unchambered the round.

With the rifle back in the scabbard, I nudged Dusty into motion with my boot heels. At the edge of the tank below the berm, I dismounted and led Dusty to the water, where he dropped his mouth to the surface and lapped it up. When he was done, I looped the reins around a low branch and took the fishing pool and hot dog bait to the water's edge, casting out as far as I could. The bobber sat still for a while and then began drifting to my right, almost imperceptibly, pushed by a gentle breeze that faintly rippled the surface around the bobber. A fish jumped further out, so I reeled in and cast out as far as I could but didn't reach the spot where the fish had cleared the surface. I didn't catch anything, but it was good to relax out there with Dusty as the sun set. The armadillo didn't return.

~

The morning of the third day by myself on the ranch was spent poisoning the last of the mesquite sprouts and saplings. The ones from two days earlier were already turning a blackish brown from the poison and the sun and the heat. I was glad to be done with the diesel and weed killer. If I got even a little bit of the fumes it made me slightly light-headed, so I had learned to take breaths upwind of it. Added to the smell, I didn't like the idea of it doing to me out here in the sun what it was doing to the mesquites. The last thing I wanted was Jack to find my desiccated body lying out here in the A&M-grass pasture with the truck parked nearby.

After a light lunch, I went to the barn to get the chainsaw and went to Dusty's stall to say hello. He looked at me expectantly, having gotten used to, and, it seemed to me, enjoyed our daily afternoon rides across the ranch.

"Sorry, buddy, not yet. I'm going to go cut up some of the fallen mesquite trees. We'll go fishing at Bucky's Springs this evening. Let's catch that ol' outlaw William." I laughed and Dusty nickered. He was game. By damn, I do believe that horse understood me. I gave him one last stroke on his muzzle and patted his neck, then went to find the chainsaw. I put some gas in it from the old tin gas can, hoping that the gas wasn't as old as the can, and checked the chain oil. It was full, and the chain was good and lubed, which gave me some confidence about the gas.

After saying goodbye to Dusty, I stowed the chainsaw and a long-handled axe in the back of the truck and drove to the back acreage above the streamlet of Tonkaway Springs, where about half of a mesquite tree had broken off of the main trunk. I stopped the truck away from the trees so that none of the wicked thorns would get to the tires. Luckily, the saw fired up after a couple of pulls on the cord, the engine already warmed from the sun. With my gloves and glasses on, I set about lopping off the smaller, thorn-bearing branches from the dark brown, almost black, twisted fallen trunk. Then I set to cutting the thicker branches and trunk into logs and sections. The sections closer to the split from the main trunk were too big for me to lift by myself, so I set to splitting them with the axe, driving the axe head into the stumps and then pounding it with a solid club-like chunk of mesquite until it split the stump deep enough that the splits either came apart themselves or I could tear them or kick them apart.

I paced myself in the heat and took breaks to rest and drink water, leaning against the truck's lowered tailgate, relaxing and looking around. Sweat darkened my shirt and came down into my eyes, stinging them. I could taste the salt from my upper lip. My muscles stayed loose in the heat.

It was hot and tiring and satisfying work, and it took me the rest of the afternoon. I had some really good, thick logs that would be good for a slow burn in Jack's pit or in his smoker. Once I was finished, I drove back up to the ranch house, where I filled the rack by the back patio and set some inside the pit's firebox on top of the tinder. It would be ready to go for Jack's next cookout. I drove the remaining logs over to the rack by the barn, unloaded them, and parked the truck inside. I said hello to Dusty, and he nickered back.

I stroked his muzzle and the side of his neck. "I'm going up to the house for some water and some food, and then we'll go fishing." I gave him a pat goodbye and made my way through the dust and heat up to the ranch house, where the cool air conditioning was welcome. It was a real luxury. I sat at the table, sipping at my ice water before I ate. When I had cooled down, I made myself a steak sandwich from last night's leftovers, which I had sliced as thin as I could. The steaks sent with me by my girlfriend's father were very good, and I wasn't going to waste a bite. I cut an onion, putting a few rings on top of the steak slices, and dribbled some juices onto the bread. Boy, it was good. No need for steak sauce. Sitting at the kitchen table, I thought, *I am living the life.*

When I was rested and no longer felt affected by the heat and the exertions of cutting up and moving the mesquite logs, I chopped a hot dog from the refrigerator for bait, picked out and tested a fishing pole, and then made my way out to the barn. Dusty was ready to go, neighing his hello and stamping in a circle around the inside of his stall. I got his saddle on, cinched on the rifle scabbard, put the drilling inside, and then tied on my broken-down rod. I led Dusty outside and mounted up, turning him toward the trash pit. I wanted him to have some exercise, and the sun was still a good way above the horizon.

After checking on the pit, I nudged him into a trot, and we headed off to Bucky's Springs. The bottom of the hollowed-out cleft of the Springs were mostly in shade, the water still and dark, and the slight breeze reaching my neck and under my shirt felt almost cool. I dismounted and casually flipped the reins around a low branch of the tree.

My first cast went long, as far out as I could get it. Pausing, I let the heavy, flashy lure sink into the darkness of the Spring then reeled in, hoping it had gotten close to the bottom. Tip up, I paused in my retrieval, then reeled more, jerking and halting, and then pulled it in. I cast out a few times more with maybe a tentative strike, but nothing more. I took a hot dog piece and secured it well on one of the lure's treble hooks and cast back out. It plopped down on the surface, sending up a little splash and pushing out a ripple that spread across the surface, and vanished. Once I started to reel in, a fish hit the lure hard. I paused before setting the hook, knowing the fish wouldn't spit it out right away because of the hot dog, and then set the hook as hard as I could. It stuck, and I knew I had something. The fish fought the bite of the hook, thrashing and trying to rid himself of it, then dashed deep and away from the pull. I held on with the tip of my rod up and then began to reel in. The fish came to the top, churning the dark surface to white splashes with its thrashing dance. Under the shade of the tree on my left, Dusty nickered and stomped the ground in a pawing motion, his shoes clinking on the rocks. The fish fought to get away, and I kept the line taught, rod bending, steadily bringing him in. I stepped out into the shallow water to lift him out of the water. I quickly unhooked him and settled him back into the water, where he rested for a moment. I tickled his underside and he jetted away, back into the dark depths. He was nice, but he wasn't William.

J. KENT GREGORY

I moved to my left to try an area that was undisturbed by the fight and maybe was shallower. Dusty looked at me, curious as to where I was going, hoping that I wouldn't leave him out of the fun.

"Just going over here a bit, Dusty. You enjoy the shade."

I got to a spot that seemed good and changed to a smaller, worm-like lure that I baited with another hot dog piece. I cast it out and let it sink to the bottom and then began to reel in, the motion and angle lifting it just off the bottom. I could feel little darting nibbles that were different than the bumps on the rocks, so I slowed the retrieve down a little. It was hit, and I set the hook. Again, there was a fight: lively, but less powerful, and not as weighty. The fish, a bluegill came in. I kept him, putting him on a stringer that I secured around a log that I had set into the water. I kept fishing here, aiming at the same general spot, and caught four more bluegill on the worm lure loaded with hot dogs. They must have been hanging out around one of the springs that helped feed Bucky's Springs with cool water.

Doves were flying overhead, some stopping to sip water and to peck at the rocks on the other side of the Springs. I thought to myself that I needed to call and find out whether it was dove season here and to get a license if it was. I caught another small bluegill that I let go and cast again a few times out to the deep. I got nothing but some nibbles, tentative strikes. I was losing confidence and wondered whether William was still out there. I reeled in and drew the stringer out, gutting the bluegills and tossing their entrails out into the Springs and cleaning their insides in the tank's shallows.

When that was done, Dusty and I sauntered back to the barn. I took a wandering route to give Dusty some exercise and to check on the property. Some crows were busy picking at something down in the trash pit and were completely unbothered by us. We moved on through the boulder and rock-strewn area near the front acreage, where boulders and slabs of rock were imbedded, some almost vertically, in the ground. The cattle were in the front acreage near the gate at the road. I let Dusty have the reins, and he galloped back to the barn, tossing his head and neighing when I pulled him up. I led him inside to his stall and hung the fish from a spike in a beam while I unsaddled him, rubbed him down with hay, and then brushed him. I gave him his feed and refreshed his hay and water. Then I rubbed him between and behind his ears as I said goodbye for the day.

Inside the cool ranch house, I finished cleaning the fish and breaded them in flour I had found in the pantry and then fried them in the cast-iron skillet. I took them out to the front porch on a tin plate with some beans. The fish were good, warm and delicate, almost not enough, but the barbecued beans filled me up. By now, the sun was below the horizon. When I was finished, I went back inside to clean my dishes. I scraped the skillet and reoiled it with bacon grease. I poured myself a tall gin and tonic and went back outside to the porch, propping my feet up and watched the sky darkening and the blue-silver lights of the stars come out while I listened to the night sounds. When it was almost fully dark, meteors flashed and streaked across the sky high above the horizon.

The evening gin and tonic was a soothing and refreshing ritual at the end of the day. The chilling of the ice, the tart perfume of the lime, the bitter effervescence of the tonic, and the juniper and botanicals of the gin, at the same time, woke me and my senses up and, a few sips in, began to sooth me to an approaching sleepiness.

The meteors kept me out, standing on the porch, leaning against a post with my drink in my right hand, looking up at the black-blue night sky. The cattle were quiet, and I could hear the coyotes calling to each other in the distance. Their haunting calls reminded me of those of the loons up on the forested lakes of northern Minnesota. When there seemed to be an end to the meteors, I went back inside to shower and get ready for bed. I washed and dried my glass and put it back into the cabinet by the sink. It felt good to keep things ordered and tidy, which was an easy thing to do since it was just me.

The shower was a true luxury. It had been recently installed and was a walk-in with jets built into the white-tiled walls that shot water at me from the sides, and one directly above. I scrubbed off the sweat and dirt from the day. The hot water blasting against my body was a pleasant massage after that afternoon's mesquite logging. I hadn't realized how fatigued I was from cutting and stacking the logs. I toweled off, and as I was stepping out of the shower, I noticed a large black scorpion that had halted, tail and stinger erect, where my foot was about to land. Carefully skirting the critter, I walked over to my boots, put them on, and took care of it.

Well, I thought to myself, *you do have to be careful about* scarpions—which was how I now thought of them—*in the house.*

I was more careful when I shook out my bedroll, and sure enough, a dried-up scarpion fell out. I wondered how long it had been in there and, too tired to think much about it, went to bed thinking of meteors and doves. I would go to the store tomorrow to get a hunting license.

~~~

The next morning, I woke up a little fuzzier in my head than the day before. I figured it was last night's gin and tonics after the mild dehydration from cutting up the mesquite tree. I started the day with Dusty. We rode the range and checked on the cattle and looked for any new mesquite sprouts. There weren't any. There were some fallen tree branches to cut up, so after giving Dusty and myself a good ride, I took him back to the barn and set him loose in the corral. I made sure his water tank was clean and full before he drank. Then I drove the truck to some fallen branches up against the trash pit, where a fox was hunting. Intent on his work, he wasn't bothered by the sound of my chainsaw. The friction from the chain as it ground through the wood gave off a cooking smell, as if I was running a barbecue pit. The smell of the heated mesquite was good and made me vaguely hungry. I tossed the twigs and slender branches into the pit and brought the rest back to the barn, where I loaded them onto the rack with the other logs. With that finished, I went back into the ranch house for a quick lunch of a steak sandwich that I made from the last of the steak I had cooked the other night. Then I drove the truck to the supply store down the road, hanging a right out of the gravel driveway and then another right further down at the T-crossing.

The store was really a big pole-barn warehouse filled with everything for your ranch from planking to feed, tools, and guns. I was greeted by tipped hats and "Howdys," which I returned, and had a conversation with the older bushy, gray-white mustached gentleman behind the counter, who, like the rest of us was dressed, in jeans, chambray, and a wide brimmed hat.

"How are you doing over at Jack's spread?"

"I'm doing all right, just keeping an eye on the cattle and cutting up the mesquite."

"Yes, sir, that's pretty much what goes on. Do you need any help?"

"No, but I thank you kindly. I've got it under control. It sure is nice over there."

"Jack sure does have a nice place out there. He said you were from New Orleans."

"Well, that's where I've been living. I'm originally from Kentucky."

"Nice horses in Kentucky."

"Beautiful. There are nice horses here too. I've been riding a real good one out on the ranch."

"Well, sir, what can I help you with this afternoon?"

I bought my Texas dove license and two boxes of shells for my 12-gauge that I had brought with me to the ranch. I spent the rest of the afternoon doing light work around the ranch house, cleaning inside and weeding and sweeping outside. There were some bags of cypress mulch in the barn that I spread around the flower beds. As the afternoon sun approached evening, I took my shotgun and shells over near the front tank, where I set up just under the limbs of a tree to wait for the doves. It was hot even in the shade, the dried earth seeming to make its own heat. In my experience, there was something about dove hunts that caused them always to take place in blistering, suffocating high heat. I had come to think of them as mini-Bataan Death Marches. Still, I was addicted to them. I was glad I had a jug of water with me.

Pretty soon, thankfully, the doves started coming in, first singly, then in pairs, and then groups with flights of singles and pairs mixed. They were fast, and my first couple of shots missed behind the birds, but then I got the feel back, got into a rhythm, and hit them. They fell in arcs, their speed still carrying them forward, dropping onto the baked ground. As each one fell, I retrieved it as other doves streaked overhead to land by the water's edge or to perch in the trees around the tank. When I reached my limit, I sat down at the edge of the water and breasted them out, leaving the remains for any scavengers that wanted them.

Back inside the cool, cave-like refuge of the ranch house, I washed the last bit of feathers off and picked out what shot pellets I could find. There were some jalapenos, and I stuffed them with the queso I had brought with me and wrapped the breasts around them and then bacon around each roll. I set them in a big bowl that I found in the cupboard and poured over them a mixture of soy sauce and salad dressing. I covered them in tin foil and placed the bowl in the refrigerator to marinate until tomorrow's dinner. They would be good. I was hungry for them now, but I knew they would be much better in a day, so I waited. I thought of my Texas friend who, a few years back, had brought dove breasts marinating in the back seat of his truck all the way to Virginia. He had pulled up to the house out in the country and we put the breasts on the grill right away. I still remember how good they were.

I called Jack to give him my daily report. He said that he and his wife were beginning to feel better, so he would come out the day after tomorrow to check on things, and that he had some work for me back at the house in town.

Well, I thought, *the solitude will be coming to an end.* After just these few days out there on the ranch by myself, taking care of it and watching over it, part of me was beginning to think of it as mine. So, I fixed myself a gin and tonic to enjoy on the front porch and to savor the last evenings of being alone. Slowly rocking back and forth in my chair, I went over what I needed to get done before Jack came to the ranch. There just wasn't much else left of what he had given me to do. I hadn't killed any varmints, but I had taken care of the mesquite in the front pasture. I thought that I could tidy up around the ranch house and cut up some more mesquite logs to top off the woodpile, but that wasn't much and wouldn't take long. I figured I would do the logs late morning but would go fish at Bucky's Springs first thing while it was cooler and the shadows covered the surface.

The breeze was nice and the gin and tonic was beginning to go to my head, so I slowed down and took a drink of ice water, crunching on the cold ice. When the sun touched the horizon, still gold, but turning red as it sunk further, making the shadowed hills on the horizon darker and then a deep purple-blue, I lit the grill and went inside to get the last steak I had brought with me. After dinner, I stayed on the porch and watched the night sky for meteors.

The next morning, after a quick breakfast of eggs, bacon, and toast, with coffee, I gathered the fishing gear and went to the barn where I saddled up Dusty. He nuzzled me as I checked his hooves and hoisted the saddle onto his back. I didn't go directly to the Springs but let Dusty get some exercise. In the flat spaces, I set him trotting, and he kicked up dust from the cattle and other animal trails. We ended up on the far eastern border of the land marked by a double strand of barbwire. The other side was land owned by a cousin or nephew of Jack's wife, I can't remember which, but had once belonged to the patriarch, Jack's father-in-law. Dusty and I rode the fence line. One length, running across three fence posts, had sagged to the ground. The base of one post had gotten loose enough for the post to tip over, bringing the lines down with it and putting weight on the posts some feet, about six I guessed, on either side, stretching out the wire and making it pop out from under the nail that had held it down. I glanced around to check for the cattle, but they weren't nearby, and it didn't appear to me that there were any across the line on the other property, so that was good.

I dismounted and looped Dusty's reins around a dried-up bush, more as a way of saying to him, "Stay here and wait for me to get done," than to hold him. My boots scuffled and scraped across the rocky baked-white ground. I set the tipped-over post pack upright and scooped some dirt and gravel back in the hole, stomping it all down with my boot heel, and then packed in some rocks on top, stomping them down too. Dusty watched it all with what I took to be a bemused expression.

"Well, Dusty, this fence stuff is funny, but I suppose it's gotta be done," I said aloud.

Checking my leather gloves and where I set them on the strands, I pulled the top strand to make it as tight as I could, leaning back and setting my legs firm on the ground, and looped it around the top of the old mesquite post, smooth and aged silver by its long time out here in the Texas sun. I didn't have a hammer with me, not expecting that I'd need to fix the fence, so I found a hand-sized rock that didn't look like it would crumble into dust, stretched the bottom loop of the top line below the old nail that was still there, and hammered that nail over the loop of barbwire as best as I could. The bottom strand was trickier because of the slackness on either side of the post, so I pulled on each side in turn and wrapped them as best I could around a nail near the ground. It wasn't perfect, but it seemed like it might hold. The job seemed to be similar to work on the other posts.

The sun was rising higher, and I wanted to get down to Bucky's Springs before it got high enough to hit the waters and heat them up, so I mounted up and turned Dusty in that direction, leaving the checking of the rest of the fence line for later.

We came down to Bucky's Springs from above and stopped on the rocky embankment, looking at the waters. In the windless morning, the waters were still in the shadows, and the sun had not hit the tops of the dried earth and rock banks. They were a black stillness, peaceful and cool. For a few minutes, we watched the waters, and I enjoyed the silent solitude of this spot. As I had figured out after riding the ranch the past couple of days, Bucky's Springs was deep in Jack's property and was isolated by the open lands of the neighboring ranches. There were no sounds of machines or people and no airplanes or their contrails in the air. Just the rising and soon-to-be-baking sun, the dark waters, and the quiet. It was a good place.

A ripple appeared in the middle of the Springs, the rings spreading across the black surface. Then a soft splash entered the silence with ripples spreading out from that spot on the surface too. The fish were moving. I knew we should get started, so we walked down to our tree. I let Dusty drink before dismounting and then looped his reins around a branch in the shade of the tree. After untying the rod from the back of his saddle, I secured a large fish-looking lure to the line and baited the treble hook under its belly with bacon. *Anything to increase my odds*, I thought. Funny how I would do this for bass but not when fishing for trout.

I cast out as far as I could to where I thought the splash had been. The line, with my bacon-enhanced lure, sailed in an arc over the still-dark waters to plop down through the surface, sending out its own ripples. I paused and didn't move, forcing myself to be still while the weighted leader carried the lure toward the bottom. The waiting was hard and tense for me. I began reeling it back in, feeling the fish-like tug of what must have been grassy weeds. The lure was near the dark bottom. I had waited the right amount of time and that gave me satisfaction and then a happiness.

Slowly and then quickly, in a jerking fashion, trying to imitate how in my mind a wounded fish would swim, I reeled the lure toward me. After a few yards, I stopped and let the lure settle back down close to the bottom. I let it rest a couple of seconds and then reeled it back in, using the same herky-jerky motion. I felt what could have been tentative, testing nibbles, maybe from the little perch or sunfish that were down there. I made a couple of more casts, rebaited my lure, and felt the same touches and tests from the fish. The repetition was peaceful, calming, but it was also taking the edge off my alertness. The growing heat dulled me even further, and my thoughts wandered. I thought about William swimming free in the cool darkness of the bottom near the spring and then about William-Bucky somewhere on the Mexican coast, sitting on the balcony of his beach house and looking out over the clear, bright waves, maybe sipping at a drink.

A sudden taking grabbed the lure. Sudden but not sharp or violent, but strong and pulling away with it. Several thoughts occurred to me on top of one another: the usual *Holy sh*t! What is this?* And then, *Wake up, dummy, before you lose this! Set the hook!*

which I did, and the pulling hesitated but then continued. It didn't thrash or turn. It reminded me of the time at my cousin's when I hooked onto a river turtle, a force or a weight that owned the lure. I let the fish take it, and the line slowly unspooled from the reel, going out further and then deeper, where it settled in the cool black depths of the tank. I'm sure it was lying near a spring. I lifted the tip of my rod and began reeling in. The fish was heavy, and the line was taught. Slowly, the fish came from its refuge, still following the bottom but coming closer to me. Dusty looked up from his sloshing and watched me straining and coaxing the line in. The ponderous plodding movement was unlike any bass that I had hooked, which was usually sharp and aggressive. This was unhurried as if the fish was unbothered by the pulling at its mouth, unconcerned. In a pause, I realized that I had hooked William. He came in slowly and I didn't force it, concerned as I always was about breaking the leader or knot. Although it was almost leisurely, with an occasional thrust to a side by William, I was tense and my heart beat fast. Without any conscious reason, unthinking, I really wanted, needed to bring him in, this trophy outlaw. And he came in as I pulled. There was no structure, no big or sharp rocks in this tank, just some weeds that lived in the few shallow yards before the white dry bank. I felt the weeds through the line that pulled against and through them. William was close, and then his back appeared above the surface, and I stepped into the shallow weeds to land him. His left eye came up above the water, and we saw each other. He dipped his head beneath the surface and shook himself in a wave from head to tail and was gone, back to his home in the cold, deep-dark part of the tank where it was fed by a spring.

I stood there, unmoving for a while, with my boots in the water. I folded my arms, cradling the rod with the line drifting on the surface and gradually being pushed to my left by a breeze. There was no depression as with other lost fish, no recrimination or emptiness.

There was a recognition, I don't know, maybe an understanding, that this was the right way of things. William deserved to be left alone; maybe he had earned it. Good ol' William. I'm glad we met. Good for him. And I thought of William-Bucky down in Mexico or South America, drinking a mojito or margarita on the balcony of his house on the beach, warm blue waves foaming onto the white beach. Like him, I had landed William. I thought about us being the only two to know William. Those two were free. I thought about that.

So that was done, the fishing for William.

I broke down the rod and tied it across the back of Dusty's saddle. Then I mounted up, and we rode the property, in part, looking for things to do, but mostly to enjoy the riding and to be out there on the land. There were still no rattlesnakes—or any other snake, for that matter—to be seen. The cattle were grazing in the green grass of the front pasture, with here-and-there mesquite saplings now turned dead-white by my spraying and the sun. To the south, over the hills and just above the horizon, a storm of spectacular blue-black, deep gray clouds were slow-motion boiling and spreading to the north. The cutting of the extra mesquite logs would have to wait. I turned Dusty back to the barn.

After getting Dusty unsaddled, I went back to the ranch house to make an early lunch. Standing on the front porch with a sandwich and a glass of lemonade, I watched the storm clouds move in, preceded by gusts of wind that were soothingly cool with the storm's moisture, and that made the A&M grass move like ocean waves. The clouds were thick and, once overhead, blocked out the sun, covering the land thereabouts with a night-like darkness. Nearby lighting flashed spectacularly, streaking down to my front, and briefly lighting up the darkness.

The rain and wind continued through the afternoon, sometimes falling and blowing like the wrath of God, with fierce lightning lighting up a world that had closed into what could be seen through the falling black sheets, gray in the lightning. I stayed on the porch throughout the afternoon, enjoying the weather, the cool, wet wind blowing into and across the veranda, with a thrill in my stomach and chest from the drama. Mostly, I just enjoyed and, frankly, was entranced by the meteorological show, but, at times, my thoughts turned to William and William-Bucky, both free and alone. Sure, they were surrounded by others; William by other, smaller fish and fry, and William-Bucky by other people, locals, I imagined, but both were essentially alone and, in my mind, living peacefully. In the case of William-Bucky, I imagined he was relaxed and at peace with where he was. I thought again to myself that I was really liking being out here by myself with just Dusty.

By the very late evening, the storm had passed, a strong breeze waved the grass, and a barely noticeable mist-like drizzle floated down with only a featureless gray sky above. The air and ground were cooled by the rain and the cloud cover, and the remnant breeze kept the humidity down. To make the most of my last night out here before Jack came in person to check on me, I set up the grill and lit the charcoal, the burnt coal-like smell rising up and swirling back on my face. I let the flames take and then die down before putting the cover back on with the flue a quarter open. I wasn't in a rush to cook and wanted to enjoy the quiet. The mist evaporated from the red metal dome as it heated up.

In the kitchen, I got some hamburger meat out from the refrigerator and mixed it up with some pepper and a little salt to bring out the flavor. I decided that I wanted my burgers really juicy, so I put in some Worcestershire sauce and a big dollop of barbecue sauce from the pantry. The mixture was so wet from the sauces and warm from working my hands and fingers through it that I could just barely make it into patties. That was OK, because I wanted them to be wet and warm with plenty of juice to soak into the buns.

I smiled. They were going to be good. I washed my sticky hands and then brought the two patties and buns to the porch along with one of my gin and tonics. The coals weren't glowing yet, and that was good. I set the plate down on the stump and covered it with my bandana, the breeze billowing the faded blue cotton cloth up and then settling it down. I leaned against one of the porch's posts and took a large sip of my sweet, bitter drink. Reaching up to rub my hand through my sweaty hair, I realized that I hadn't taken my hat off. I hung it from a post, and the breeze brushed over my sweat-flattened hair. It was cool and felt good.

I looked out across the mesquite-cleared pasture, its pale green grass moving like ocean waves with the wind blowing over it and down onto it, and then I looked far out to the tank with the berm where I had passed over the armadillo the other day. From there, I looked out to the front, following the chalky-white gravel driveway down to the metal bar gate that opened onto the road, then across the road and up the hill, behind which I could see the remnants of the gray storm clouds breaking up into white wispy edges with a pure robin's-egg blue sky behind. To my left, the breezy gusts moved through the untouched field strewn with rocks and boulders, some of them slabs sitting, driven somehow, vertically into the ground. I idly wondered how they got there: some naturally there, I supposed, others dumped from clearing another field some time ago, maybe by Jack's father-in-law, Jack.

The peace, along with the fading, quieting drama of the storm, moved a thrill within my chest and gut. The solitude deepened the thrill, as if the land that I saw, the wind I felt, and the smells of the freshened earth and grass and rocks were mine, alone out here with Dusty, William still down in his tank, the cattle, the armadillos, the turkeys, that rogue pheasant, the distant coyotes, and even the scorpions.

The quail began their peeping in the wet grass along the fence line.

I went inside and fixed myself another drink and came back out to put the burgers on the grill. The smell of the charcoal mixed with the cooking meat and the caramelizing sauces searing on the metal. I flipped them quick to keep them juicy, timing them by sips from my beading glass. The feathered wisps of the clouds grew towards me, and the clean blue sky darkened to evening. My land remained shadowed but yet lit; the grass and rocks and fences were sharp and clear and clean-edged. The gravel down to the road glowed like a phosphorescent white ribbon.

The burgers were tasty and the right amount of tangy fatty juiciness soaked into the buns. I hadn't realized how hungry I was, and they hit the spot. Sitting on the railing with my drink next to me, it was satisfying to think that pretty much all the work that Jack had given me was done. I had hit every mesquite sprout and sapling in the pasture, even beyond its edges to make sure, thinking that would give some more land for the grass to expand to. Most of those I had gotten were a dead, ashy-white already. I had even cleared up some fallen mesquites and stacked up enough firewood to last Jack and his wife for a while. It was a good feeling that everything I had been given to do, and more, was done. I wondered what else he would want to give me.

The dinner was good and left me with a full, satisfied feeling. The last feathered clouds vanished as the sky darkened to a deep, rich blue and then to a black with the silver motes of the stars and planets suddenly appearing after the quick sunset. I covered the grill and moved a chair out from the porch. I stayed out later than usual, watching and enjoying the clear night sky, thinking that this might be my last night of my last day alone. This was better than sitting at a bar in town with other ranch hands.

Part II—Madness

The next morning, both Jack and his wife came crunching down the gravel driveway in their older-model green Chevy truck, dust from the already dry rocks kicking up in a plume behind them. I waited in front of the house on the gravel until they stopped, and then opened the door for Jack's wife. Her hand was cold and light in mine as she shifted out of the truck, a sour look on her face and mouth like she had just bitten into a lemon. She mumbled a hello as she ducked her gray bouffanted head with its blue tint out of the cab.

Jack opened his door, the hinges creaking with use and age. "Good morning, Jack," he said in his happy, nasally voice. "The front looks real nice."

He had just called me *Jack*. I didn't catch it right away, as I was helping his wife out and closing her door, and then it was too late to correct him, which I wasn't even sure exactly how to do. At first, I thought to myself, *Oh well, it is my first name, maybe it was just a slip on his part,* but it wasn't that because he *kept* calling me *Jack*. After several *Jacks*, it was just too late to correct him. The more I thought about it, the more puzzled I became, because I couldn't figure out how he would have known my first name. I always went by my middle.

Later that day, after giving him a tour of the ranch and showing him what I had done, we were back in the ranch house with the rusty nails he had fixed for us and listening again to "The Lion Sleeps Tonight" on a loop, it was as if some train of thought or reasoning had gone on in Jack's head, and for a bit, I had become the other Jack, his father-in-law, the man he and his wife had inherited the ranch from long ago when they were young. The change was subtle, or maybe I was just slow to catch it, but it was unmistakable when he thanked me for the ranch and was proud to have it and promised that he would take care of it.

Jack, sitting in his recliner, settled into a quiet reverie with his eyes half closed. "The Lion Sleeps Tonight" kept playing, and I did my best to drink my rusty nail. I was a little unsettled and didn't know what to do. I can't say that I had an immediate concern for him; I was a little embarrassed and, strangely, honored that he would think that I was—had become—his father-in-law.

We sat in silence until his wife came in and called us to dinner in the kitchen. She had heated and served up some chili she had brought out from town. I cleaned the table and joined them on the porch. She was drinking water, complaining that her stomach was still a little off, and Jack, had moved on from the rusty nails, thank God, to a beer, and offered one to me. After going over again—for his wife's benefit—what I had done, Jack decided that the next morning I should come out to their house in town to do work there since there wasn't much else he wanted me to here. I offered that there were some mesquites that I could still cut up and that I would exercise Dusty.

"Naw, you just come on to town. We've got some things for you to do," he said. So, my quiet, solitary routine was ending, at least for tomorrow.

With Jack having said his piece, he returned to his beer, and I continued to nurse mine, tiny beads of moisture on its brown neck. Jack's wife took over the conversation with her slow Texas twang, like Jack's. The talk drifted from my girlfriend to her sisters and then to my girlfriend's father, and then it turned sneakily critical of him. First it was issues with his now wife, whom he had married after the death of my girlfriend's mother, Jack's and his wife's daughter.

"What do you think of his blonde wife? Pretty little thing. Seems to fawn on him, bless her heart," Jack's wife mused.

"She's been very kind to me," I said. Uh-oh. I'm from the South, so I knew the meaning, the criticism, and the condescension of the phrase *bless her heart*. That's what woke me up, so to speak, that this conversation was taking a bad turn.

"Do you think she's high strung?" she asked.

"Not that I've noticed," I replied.

There was a little pause as we sipped at our drinks and looked out on the front stretch to the fence line along the road. A hot breeze was blowing from that direction. Although hot and dry, it was refreshing, cooling my sweating under my loose denim shirt, and carrying the scent of dirt, dust, dried grass, and mesquite. It was clean and simple.

Jack's wife started up again. She started talking about religion, a topic I tended to avoid.

"Where do you go to church in Waco?" she asked.

"Well, I go to this little place in the center of town."

"What's its name? We know some folks over in Waco. Maybe you pray with them."

"Saint Mary's."

"Oh." Pause. "There must be a lot of Mexicans there."

"Well, yes ma'am, there are. It's a good place." I had found that admitting to being Catholic in some places brought a religious conversation to a halt. I never really understood why, maybe because it was so foreign to folks who had only known Baptists, Methodists, or some of the more evangelical congregations; or maybe it was because they thought Catholics were beyond conversion and redemption. Probably a little of all that.

So, the discussion about my religious inclinations stopped short, which was a blessing, but Jack's wife turned it toward the religion of my girlfriend's father, which is where she wanted it to go anyway.

"Have you ever been to church with him and his wife?"

"Well, yes ma'am. They were kind enough to take me when I was at their house over a weekend earlier this summer."

"Well, we've been too. A little different, don't you think?"

"I don't know. I thought it was a nice service, and the folks were very friendly." Since I didn't have a good feeling about where she wanted to take this conversation, and though from my Catholic perspective that service had been pretty strange and uncomfortable for me, I was darn sure that I wasn't going to admit that and be drawn into whatever was going on here.

Jack's wife, as she rocked herself in her chair on the porch with beads of moisture dripping off her glass, let out her scorn about her son-in-law's religion—again, in what I thought was a sly, understated way. She talked about how it was extreme and weird, and how he had found this congregation after the death of their daughter. Jack grunted or nodded in agreement whenever she looked at him.

I just kept rocking in my chair, paying attention but trying not to be drawn in. I liked my girlfriend's father, and his religion was his business. Shoot, the way I looked at it, pretty much whatever that man did or needed to do to make it through the devastation of his wife dropping dead was OK by me. Heck, he could have turned to worse things and didn't, and he had raised four daughters from that point on all by himself. I wasn't going to find fault with him, or anyone, about their religion.

I did not like that conversation and was glad when it was over and Jack and his wife drove back home, telling me to come to the house in town the next morning. I thought about Jack's wife as they drove back down the gravel driveway to the front gate, the pickup bouncing and kicking up gray-yellow dust behind them. The dust hung in the hot, dry, windless air after they passed through the gate and turned right back into town, the sound of their engine quickly vanishing behind the dry hills.

I took the rest of the day off. I grabbed my fishing gear and saddled up Dusty. We trotted through the back acreage to let Dusty exercise and for me to clear my head of Jack and his wife. I think that's why I didn't choose to make our way to the tank in the front part of the property. We came upon the cattle, who were silent in the early evening heat, slowly ambling along one of their paths that led between a cluster of mesquite trees down to Tonkaway and Bucky's Springs. Enjoying being outdoors touring with Dusty, I pulled him up to a slow walk to follow the cows.

I wasn't in a rush to hurry along the rest of the day, having this feeling that the peace of the past few days had come to an end; the solitude of doing my work, riding the range in the heat with Dusty, and ending my days by cooking and eating my dinners alone on the hot breezy font porch were all mine in a way until the arrival of Jack and his wife and her marring it with her talk. I didn't like thinking about that and tried not to, instead just enjoying the sway and bouncing of Dusty beneath me and between my legs, and the musty sweet smell of the cows ahead of us.

Eventually, without any prodding from us, the cattle spread out into the mesquite-shrouded grass on either side of the path, so we trotted through before they closed up again and turned down the dry pale brown path to Tonkaway Springs. It didn't seem right for me to disturb William down in his dark peace at the bottom of Bucky's Springs.

Tonkaway wasn't shaded like the spot I liked down below at Bucky's, but it was getting late in the day and the sun was nearing the horizon, so the heat was declining. We came down off the rocky hill to the more level side where I swung off Dusty, not bothering to tie him up because I knew he would stay close. He stepped to the edge and slurped at the dark water, sending ripples that softened and then faded before making it out to the middle of the smooth, dark surface. Some crickets, cousins of the summer infestation in Waco, floated out over the water and dropped onto the surface, creating little ripples. Fish rose to take them; bass and perch snatched them without any finesse, as they do, not at all like the smooth sipping or engulfing by trout. I had my flyrod with me and decided to give it a try. Flyfishing was what I had learned on my own up North, and I often found myself, by reflex, gravitating to that, even in situations that weren't the classic fly-casting setup. I suppose it seemed that I had nothing more to lose, and nothing more to gain, as I sensed the ending. I had hooked William. And something about the rhythm of casting always calmed me, and I wanted that now.

I untied the waxed canvas case from the bundle behind the saddle, removed my rod from its cotton sleeve, and jointed it, lining the eyes up and then running the pale green line through each of the small metal loops, careful not to let weighted line pull the thin leader and tippet back through. The tippet was old and shorter than it should be from use. I bit it off, coiled up what remained of it, and pushed it down deep into the front left pocket of my jeans. Then I tied a long tippet onto the leader, knowing that I needed as much length on the line as I could get. I ran the leader and tippet through my fingers, stretching and straightening it. It took a long time, even in the Texas heat and with my sweaty hands. It had been a long time since I had used my flyrod. With the ritual completed, I moved off to the other side of Tonkaway closer to the surface where the fish were taking the crickets. It would be a real stretch, but I thought I might be able to reach my fly out there.

Inside my gray tin fly box, there were two old hoppers from the last time I had truly fly-fished, two summers ago when I was up in Wisconsin, fishing the section of the Kinnickinnic that was upstream of the two-lane highway and past the cliffs where it flowed through fields, its sides overhung with willows and long grasses from whose bent-over green blades when stirred by the breezes grasshoppers fell.

I had tied these hopper imitations at my basement desk, and they had worked up on the Wisconsin river. Maybe they'd work down here too. The hopper with the dark turkey-feather wing covering and legs with the pale-yellow yarn body looked like the best. I tied it on and spit on it for good luck and began false-casting to get my line unfurling out long enough in the air and then let it go on a forward cast, the weighted line pulling out more of itself from the length I had been drawing out as a reserve.

That night, I had the dove breasts. I thought about my Texas friend and his marinated dove breasts that we had in Virginia.

The next morning, after a quick breakfast of coffee and pancakes, I checked on Dusty to make sure he had his feed and water and also to spend some time with him before driving into town. Once there, Jack's wife put me to work in her flower garden, cleaning out the weeds. She and Jack stayed inside. It was shady under their pecan trees, and there was a pleasant breeze blowing, cool and soothing, compared to the virtually shadeless ranch. The garden had gotten pretty overrun with weeds, so I spent the entire morning there, sitting down on the gravely earth after my knees began to ache. My mind wandered back to the ranch and the fishing and to William and Dusty. I looked forward to getting back there this evening.

By lunchtime, I figured I was done, having bagged up the weeds and twigs, but Jack's wife told me to lay down bags of mulch before lunch. I was hungry and didn't understand why I couldn't do the mulch after, but she was the boss. It took another hour to lay down the sweet-smelling bronze-colored cypress mulch and sweep up everything afterward. I was tired and hot, not to mention pretty hungry and thirsty by the time I finished. The air-conditioning inside was welcome on my sweat-covered skin. That was something I liked about Texas, how refreshing and relaxing air-conditioning was after being out in the Texas summer heat. Jack's wife had set out a plate with a peanut butter and jelly sandwich with some potato chips and a glass of ice water for me. Jack joined me at their round kitchen table.

"Thank you for your work here and out at the ranch. You're a good hand," he said in his slow drawl.

"Yes, sir, you're welcome, and thank you. I've enjoyed the work."

"After you finish here today, why don't you take some time off back in Waco?" One of Jack's long pauses followed. "Ol' Bobby and his family are coming out to enjoy the ranch for the next couple of days."

"Thank you. That would be mighty nice, but I'm happy to keep on at things out at the ranch. There are some trees that could be cut up. That mesquite sure is good for the pit and smoker." I did not want to leave the peace and simplicity of the ranch, and I did not want to go back to Waco, where things were ending.

"No, you should take a couple of days off."

"Yes, sir. I see." The father of the thief was bringing his family out there and there wouldn't be room for them and me. I had met this Bobby, maybe last year. He was a big, lumbering, gap-toothed fella with crazy eyes. I had seen his kind before, coming as I did from Kentucky, and he knew it. I did not like being around that dude.

Jack let me know that they would be having the family, namely my girlfriend, her father, his wife, my girlfriend's three sisters, the eldest sister's fiancé, and the fiancé's father over for a get-together at the ranch at the end of the next week. There would be jobs to do out there in preparation for the gathering.

After our lunch together, Jack set me to cleaning out the gutters, which were stuffed with decaying leaves and other debris, mostly dry. The gutters really needed it; there were black-brown stains from months of rainwater overflowing and washing the decaying debris down the sides of the gutters and walls. I kept at it, scooping the dried, rotting leaves and sticks into a garbage bag, shifting my aluminum ladder down every few feet, until I came across a long, grayish shed snakeskin. I couldn't figure out what a snakeskin was doing up here in the gutter, and I couldn't tell what kind of a snake it came from, but I knew I didn't want to find out. There was a lot of debris up there in those gutters, and I did not like the thought of scooping my hand through it to find a live snake. I decided I was finished with the gutters. I climbed down, bagged up the trash, stowed my ladder in their garage, said goodbye to Jack's wife and shook Jack's hand, and drove back to the ranch with my windows down, letting the hot wind wash over me. The closer I got to the ranch, the more the land smelled, now almost home-like, with the baked gravel dust and mesquite.

I drove through the gate and down the gravel driveway to park in front of the house. I first walked over to check on Dusty. He nickered to me when I stepped into the barn. He tossed his head and neighed, happy with the rub-down and scratches behind his ears. I led him out to his little corral.

"Just let me grab a quick bite to eat, and then we'll ride the range." The sun was still hot in the late afternoon, but it was approaching the horizon. I made myself two good-sized bean-and-cheese burritos and washed it down with water. The burritos were good, and they filled me up. The water was cool and refreshing. I wasn't in the mood for a beer or cocktail. After washing up, I went back out to Dusty and saddled him up, strapping on the scabbard with the drilling inside. I stowed some shotgun shells and .22 cartridges in my breast pocket, in case I saw a snake or maybe some other varmint. I had already decided that I wouldn't be shooting any armadillos. I swung up onto Dusty and turned him towards the front tank.

We spent the next few hours riding the property, stopping along our lazy way to watch the land and the sky. The front tank was flat and quiet as the sun began to sink below the horizon. We picked our way through the boulder field, where thin, tiny lizards scurried around the rocks or off their warm surfaces into the shadows. As we sauntered over to the trash pit, I saw a fox prowling its rim, so I pulled up Dusty, and we watched him hunt for his dinner in the declining light. When the fox left, having had his sport and gotten his fill, Dusty and I moved off to the tanks. The last edge of the sun had sunk below the horizon, and already, I could feel the drop in the temperature beginning. There weren't any clouds in the sky, and it gained a deep robin's-egg blue with the sun gone. There was a rose-to-orange cast to the air above the horizon where the sun had disappeared, and then there was one of those rare sunset flares that shot up and stayed vertical from the sun that was gone. It was like a white-gold spotlight that shone, glowed straight up into the sky and held that way. I halted Dusty to watch the beam as it grew in strength, held, faded. We moved on through the gloaming towards Tonkaway and Bucky's Springs.

Nothing was moving at Tonkaway Springs. There was a quiet, uninterrupted even by the cattle who were somewhere off in the distance. Dusty shared my mood, happy to be alone out on the good land. Bucky's Springs were still and flat in the growing night. We stood on the low hill just above the Springs. No breeze stirred its black surface. I tried to look into the depths, trying to see fish, maybe even William, but the water was an impenetrable black whose surface reflected the stars and then the risen moon as the sky became night. The surface became a mirror of the sky above, seeming to hold the stars in its depths. We stayed there on the hill into the night, watching the land and the sky and the sky in Bucky's Springs.

Finally, we strolled back to the barn on the beaten cow path that glowed white under the moon. I unsaddled Dusty and rubbed him down and then went to bed.

The next morning after breakfast, I spent time in the barn with Dusty, rubbing him down and brushing him. He trotted and played in the corral while I cleaned out his stall. I made sure that he had water and food; I didn't know how much care he would get from the family that was coming in. I sat on the fence posts while Dusty played in his corral. He came over to me and bent his neck to nuzzle my legs, asking for ear scratches.

"You hang in there, my buddy. I'll be back in a couple of days and then we'll ride together again," I said as I rubbed his neck and scratched behind his ears. Yeah, I didn't want to leave.

I led him back into his stall and began the hot drive back to Waco. I left the windows down, enjoying the heat and the smells of the country along the two-lane highway. Through my sunglasses, I could see the heat rising from the highway's surface. Jerry Jeff Walker played on my radio.

About halfway through the two-hour drive, sweat coating my skin, I began to feel an itch on my legs under my jeans. The itching quickly grew and spread to my stomach and up my chest. Under the sweat on my body, the itching became a torment, a madness that took hold because I couldn't do anything about it and didn't know what it was from. The two-lane highway that I was racing down now through the heat shimmers, had stoplights every few miles that were clustered more densely around towns, but unfortunately, they all stayed green. Normally, that would have been a welcome blessing as I sailed through, but now it was a curse. It didn't occur to me to pull over, the madness was taking hold. I just wanted to get to the end, where I hoped to find relief.

Finally, there was a red light. Carefully, and hoping not to gain any attention at what would seem weird or obscene to the older man in the beater truck beside me, I unbuttoned my jeans to look at my waist, where the itching was worse. Small raised red pin-pricks ran around my waist and reached across my skin as much as I could see. I raised my shirt, and there they were, too, on my belly.

"Goddammit," I shouted. I had chiggers. They were all over me. Where could I have picked them up? It would have to have been in the last day, no more. Then I realized: it was the garden. The garden at Jack's house in town. It had been pretty overgrown with weeds, and I had been doing a lot of sitting or kneeling down in it. Goddammit. The chigger bites were driving me mad.

There was a honk from the car behind me; the light had turned green. The man in the beater pickup looked at me as he drove past me. I waved and mouthed, "I'm sorry."

It was hard not to itch, but I knew that would only make the now-burning itching worse. I pulled over at the next drug-cum-convenience store, where I found calamine lotion. I bought two bottles. The thought of slathering the lotion on, rubbing it in once I got to my girlfriend's apartment, gave me some hope. I sped on down the highway, hoping not to be caught by the highway patrol.

Finally, the itching horrible now, I pulled up at my girlfriend's apartment, which was set back in something like a park with a groomed lawn under the cover of tall spreading pecan trees. Not bothering with my canvas grip, I grabbed the bag with the calamine lotion and rushed to her door. After a few hurried nocks, she came to the door. She was tall, taller than me, a willow-like blonde with blue eyes who was looking forward to something other than me with a parasitic rash.

Giving her a quick hug and a peck on the cheek, I said in a rush, "Chiggers," and raced to her bathroom. I stripped down to nothing while she watched in at the door and saw, not unexpected, but somewhat to my horror, that the red pin-pricks covered me from the waist down and that a good many were on my belly and lower chest. Some, unnoticed until now, were on my forearms above my wrists. *Ah, above my gloves,* it occurred to me.

"Goddammit," I said aloud.

"You shouldn't take the Lord's name in vain," she said.

I looked at her sideways as I opened a bottle of the calamine lotion. As I fumbled with the lid and the seal, several less-than-high-minded arguments occurred to me, that *God* was not His name, but that if we were being textually accurate, *Yahweh* would be it, or … I mean, for Christ's sake—and I certainly didn't say that out loud—I got them at her grandparents' house.

The calamine lotion was working, and my madness and annoyance subsided. I just stood there, letting the soothing lotion do its thing. I pulled my clothes back on after it had dried. Then we sat in the kitchen, the firm chrome chairs somehow more soothing than the stuffed couch. The ice-cold Shiner beer was good. I was better. There was still a vague itching, but the beer took my mind off it.

"Where did you get the chiggers?" she asked between sips of her own beer.

"I'm pretty sure that I picked them up at your grandparents' house yesterday."

"What were you doing there? I thought you were out at the ranch."

"I was, but I pretty much finished everything up there. I took care of all the mesquite sprouts and saplings in the front area, chopped up a few mesquites that had fallen on the property, and filled up all their firewood stacks. I made sure to comb and exercise Dusty.'

"The old horse? I'm glad you did. They don't do much with him." I raised my eyebrows at that, but I guess I shouldn't have been surprised.

"He's not that old. He's a good horse. Anyway, your grandfather asked me to come to the house since things were done and quiet."

"What did he have you do?"

"I cleaned out their gutters and weeded and fixed up your grandmother's garden."

"I'm sure that's where you got the chiggers."

"Yeah, that's what I thought too."

"She had let that garden go because she got chiggers out there a couple of months ago. She didn't let you know?"

"No."

"I'll give you a bottle of nail polish. You should put that on the chigger bites. That should help."

"Really? Thanks."

While we drank our beers, I told her about the ranch, and she let me know that we would be going to a birthday party at her friend's apartment that night.

It was a good party with plenty of Tex-Mex food and Texas beer. The nachos, piled high with chili beef and beans and queso, were really good. We got home late, and I painted myself with nail polish and we went to sleep in the cool air-conditioning under the fan.

In the early morning hours, I woke up with my stomach rumbling. It moved to and stayed in my intestines. I couldn't fall back asleep, though I lay there hoping the feeling would go away. It didn't, and I rushed to the bathroom. It was coming out both ends. Soon, there was nothing left. For the next two days, I didn't leave the bed other than to put on calamine lotion and paint myself with nail polish. I couldn't keep anything down, not even water or crackers. At first, I thought I had food poisoning from the Tex-Mex food or that it just didn't sit well with me, but later on, that first day, I realized that I had the same intestinal bug that Jack and his wife had. I figured that I got it from them, maybe when I helped Jack's wife out of the truck when they visited the ranch, maybe when I was in their house in town.

The calamine lotion ran out and I had gone through three bottles of nail polish. My girlfriend was happy to share the second bottle with me, but by the third bottle, she was not happy. I had also smelled up her apartment pretty badly. For two days, lying there in bed, I would watch my stomach and abdomen inflate like a basketball. It was painful, and my only relief was to force myself to pass gas. But it was only a temporary relief because my abdomen would start inflating again right away. My gas in the bedroom became so bad that it set off her carbon monoxide detector. By the end of the second day, she was complaining to me about using up all of her nail polish and told me she was disgusted about the gas. I thought that was unfair, seeing that I had gotten the sickness from her grandmother and that that woman hadn't even bothered to tell me about the chiggers in her damn garden.

By the third day, I was beginning to feel a little better and was anxious to get back to the ranch to check on Dusty and because I had promised Jack that I would be back to help order the ranch in preparation for the family party that coming weekend. My anxiety to get back grew through the day. My girlfriend wanted me out of her apartment. I felt that I needed to get back, and I took that as a sign that I was gradually getting better. I still felt awful, but my stomach and bowels weren't inflating like they had the past couple of days, and I was able to keep down water and crackers. I also figured that Jack, having had the same sickness, knew what I was dealing with and would give me some relatively easy jobs.

That evening he called and spoke to my girlfriend. Afterwards, she and I spoke.

"Bobby said that he wanted to use the truck but couldn't because it had a flat tire. Pawpaw wants to know if you did anything with it that you shouldn't have."

"No. I only used it when taking care of the mesquites. The rest of the time, I was on Dusty. The tire wasn't flat when I left."

"You need to tell him that when you talk to him. Remember to look him in the eye so that he knows you're not lying."

"I'll make sure that I do." I don't know that I needed this advice but was glad of the reminder.

"I'll bet it was Bobby and his kids who did it."

"Yeah." At least she still believed me. I didn't add that it fit my opinion of Bobby that he would try to toss the blame on me. I think she thought the same of him.

The next morning, I said goodbye to my girlfriend and made the drive back to Jefferson to meet Jack at the house in town. I could just stomach the peanut butter and jelly sandwich that my girlfriend had made for me. I had a big cup of ice water and an ice-cold soda. The drive was harder than I thought, and I kept the windows up and air conditioning on because it felt unusually hot. It was a hundred degrees when I got to Jack's house; it would turn out to be 110 out at the ranch. The water was good, but the soda was better—that cold, sugary carbonated water sure tasted good, and the carbonation also helped to settle my stomach.

I pulled up at the house in town, glad to have made it and to be in the shade and out from on the open highway with the sun burning down. I was also glad to be closer to the ranch. I was anxious to meet with Jack and get the flat-tire thing behind me.

I climbed out of the driver's seat and took a breath to settle myself. Jack opened the door and led the way inside to the kitchen table. The inside coolness felt good. His wife wasn't in sight, but I thought I could hear her moving around somewhere else in the house. It didn't matter to me. I was just trying to keep myself together long enough to make it through the interrogation that was coming. We sat down, and I drank some ice water slowly.

"I'm glad you came back," Jack drawled out.

"I'm glad to be back. I'm still a little shaky, though."

"Oh? From what?"

"Oh, I thought you knew, that she told you." I had to go slowly.

"No, sir." I was glad it was going slowly; I could catch breaths between my talking.

"Well, I must have had what y'all had. It hit me hard. I got back as soon as I could. Still shaky though."

The sickness didn't seem to matter to him, he got right to the point. "Ol' Bobby found a flat tire on the pickup. He said that he and the family couldn't ride around in it." He looked me in the eyes. I held his gaze and didn't let up. It was hard with the slow talking.

"Yes, sir. I had to call a neighbor over to change it and get it to town to be patched up," Jack continued.

"I'm glad that you didn't change it." I couldn't understand why Bobby didn't change the tire; it's not a hard thing to do. I didn't ask because I knew the answer, and I think Jack did too. I was right about Bobby.

"Tell me, did you do anything with the truck?" We were still holding each other's eyes.

"No, sir. I only used it when spraying the mesquite shoots and saplings in the A&M pasture and when I took it to load up the mesquite logs I'd cut. But then, I stayed to the track. And I checked the tires afterwards. I spent the rest of the time riding Dusty." Still, holding our stares. I made sure not to flinch. There was a long pause, like Jack was thinking it over or testing me with his stare.

"Well, sir, I believe you, and I thank you for taking care of the truck and for riding Dusty. He needs the exercise. I can't ride him anymore."

He stood up and walked me to the door. "You go on out to the ranch. I'll be out there after lunch."

"Yes, sir. Thank you."

That goddamn Bobby, I thought to myself as I drove. He had probably been off-roading in the truck and picked up a thorn or did something. I hoped he hadn't done anything with Dusty.

At the ranch, I parked on the gravel and threw up when I opened the door. I stayed doubled-over while I spit out the last of the bile and caught my breath. I felt a little better. It was hot, so I brought my grip inside. The thermometer on the veranda read 110. That seemed about right. I found a carrot in the refrigerator and took some sugar cubes from the cabinet above the coffee maker.

I walked over to the barn to check on Dusty. He tossed his head and came to the window of his stall when he saw me. I hugged him around his neck, scratching him around his ears. He chomped the carrot down and nickered at me. I let him nibble the sugar cubes from my hand, his lips tickling my palm. He needed food and some water, and his stall needed to be cleaned out. I took care of that while I let him run in his corral. He needed, wanted to get out and run. The work was hard, but it needed to get done and it was for my friend. It didn't look like Bobby and his family had done anything for him while I was gone. Hopefully, Jack had checked in on him. I had to pause several times, and I was glad that I wasn't out in the sun.

When that was done, I led Dusty back into his stall and I went inside the ranch house to rest in the air-conditioning. It felt good. I drank some ice water, but my stomach was upset and I was light-headed from the heat and work. I opened a large plastic bottle of soda and tried not to guzzle it. That sugary drink was really good to me. I sat there in the kitchen, trying not to move too much and to keep it together. I felt like I was on the edge of passing out and throwing up.

As I rinsed my glass at the sink, I could see a long wire-cage trap just on the other side of the fence that ran around and made the yard of the ranch house. There looked to be something in it. *What the hell?* I thought to myself. *What's a trap doing out there?*

I walked out through the backyard to the fence. There was a fox lying on its side in the trap that was sitting there in the full sun of high noon, just outside the shade of a mesquite tree. It could have been the same fox Dusty and I had watched hunting around the edges of the trash pit. I wondered what the hell was going on. Who had put the trap there and just left it? That fox wasn't doing well and would die a pretty unpleasant death, dehydrating and cooking in that heat. I bet that damn Bobby or one of his brood had put it there and forgotten about it. I put my gloves on and hopped the fence, thinking I would open the trap and let the fox go. But the moment I hit the ground in my boots, the fox jumped up and began a vicious snarling, its teeth bared.

That was not what I was expecting at all. The fierceness was shocking from what I had thought was a nearly comatose fox.

"It's OK, little buddy. I'm gonna try to help you." More snarling and now a kind of barking, yipping from the animal.

"It's OK; it'll be OK. Just let me help you. I understand. I'd be mad too. Don't be afraid." The closer I got, the more crazed the fox became. I began to reach for the lever to spring open the cage door and the fox went bananas, knocking against the sides of the cage, trying to bite my gloved fingers. This wasn't going to work. I didn't want to open the trap just to have the fox come out after me in his anger and fear and sun-madness.

I went back inside the kitchen and made two jelly sandwiches out of the white bread that I soaked with water from the tap. Hopefully, the water in the bread and the sweet jelly would help him, keep him alive while I thought about what I could do. The fox began his snarling again when he saw me. I tossed the soggy sandwiches onto the top of the cage. They were so wet that they broke up, almost melted, and dripped through the gray cage wire. When I turned away, the fox lapped up the sandwich pieces that had dropped through and then licked off what remained on the cage above him. Poor little guy. Damn.

At the barn, the sickness hit me again. I had forgotten about it; it had receded while I was busy with the fox. I stopped and leaned against the hot wood of the door. I caught my breath and breathed deeply. My stomach calmed. I needed water, but first, I had to figure out how to help the fox. Maybe I could get a pole from the barn and use that to reach across from behind the fence to spring the release lever. I thought that might work.

The sickness passed. Inside the barn, rummaging around in the corners and along the walls, I found a couple of poles that would do the job and some twine that I could use to lash them together. That would be good. There was the sound outside of a truck crunching across the gravel path towards the ranch house from the road. I went outside with my poles and set them against the wall. I stuffed the twine in my back pocket. The fox would have to wait. I hoped that he would hang on.

Jack pulled up in his truck, and his wife was with him. I don't remember that she even said hello when she got out. I was still too sick to even think about those things. The sky was free of clouds and was almost a yellow from the glare of the hot sun with barely a hint of blue in it. It was directly overhead now. Jack said he had a couple of jobs for me. I hoped that they would be easy, that he was mindful that I was recovering from the stomach bug that they had given to me.

"Someone set a trap out back and there's a fox in it," I said.

"Oh, good!" he laugh-cackled. "I caught the fox that's been eating the peaches from the tree."

"Pardon?"

"Yes, indeed, that fox has been climbing up into the peach tree in the backyard and eating the peaches." Jack had lost his mind.

"Climbing? Peaches?" Maybe I shouldn't have shown my doubt, but I was shocked by the absurdity. "What are you going to do with him?"

"Well, sir, I'm going to keep him out there to show him to the family tomorrow and then I'll pop him." That was cruel and bizarre. I needed to help that fox out.

"Meet me over yonder where the boulders are. I'll be there shortly with the bobcat." I didn't like where this might lead. I was beginning to envision what he was going to have me do, so I went inside and had some water and a lot of the soda. The first liter was almost gone now. There was another in the pantry and some cans. I moved them to the refrigerator to get them cold.

Jack rumbled into the boulder field, sitting in the cab of the bobcat with a spade and a long, heavy crowbar in the front bucket. Oh no.

"I want to clear this field of boulders. I'll work the front-end loader, and you use your crowbar to pry the boulders up and out and into the bucket."

"Yes, sir." This was not what I was hoping for.

"Alrighty, let's get it."

For the next couple of hours, I was on my knees on the hard ground in the heat and diesel fumes and dust kicked up by the bobcat as I pried boulders out of the ground and tipped, slid, or tumbled them into the bucket. It was hot. I was weak, and the nausea was there. The boulders were heavy and awkward, and some were embedded deep in the ground, and I had to dig with the spade to get to the bottom edge of the rock. The ground was hard, a baked chalky limestone like the rest of the ranch—nothing that

I would call earth, certainly not beyond the first inch or less of soil that held the scrub grass roots.

Jack sat in the cab, a little white fan attached to the roof-shade strut, blowing air into his face. He worked the front bucket jerkily with the controls, almost knocking into me or tipping a rock slab back on me a few times. I was lucky to jump out of the way. We didn't stop for breaks, and I was sweating like I never had before. I was still weak and sick to my stomach.

He would shout at me, "Harder! Pull harder! No, not that way! Watch out! You're not doing it right!" Leaning on my crowbar as I caught my breath and steadied myself between rocks while he shouted at me, I began to have very un-Christian thoughts regarding him.

Finally, we reached a stopping point. Jack seemed to think that we had cleared enough of the field, at least for the time being. It didn't seem that we had cleared that much of an area, at least not enough to seed more of the A&M grass. When I looked it over, it just seemed pointless.

I went inside and drank some cold ice water, more ice than water, just to cool off. I could feel the liquid going down my throat and into my stomach, cooling me from the inside out. I then guzzled down the last of the soda from the liter bottle. That tasted good. I sat there in the cool and quiet, glad to be alone and to rest. It felt good to be inside and to have made it through the boulder work and to be done with it.

Jack came back inside. I was still in the kitchen. He turned on the sound system. This time it was "Blue Bayou" on a loop.

"Well, sir, it's a hot one out there, shooo-weee!" he exclaimed as he came into the kitchen. "I've got one more job for you before we head back to town."

I nodded as I looked him in the eyes.

"I want you to rake the driveway gravel smooth from the house to the road. It ought to look nice for when everyone arrives tomorrow."

"Yes, sir," I said as I stood up from the table and pushed my chair back. He showed me where he had put the rake on the front porch. I put my hat on and looked at the unshaded quarter-mile-long driveway with heat shimmers coming off the cooked-gray gravel.

Jack and his wife sat in the rocking chairs drinking sweet tea and listening to "Blue Bayou" on its loop while they watched me rake the gravel. I thought about the fox and hoped he was hanging in there. I knew that I could free him once they were gone. The sun blazing down was a hard thing.

It took me until late afternoon to get that driveway done. It was another pointless task. There wasn't much gravel anyway, so there was no smoothing it out, and very little had spilled over the sides. Once I got far enough out from the porch, I just went through the motions of raking. I was anxious to get to the fox and I figured that the old people would leave once I was finished. They did, and once their truck turned right onto the road toward town, I set to work.

Quickly in the kitchen, I filled a bowl with cold water and made another jelly sandwich. I took these outside with me to the fox. He was lying on his side in the cage. I noticed two buzzards circling up above now. He didn't move at all when I got close. Kneeling down next to the cage, I could see that the fox was still breathing. He opened his eye and looked at me, just ever so slightly tilting his head. I tore off a bit of the sandwich and dipped it into the water and dropped it into the cage. I didn't get it close enough for him to reach it, and he didn't even attempt to stretch to get at it.

I can't say it was the wisest thing I've ever done, but I decided I was going to do what I could to help that fox, to free him. It did not sit well with me that Jack had trapped him for stealing peaches and was going to kill him to show off to his family. It also didn't sit well that he had left him out in the sun all day. I rolled down my sleeves, put on my gloves, opened the trap, and dragged the fox out by the scruff. I was relieved that he didn't seem to mind. I shaded him with my body and dipped my bandana into the water. I tilted his head up with my right hand and squeeze-dripped water onto his muzzle with my left. He licked at the water. We kept at this for a while. It was hot, but the sun was declining, thankfully. He opened his mouth, and I dripped streams into it. I stroked his fur. Slowly, I fed him bits of the jelly sandwich soaked in water. It took a long time in the sun and on that hot ground, but he was reviving. I stopped giving him the jelly sandwich and dripped more water into his mouth. I moved the bowl next to him and helped him lift his muzzle to it. He softly lapped the water. I stroked his back. He made attempts to stand and he made it up, standing still as if to make sure he could do it. I backed away and left him to the water and the sandwich. He took a while, but he finished them. Then he looked back at me and trotted off.

"Be free, my friend."

That evening, my stomach and insides were feeling better, and the next day looked to be a much better one. I was tired and still feeling a little dehydrated, but the sickness had passed through me, or maybe I had even sweated it out. I rode Dusty around the property as the sun set, enjoying the land and the waters and the sky for what I knew would be my last time alone. The sadness of leaving and that separation hit me, but my time there was up, and I needed to get away from Jack's unsettling craziness and his wife's unspoken meanness. I wished my stomach was feeling better, but since it was not, I had a peanut butter and jelly sandwich and ice water on the porch while I watched the stars come out and listened to the now familiar, welcome night sounds.

The next morning, I got dressed and made pancakes and bacon for myself and had them with my coffee back out on the porch. My sleep had been restful. I could remember a dream of riding Dusty at night and looking down at the white-blue stars in the deep, black depths of Bucky's Spring's, waiting for William-Bucky. He appeared and cast a line out into the middle. He brought William, the fish, in and then released him. The fox came trotting along the ridge and then disappeared back into the night, sauntering off in the direction of the trash pit.

My breakfast tasted good and felt good in my stomach. I was happy and relieved that the sickness was finally and fully over. The morning sounds were there: the cattle lowing in the distance, the quail peeping in the grass along the fence line. I spent much of the morning tidying up the ranch house and sweeping the back patio. Everything was clean and ordered, ready for the family's arrival that afternoon. Jack and his wife pulled up at lunchtime. She didn't accept my hand when I opened the truck door for her. Jack started calling me by my first name again.

"Your ranch is looking mighty nice, Jack," he said in that slow nasally drawl. Was he confusing me with his father-in-law again? I showed him the back porch, and he saw the fox cage beyond the fence, lying on its side.

"Well now, what happened to the fox? I was looking forward to showing him to all the folks when they got here."

Looking him straight in the eye, I said, "I don't really know, sir. I noticed the trap on its side just now too. There were buzzards circling yesterday."

"You don't say, now. Well, maybe they got him."

"I wonder."

He stood there looking out into the distance beyond the trap. I asked him if there was anything else I could do.

"Well, no, everything looks nice. I think you're done here. Everyone should start arriving soon. Why don't you take Dusty riding, or whatever you'd like?" At that point, I was no longer the father-in-law to him, and I wasn't part of the family gathering. I was glad he liked the work I had done, but at that time, I was just a good hired hand to him.

Riding sounded nice to me. I also didn't want to interrupt the family time. I recall that this was going to be the first time that my girlfriend's father and his wife met his daughter's future father-in-law; the same for Jack and his wife. I made myself a couple of sandwiches and wrapped them in wax paper, which I stuffed into the breast pockets of my chambray shirt. I got two Shiners from the refrigerator and put them in a plastic bag and dumped some ice on top of them. I was definitely better now. Those Shiners would taste really nice that afternoon while I fished. In the barn, I brushed down Dusty and saddled him.

"Looks like this might be our last ride together, buddy," I said as I patted him on the neck. He tossed his head. I swung up into the saddle, and we trotted through the front A&M grass and then picked our way through the boulder field, then on the down to the trash pit where we saw the fox. He was prowling the edges where the grass was long and the ground sloped into the pit. On our way to Tonkaway Springs, we saw a rattler slither off into the brush. He was long and fat. He would have made a real nice belt, but I didn't have the drilling with me, and I don't know that I would have shot him anyway. Now that my time there on the ranch was ending, I didn't want to take anything from the land; it was enough to have seen or touched it and to hold the land in my memory.

We stopped at Tonkaway, and I slid off Dusty and wrapped his reigns loosely around a scrub bush that was soon to become a tumbleweed, under the shade of a spreading tree. It was cool and pleasant in the shade. I reached into my saddlebag and pulled out one of the Shiners and popped its top. It tasted good and felt good, still cold from the ice. In the shade, looking out over the still waters of Tonkaway, that beer was good. The best beers are the ones that are drunk ice-cold after someone has been in the heat and gotten a little dehydrated. I suppose these Texas beers were made to be that way.

After the beer, I rigged up the spinner rod and tossed a heavy lure out as far as I could and let it sink as much as I dared before cranking it back in. I could feel it bump on the bottom and catch light snags, maybe on some weeds down there at the bottom. I spent much of the afternoon out there, not bothered that the family was arriving and not feeling a need to be among them. I caught a couple of bass who put up nice, exciting fights, as bass always seem to do. I let them go and watched them swim off into the dark cool depths to their homes by the cool fonts of the springs.

When the sun was far down on its decline, I rode Dusty over to Bucky's Springs to say goodbye to William. We rode down to the edge and watched the water. I was a little surprised that it wasn't lower, despite the lack of rain. I figured it was still being fed by springs from an underlying aquifer. It was a good home for William. I stayed on Dusty and slowly drank the last beer, enjoying it and the quiet of this desert-like land. Then we rode off, sauntering past the cows and back to the barn, where I unsaddled him and rubbed him down again in his stall, making sure that he had enough food and water.

All the family was gathered in the kitchen of the ranch house, watching the fiancé and his father prepare a leg of lamb. My girlfriend's father shook my hand when I came in and introduced me around. I got a brief hug from my girlfriend. As I found out, the fiancé had had formal training as a chef, and his father was a thin, somewhat high-strung fellow. The fiancé's father, having taken over the kitchen, was making quite a show of it, which was somewhat out of place there at the ranch among my girlfriend's slow-talking, generally relaxed family, and there was a tone to him as if he was talking down to them, me included. My girlfriend's father kept him going with questions. Though it's been a long time, every time I think of or have a leg of lamb, I think of that guy and the fiancé making the lamb with crushed pistachios and mint jelly.

When the lamb had been put into the oven, the women all went into the living room with their drinks. The fiancé went with them. My girlfriend's father and I, Jack, and the fiancé's father stayed in the kitchen. I finished my water, and my girlfriend's father handed me a beer. I sipped it slowly, having already had two out in the heat.

Her father led the conversation and drew me in. He had been plying the fiancé and his father with questions. The fiancé's father liked to talk, it seemed, and really liked talking about himself, but my girlfriend's father changed the course of the conversation.

"How has the ranching been?" he asked as he turned to me.

"I've enjoyed it. Hard work, but there's a beauty out here, a peacefulness."

"Yes, I like it out here too."

The talk turned to what I had gotten done and what I had been doing in my off time.

"How was the fishing? Did you try catching William?" he asked me.

"The fishing was real nice. Dusty and I would ride down there or to Tonkaway in the evenings. I caught some good bass but never got William. Tried a few different lures and baits."

"Never a bite that might have been him?" He looked me in the eyes, and I caught a hint of a smile.

"No, sir. I believe he's no longer there. Maybe he got washed out and down somewhere during one of the floods."

Jack piped in, "Well, shoot! I guess Bucky would be glad to know that he was the only one to have caught him."

"Yes, sir," I responded. "Bucky's the only one. That's real good for him. That ol' William is a legend to me."

The fiancé's father couldn't stand being left out and asked, "Who or what is this William?"

"He's a big ol' bass that has been down there in Bucky's Springs for years. No one's been able to land him. Bucky caught him a couple of years ago before he went away, but the fish broke off before he could land him. He said it was the biggest, fattest bass he'd ever seen. Bucky had seen a lot," Jack answered.

"Who's Bucky? I thought that was the name of the pond," the fiancé's father said. I was concerned. He was getting interested in the fish.

"Bucky is my other daughter's husband. He went away a few years ago. He's down in Mexico, the last we heard."

"I heard he's doing well. His real name is William. The fish he tried hard to catch is named after him," my girlfriend's father added.

"I wonder if I could try it down there. I'd like to try to catch him," the fiancé's father said.

"You could try, but if Jack here (so I was back to being Jack's father-in-law) says William's gone, then he's gone," Jack said.

"Yes, sir, I'm pretty sure he's gone. I would have liked to catch him, like Bucky, but I'm glad that William is wherever he is and that Bucky is the only one who got 'im," I put in. The fiancé's father seemed to get the picture and didn't push it.

"Well, tell us about the ranching. What all did you see? Were the snakes crawling?" my girlfriend's father asked me.

"No, the snakes didn't seem to be crawling. I only saw one, just today, down near the tanks, but that was it. Saw some turkeys strutting along the fence near the road. That was nice to watch them. I also saw a pheasant, of all things, also in the grass along the driveway, up near the gate."

"A pheasant?" the fiancé's father asked incredulously.

"Yep. I was sitting on the porch, and I saw him near the fence out in the grass—pretty much in the same spot where the turkey were. His colors stood out."

"You couldn't have seen a pheasant. It's too hot down here for them."

"Well, I was sure surprised to see him, but that's what it was."

"You must have seen some other bird. It couldn't have been a pheasant, not down here in Texas." the fiancé's father just wouldn't let up.

"Well, maybe, but I'm pretty sure about what I saw." I decided that I didn't like this know-it-all guy.

My girlfriend's father jumped in. "There's a game farm not too far away. I hear they keep pheasants for some put-and-take upland-style hunts. My guess is that the pheasant escaped from there." He winked at me.

We had dinner. The lamb was really pretty good. The fiancé and his father had done a good job; they both enjoyed everyone's compliments. My girlfriend and her sisters had made a peach cobbler.

A little later, while the rest of the party was inside, my girlfriend's father and I were alone on the front porch, our boots up on stumps, sipping away at our Shiner Bocks. The sun was still above the horizon and hot, but was declining swiftly. We listened to the late-evening sounds, crickets chirring, and the quail just beginning their gentle peeping sounds that I had come to cherish.

"You've done a real good job out here," he said. "Jack told me how grateful he was."

"Thank you. I tried my best. I appreciated the chance to come out here; I enjoyed it. They have a nice piece of land here."

"It is a good place."

There was a pause while we drank our beers and listened to the evening sounds that were coming awake with the gentling of the heat.

"I'm glad you didn't land ol' William," he said.

I looked over at him. So, he knew.

He smiled, and there was something in his gaze. I saw it. "I won't say anything. We all deserve to be free and happy wherever our homes are." I've often thought about this over the years. It applied to William, the fish, and William-Bucky, the man, but I also believe that he knew things were ending and that he was OK with it, and so it applied to me too.

I didn't say anything. And I don't know that there was anything to say, so we just relaxed there on the porch, sheltered from the last heat of the Texas summer sun, drinking our Shiners, their brown glass bottlenecks sweating above the coozies.

~

I drove away from there the next afternoon right after lunch. Before I left, Jack sat down with me in the room that had been mine and went over the hours that I had logged in my notebook.

"Thank you, Jack. You did a real fine job out here and left us with a ranch that is in really fine shape," he said, patting me on the shoulder and resting his hand there as he gave me the check. It was for the agreed-upon hourly rate, and he had rounded up.

"Thank you. I'm glad I was able to help out. You have a fine place."

We shook hands, and I went downstairs to the kitchen to say my goodbyes to my girlfriend and her family. Just before I entered, I heard Jack's wife saying something like, "He drank all of our sodas and ginger ales, and he didn't even ask." I stayed at the bottom of the stairs, not wanting to intrude on this at all.

"Mamaw, wasn't room and board part of the agreement?" That was my girlfriend.

"Hmmph. Not that much, it wasn't."

"Well now, I understand he came back still sick from the same thing that y'all had. Maybe he was just trying to stay vertical. Now, what do you think?" That was my girlfriend's father.

I backed off quietly, staying to the carpet in my boots, and went out the front door to my car. I put my grip in my trunk and then came back inside, making enough noise so that they knew I was coming. I hugged my girlfriend, her sisters, and stepmom. Jack's wife was like a statue when I went to give her a goodbye hug. I shook hands with the fiancé and his father. Last of all, I shook hands with my girlfriend's father. He gave me a firm, warm grip with his sun-browned leathery hands.

"You feel free to spend the night at our place on your way back, split up you trip. You know where the key is," he said.

"I thank you, sir. That is really kind of you, but I think I'll make the whole drive back tonight."

"I understand. We appreciate what you did out here." I think he knew that I had overheard.

"Thank you. That means a lot to me," I said as I shook hands with him again. I think he and I both knew that this would be the last time we'd speak.

The gravel crunched and slid under my boots as I stepped over to my truck, left my hat on—the wide-brimmed straw hat that I had been wearing since my first full day when I put it on after being out in the sun—and drove off, kicking up dust and spreading the gravel even more. Once I turned right on the road, I took a deep breath, turned on the radio, and tried to unwind from the awkward goodbyes, glad to be leaving some of those people. But still, an unease stayed with me. I drove south and then east across hot, heat-shimmering two-lane highways and interstates, thinking about my time on the ranch and missing Dusty and what the ranch had been, but glad to leave. It was a leaving that was more like fleeing, escaping. I felt bad about leaving Dusty, that I had abandoned him, and that bothered me, and I thought about William and Bucky's Springs. I was happy that I had hooked him and that he was still there and maybe safe from others. I thought about the fox and was glad to know that he was free too.

The road and wind through my windows were hot all day and through the night. I drove hard, only stopping for gas, wanting to put distance between myself and the people at the ranch and get back to my apartment in the city that I had heard someone call the Land of the Lotus Eaters. I pulled up outside my apartment around eleven o'clock and got out to the sound of a foghorn on the river and the scent of night-blooming jasmine floating in the humid air. I took a deep breath of the jasmine and carried my grip and bedroll inside.

Epilogue

The warm blanket of the New Orleans night air was heavy and humid as I walked the couple of blocks to my neighborhood bar under live oaks and past banana and fig trees, wafts of the sweet olive, camelias, and jasmine enveloping me. I wasn't ready to go to bed yet, and I wanted to stretch my legs after the hot drive across a good swath of Texas and the width of Louisiana. The bar would be a way to ease back into New Orleans.

While I sat there in the cool dark, I felt glad to be back home but kept thinking about Dusty. No one rode him anymore, and only Jack was making sure he was fed and had water. I wondered how long that would last. I figured that pretty soon they would sell him. That realization decided it.

Two weeks later, having talked to Jack and having set things up with a stable on the North Shore, I drove back across Louisiana and Texas with a rented trailer hitched up. My girlfriend and I had finally ended things over the phone, so I bypassed her father's house and her apartment and stayed the night in a motel outside of Dallas. The next morning, I finished the drive out to the ranch. It was Jack's wife who met me there. She let me know that Dusty's price had changed.

"Yes, ma'am. What is it now?"

The price she named was exactly what Jack had paid me. Well, she had me, and she knew that pretty damn well. I wasn't going to leave without my friend, Dusty.

"That sounds fair enough," I said. Which it wasn't. It was more than they would get for him from anyone else. "But I suppose I'll be wanting the saddle and harness."

"That will cost you more."

"No, ma'am, I don't think it will."

Dusty neighed loudly when he saw me. I patted him on the head, and while I brushed him down, I spoke to him. "I'm sorry that I've been gone, my buddy. I'm back, and I'm going to take you to a new home where we'll be free to ride together."

I loaded him up, his hooves thudding dully on the metal floor, and stowed his harness and the saddle. It was a slow ride back to the stable on the North Shore. I stopped a couple of times at rest areas to check on Dusty and let him out for a little exercise. It was early evening when we got to the stable, the air was warm and muggy, and the ground was flat and lush. The stable was under the shade of pine and live oaks trailing gray-green beards of Spanish moss. Pines and live oaks also surrounded the vibrant green pasture. As I saddled him up for a ride, I noticed for the first time that the underside of the saddle had been branded *Jack*. I wondered if this had been Jack's or his father-in-law's. Dusty and I stayed out riding and watched the sun set together.

A CAFÉ SCENE

The cold was a pleasant return to winter in this winter-that-had-not-been-a-winter. The cloudless, soft-blue morning sky let the sun come down onto the brick streets with a happy golden light as he strolled alone through the open-air market, admiring the cuts of meat and cheeses found nowhere else nearby, and the fish. Odd, he thought to himself, that sea fish were here so far inland.

He bought some cheeses and an interesting, new sausage, stopping to put them in his canvas bag before walking back through the not-yet-crowded early morning briskness to the café where the young waitress with the jet-black hair and olive Mediterranean or desert complexion brought him his champagne infused with the essence of elderflower. The elderflower complemented the sun, which was now bright and above the surrounding hills. The elderflower and sun recalled past summers.

Why this yearning, if yearning it was, for summer when the cold, with its envigorating sharpness, was so pleasantly welcome? Perhaps, he mused, it was both the fond remembrance and the hope, the looking ahead to knowing again the beauty and joys.

Ahh, he sighed as he sipped from the delicate crystal flute. The champagne and elderflower were perfect, an intuitive suggestion from the young waitress. They were going to his head. Her name was Rachael.

The tarte that he ordered was delightfully delicate with a hint of salty smokiness from the bacon. He enjoyed it slowly as the café gradually became more crowded and noisier. The feeling was jovial, but as always to him, and perhaps increasingly so as of late, being alone was pleasant.

The crème brûlée came, and with it, the white wine that she brought out of the cellar for him. He continued his writing as the café became crowded with the approach of lunch.

SOLITUDE

A cold gust hit his face, stinging and tightening it as his black shadow-like dog snuffed the ground, searching, trotting ahead of him. A light snow had fallen the day before, not heavy enough to cover or beat down what remained of the corn stalks that still provided a dry, wintry shelter for the birds to hide.

The late-afternoon sky was shrouded in low clouds, so low that they seemed just overhead, a mix of dark gray and blue masses, swollen and heavy, as if threatening to drop down and engulf him and his dog. Only a thin gap of golden light declining to red-orange showed on the far-off horizon between the dark clouds above the almost treeless rolling fields below.

The light was vanishing, and the snow, like all winter snows, glowed with a blueish-white phosphorescence. Night came quickly and cold on this land in the North. He and his dog turned back to the cabin, crunching across the fallen cornstalks on the frozen ground.

They had spent several hours ranging over the field and down by the bog where the dried marsh grasses and cattails rustled in the wind, stopping a few times to drink water and to have a snack to keep them going. It had been a long and good day. They had a couple of birds. The stark, moody beauty of the winter land, with a snowstorm coming tomorrow, or maybe tonight, stirred him. The cabin, with its evening fire and a drink, called to him.

~~~~~~~~

He stepped onto the wooden planks of his cabin's porch, and his dog followed him. He sipped from his hot black coffee. His flannels and wools retained the warmth from the fire inside. In the pristine cold of the predawn, they surveyed the silent, resting land. Some snow had fallen in the night, but not as much as yester eve's clouds had seemed to promise. The clouds, still low, gave him a feeling of close comfort, a limiting and containment of his world. They had broken up some overnight, letting through the brilliant, uncorrupted starlight in the west and a gently waxing, spreading rose-to-purple in the east. The snow cover held and cast forth the glowing colors of the sky above.

He considered whether to hunt again this morning or to stay in and rest. He decided to stay in, to enjoy the quiet, the solitude before they arrived, but that he would hunt again in the fading light of the late afternoon. A gentle wind was blowing across the snow to the porch, ruffling his hair. It was clean and refreshing, but quickly became too cold for him, so he turned back inside with the dog.

He knocked coals off the logs burning in the river-stone fireplace, the gledes falling to the orange-glowing bed above the ash, and added two more aged pine logs to the fire that released their clean forest scent into the room. He poured himself a fresh cup of coffee; the beans he used were especially rich and dark and chocolate-like. The feel and taste of the coffee reminded him of the café in eastern France where he would sit drinking the café's dark espresso among the buildings whose stones held the gray cold of many years, not like his cabin with its hearth of multicolored rounded river stones and the honey-colored planks.

He pulled *Beowulf* from the bookshelf flanking the river stones and sat down on his leather couch, while his dog stretched out on the rug in front of the fire. He was absorbed, as always, by the language and lost himself, living in the ancient past among the moors and fens of the land of the Spear-Danes.

Later that morning, he came back to himself in the room and the fire burning low, the red-gold gledes accumulating, filling the room with an orange warmth. The silver-gray light from outside remained in the corners, unreached by the fire-glow. He was hungry.

He removed one of yesterday's pheasants from the old white refrigerator with the chrome handle, fileting off the breast meat and then stowing the bones in the freezer compartment, thinking he would make a stock out of them maybe for the others. He set his ancient black cast-iron skillet, its inside smoothed with long use, on the stove, and scooped a heaping spoonful of bacon fat onto it, letting the white-amber mass, flecked with burnt bacon bits, melt into a clear liquid across the bed of the skillet and then heat to smoking. He set each of the dark breast filets onto the fat and then flipped them after a quick brown sear. When they were done, he cut them into thin slices and put them onto toast and slathered them with cranberry jelly that he had made in the fall after the harvest. He gave some slices to his dog, who had rested his muzzle on his lap, the dog's way of saying, "Please." Although it was still morning, he washed it down with a thick, creamy stout. He was alone with his dog, his friend, as he liked it, and no one was there to judge his choices. That was a good breakfast. He was pleased with the meal and himself and was satisfied.

By early afternoon, he had finished the book and rose from the couch, stretching his legs and arms. He fixed himself another stout and sat at the square wooden table to tie flies. With reflexive motions and memory, he tied the flies he wanted, some from the feathers of yesterday's birds, giving him a certain satisfaction in the linear, balanced connection between the hunt and fishing, and, as if in a waking dream, he was back on the early spring rivers, still cold from the melt, the fish coming alive, out of their deep winter torpor, warmed by the growing length of the days and, this early in the spring, perceived, felt, only by them, the growing warmth of the sun's golden light passing through the surface of the waters. The insects came alive too, rising through the water, some here and there, not like the warmer summer clouds, lifting off from the surface and floating away. His tied flies landed among them, the tiny ones that were hard to tie with his stubby fingers and aging eyesight. The trout took them, as they always did in his dreams. His dog was with him, waiting with wet paws on the rocky bank, where the earth and stones gently sloped to the river's cold edge.

He came out of the dream, his imitations of the coming spring's insect-life stages laid out on the table. He stored the flies in his boxes and his father's old leather wallet and stowed away the unused feathers and fur and string. He tossed the scraps into the fire, along with two more birch logs, and moved to the kitchen. The birch, as it kindled, gave off a pleasing, soothing scent that was fresh like the wood was in the spring and the cool breeze-stirred shade of early summer. His dog rose from the carpet and followed him, knowing that it was time for lunch.

He retrieved two more pheasant breasts from the refrigerator and set each of the fillets on the skillet with the cooled bacon fat from breakfast. He looked out the window above the sink onto the land. There was no longer any clear sliver of sky to be seen. The cloud cover had become lower and heavier, more so than yesterday, blocking so much of the light it made the outside seem almost in the deep gloaming. A heavier snow was coming. He wondered whether it would fall before they came. Maybe, maybe it would. He hoped he would get one more hunt today before the snow.

He scooped the pheasant breasts out of the skillet and set them onto his plate. He let them cool while, in a different black pot, he reheated enough leftover sausage gravy to cover them. When that was done, he ladled the thick mass onto the breasts and carried them with a second plate over to the table. He poured himself a glass of water and a mug of the remaining coffee. The coffee was always reduced and aged to bitterness by the time he had the last mug, but he still liked it. He sliced up one of the breasts and set it in the other white stoneware plate on the floor for his dog so they could eat together.

When they were done, he gathered the plates and washed them off in the sink, then took another book off the shelf, a collection of Anglo-Saxon poems, a companion to his *Beowulf,* opened it to "The Wanderer," and sat down on the couch to read.

It was almost as dark as night, except for the clouds that were lit from above, glowing with a blueish phosphorescence, and the snow scattered in the field receiving and reflecting the blue-like glow. He cherished this end-of-the-day winter quality up here on the land. It thrilled him. He and his dog exchanged expectant, eager glances, and he rubbed the dog's black head. An icy gust hit them, and its biting cold expanded, intensified the thrill. A second quick gust was cold, felt colder, and began to sap at his heat.

"Time to go," he said to his dog, and they stepped off the wooden porch onto the prairie. They loped around to the back of the cabin and moved down the prairie-grass slope that descended from it. The frozen grasses waved stiffly in the wind, rigid and rimed with ice and snow. Below the short slope, the harvested cornfield began with here-and-there patches of stalks left uncut to provide shelter for the birds. He loaded his two barrels and snapped the gun closed. He sent the dog out with a "hunt 'em up," and the dog did his thing, running with his nose to the ground, sniffing, searching, happy in back-and-forth arcs to his front. He let the dog determine the path, trusting his dog and knowing that he'd find the birds. Large flurries began to fall on them, taking him back to his first bird hunt long ago.

His dog searched beyond the prairie-grass tussocks below the cabin, having found no birds sheltering there, and was out in the hard frozen black earth furrows where stalks and half-stalks still stood, shorn of their corn months ago, where brown cobs lay scattered here and there, mostly stripped of their kernels.

His dog was now far out front, a featureless black void, unless one counted his silhouette outline as a feature, moving through the stalks. The dog stopped suddenly and lifted his nose, paused, and tested the air. He broke the gun open and slow-jogged in his heavy, clumsy-for-running boots, to close the distance. The dog seemed sure now and took off at a trot, nose alternating between the ground and the air. He knew that his dog was on one. He slowed and closed his gun, walking steadily, carefully, crunching the hard ground and months-dead stalks, now dry and frozen.

His dog was slowing and moving straight now and then froze, his black outline tense, left front paw lifted. As a younger man, he would have said, "Steady" or some such thing, but he trusted and knew his dog. He moved slowly, carefully, behind the quivering stretched line of his dog's body, thumb on the safety and finger resting alongside the trigger guard. He couldn't see the bird, but he knew it was there. He was tense with excitement, like his dog, even though he had stood here behind his dog uncounted times, awaiting the explosive flush of a bird from cover. It was always a surprise, the split-second flapping and rustling as the bird fought to escape gravity and its hideout in deep prairie grass and cornstalks.

His dog took a slow, gentle step forward, nose and eyes fixed. A bird launched, and he swung left towards its rising flight, safety slid-clicked off, finger moving to the front trigger. A hen. He held off, and the bird soared in an arc toward his left, and then another bird rustled and struggled through the stalks into the air to his right front. He swung to it, a rooster, letting it gain height and distance, its colors beautiful against the gray-blue of the low clouds. He held as it flew straight ahead, on a line extended from his barrel. He pulled the front trigger, and his right barrel roared, the only sound aside from the wind in the stalks. The bird's flight stopped, wings collapsed to its sides, and it glided heavily to the ground.

He broke open his gun and his dog leapt forward, a moving blackness in the waning afternoon light, his eyes following the downward arc of the bird. He disappeared into a small depression in the field and then bounded out, happy, with the bird in his mouth, and trotted back to him. He stroked the dog on the head as he received the bird and then reached behind him to stuff the bird into his coat's game bag. His dog looked up at him expectantly, with what he always interpreted as a smile, his tail wagging. He smiled back and pressed his dog's dark head against thigh, rubbing his neck fur.

They moved off under the darkening sky, his dog casting off ahead of him and then running in a swirling arc, nose to the frozen ground. The clouds covered the entire sky, and above, beyond the clouds, the sun had touched the horizon. The snow began falling, big, heavy flakes like pieces of the clouds dropping to the ground, where they took on the whitish-blue phosphorescence of the cover already there.

The wind picked up, and the flakes, even though they were big and ponderous, fell at a slant. He and his dog pushed on. There was just enough light. He wanted to make the hunt last as long as possible, to get one more, and his dog was having fun. The snow and wind and failing light, mostly now the glow from the snow on the ground, sent a thrill through him. The search for another bird before the dark and cold became too much was part of it, but the mood and drama of the elements and sky were the main source of the fluttering in his core. It reminded him of the feeling he got just before the wrath-of-God spring storms in his youth down South when the sky clouded over with low, olive-green clouds. He smiled. It was wonderful.

His dog looked back at him and huffed in shared excitement, his breath frosting in front of his open mouth, again looking like a smile. Then the dog turned back to the hunt, his black void outline working ahead, no longer in an arc. He thought to himself, *He's on to something*, and hurried his steps to catch up, his shotgun held vertical, sheared corn stalks and husks slapping at his boots and the bottom halves of his tin cloth pants legs. The black outline stopped and he moved the gun to his shoulder, but then the shadow was moving again in a straight line, nose partly to the ground, but his eyes forward. The bird was running. This was difficult, running over the frozen ground through knee-high stalks and needing to anticipate both a hold and an explosive flight up either left or right. The end of the field was coming, but then it was long grass, so the bird could duck under the snow-covered prairie grass tussocks and hold safe. Even if they pinned the bird down, he wasn't one to kick it into the air. The bird would be safe in his refuge and remain untouched.

The prairie grass was closer and the snow was falling heavier and thicker. All that remained of light was the glow. Then, almost at the same time, but in a barely perceptible order, all happening in just a couple of seconds, the black shadow froze with its paw lifted, the rooster launched itself straight ahead, his gun came to his shoulder, his thumb flicked the safety off, and his finger moved to the front trigger. He held, held; the rooster was flying straight ahead of the length of his barrels. He held, squeezed the trigger, heard a crashing boom, and the rooster shuddered and still flew. He moved his finger to the rear trigger and the left barrel went off, fire bursting forth from the muzzle in the darkening glow. The bird crumpled and dropped; the dog launched himself after the bird. He lowered the gun and broke it open, his old leather glove covering the chambers to catch the shells as they ejected.

The crashing sound faded, and his awareness came back and broadened from the focus on the shadow's point and the flight of the bird. He noticed that the snow was falling much heavier and thicker, hitting his cheeks, some flakes finding their way under his collar to the skin of his neck. It was now dark, but the fallen and falling snow glowed with blue-white light, like the clouds. His dog trotted back and deposited the limp bird in his hand, his black feather-duster-like tail wagging, catching snow, becoming a glowing shape, no longer a solid shadow-void as his black fur collected the snow. He stowed the bird in his jacket, rubbed his dog on the head, and back to brush the snow off. His dog looked up, smiling in his dog way.

They stood there together at the edge of the field and prairie grass in the dark and the now blue-silver light of the clouds and snow. There was a deepening snow bed around them. He noticed the wind again, its cold biting and tightening the skin of his face. He thought of the warmth of the cabin, but the visceral thrill of being outside in the dark, below the moody clouds and alone with his friend still held him. He fingered two more shells, thinking that maybe there was still enough light for another bird. His dog looked up at him at the sound of the shells, his tail wagging. He smiled down at him.

His dog snapped his head up, ears alert, and gave a snort. He turned around, looking back toward the cabin. Two sets of headlights in the far distance, their beams illuminating cone-like paths through the falling snow, were making their way toward the cabin. He sighed and dropped the shells back into his pocket. His dog's tail had stilled; the dog looked up at him, the dog-smile gone. He shouldered his gun, and they walked back to the cabin.

HEALING WATERS

He stood in the cold, gray rushing waters of the McKenzie, a morning hatch of tiny dun-colored mayflies rising off the surface. Trout were rising too, to snatch the flies before they floated up into the drizzling air. He lifted his line off the water to change from a nymph to a dry fly. The heavy drizzle numbed his fingers, and he fumbled, nipping the nymph off the line and hooking it onto his vest's wool patch. He threaded the tippet end through the eye of the dry fly's hook and paused. He couldn't remember how to tie the fly on, something he had done hundreds of times and as recently as ten minutes ago with the nymph.

He tried clearing his mind and letting his reflexes take over, but that didn't work. He just couldn't remember. The mayflies continued to float off the surface of the water, and trout rose in arcs to take them. He stood alone in the middle of the stream with the cold water rushing against and around his legs, his line trailing off into the current to his right.

So this is what the bottom is, he thought.

He could feel a black despair building, rising, as if climbing up from a sewer. He closed the manhole cover as he had been doing for four months now and stood there in the middle of the stream, stunned, trying to remember how to tie the damn knot before the hatch ended.

He didn't catch any trout on the narrow stretch of the river and the rain was no longer a drizzle. He left the gray river for the little car he had rented. He popped the trunk and sat down on the fender, rain beating down on the brim of his brown felt hat. He stored his khaki canvas fishing vest, a gift from his parents, along with his rod and boots in the trunk. He hurriedly stripped off his waders, trying to stay as dry as possible, and dove into the driver's seat. He sat, thinking, still feeling lost, a lack of direction that he had never known before. It was strange, not knowing what to do; perhaps it was because he could now do anything and had not understood that yet.

He started the car and drove back in the direction of the bridge that crossed the McKenzie from Eugene. The gray, rain-slick road followed the course of the river, above the banks and against the wooded hillside of an outlying spur of the Cascades. Trees overhung the road, dripping heavy rain drops on his car. Ahead, he saw the red roadside cabin-like restaurant advertising the "best homemade pies" that he had driven past on his way out to the river. Cold and hungry, he pulled over and walked in. He sat down in a booth as far from the door as possible, wanting to avoid the damp cold. The cherry pie was still warm, and the coffee was dark and hot. He ate slowly, in no hurry to get back out on the river, enjoying the pie and coffee warming him from the inside.

After leaving the red restaurant, he drove to what seemed like a rocky, sandy landing just upstream of the bridge. The river, here, looked shallow enough to wade at least for some distance from the shore, although the river was high and rushing past swiftly, causing waves to billow over and around boulders and to race over the riffle. If he wanted to fish here, or further out, he would have to be careful. Part of his mind urged him to stay on shore, but another side won out, and he stepped into the river onto some rocks, aiming to get within casting distance of a lone boulder. As an older man, he

J. KENT GREGORY

would know to pass this by, the rush and waves too much, but now, a much younger man with still an optimism and an unwillingness to pass up what seemed like an opportunity, he was compelled to try the fishing here. He was also unwilling to give up.

~~~

Looking out the window of the airplane, down at the snow-covered mountains, he sighed with relief that he hadn't tried to drive through the northern Rockies at this time of year. He was pretty sure he could see Canada. He was glad to have escaped and was eager to get to Oregon to see Kate. He had made it and was glad to have gotten through, grateful that it was finished. He relaxed and let the excitement of seeing her and fishing the mountains and the salmon run take him. The flight attendant stopped at his seat. He smiled up at her and ordered a gin and tonic. She gave him a nice pour, mixing it for him. He sipped at it, calming down, and looked back out his window at the snow-covered mountains.

Later, the airplane landed and rumbled up to the gate. He pulled his heavy green canvas duffle and his old, beaten leather rod tube that held his new rod from the overhead bin, the green canvas worn and faded in some places and the tube's leather smooth and shiny, polished by use. He put on his brown felt fedora and stepped through the airplane door into a soft, gray mist-like rain and descended the wheeled-up staircase to the tarmac to begin the last stage of his journey to Kate.

He took a tram to the place where he was to pick up his car. With the attendant, he checked out the car and decided it would do just fine. He loaded his duffle and rod case in just as the mist became a heavier, colder rain. He hurried into the driver's seat, switched on the wipers and the heater. The heater quickly fogged up the windows, so he turned it back off. He unfolded the map of Oregon and the directions she had given him over the phone.

He looked back into the rear seat to check his duffle and rod case again. They were there. He felt tight inside, an anxiety just below the surface. He didn't know quite what to expect, and he was surprised, but happy, to find himself here. Turning back around to face out the front windshield, he sighed and began the drive down to Eugene.

⌒ ⌒

Shortly after arriving in Eugene, Kate asked him if he wanted to go jogging in the wetlands behind her house. He kept up with her, but kept tripping. Three times he tripped, stumbled, and fell. What the hell was wrong with him? Kate stopped each time to help him up, and she had no judgement or perplexed curiosity. He couldn't figure out why he kept falling.

⌒ ⌒

The morning before, he had sat alone in the coffee shop in Eugene, a cold November drizzle falling and then stopping then starting again, where Kate had dropped him off while she went to her job as a pastry chef that paid her bills so she could do her pottery. The cold, gray dampness made him glad to be inside. He wrapped his hands around the warmth of his mug of chai, breathing in the soothing spice of the turmeric and cinnamon. He had never had chai before, and its newness appealed to him as he tried on his new life. He still felt a little lost. Leaving his canvas barn coat on, he spent the next three hours drinking chai, writing, and sitting, staying warm alone. A coffee shop and chai. Both were new to him. He felt out of place and was certain he looked it, although he didn't.

⌒ ⌒

Kate drove them up to Portland from Eugene in her old Ford, the wipers passing back and forth slowly to keep the drizzle and gray mist off. Sitting in the passenger seat was new to him, and he was glad that he could watch the mountains as they passed off to his right and peer down into the rivers. The waters flowing down or dropping off the mountains were gray and white where they crashed against rocks or fell off the slopes through the air until they hit the gray-brown rivers down in the clefts where they flowed, swollen by the rain.

During the slow, nearly two-hour drive due north, she told him of her artwork, mostly pottery, working with the raw clay, free-form without a wheel. She talked of being asked to cook the perfect omelet in a try-out for a restaurant in Eugene. He wondered if *perfect omelet* was a technical term, but didn't ask. He listened to her talk about her food and pottery.

"You'll like this bookstore where I'm taking us. It's big, an old warehouse with brick walls, and the original old wooden beams and floors are still there."

They parked across the street from the store, a temple-like building downtown near the river. The rain was falling harder, and they huddled together under the umbrella as they jogged across the street. She wrapped her arm through his as they ran up the steps. At the heavy wooden doors, she slipped her arms out and pulled him by the hand through the threshold.

Inside, there were floors and then more floors of rooms with dark wooden bookshelves filled with books, both paper and hardbacks, and the walls were old raw brick. Thick wooden beams crossed the ceiling and supported the wooden floors above. Here and there, brown patinaed iron beams supported the walls and ceilings both. It was warm inside, and the rainwater dripped from their jackets and umbrella onto the old, dark wooden floor. Books were everywhere, and there was a smell of their aged and aging mustiness mixed with the old wooden and bricks.

It reminded him of the old library in France. Comfortable, ancient, filled with treasures, a sanctum. Kate took him upstairs to an inner, more dimly lit part of the building. The walls were lined with paperbacks, their colors alternating and subtly changing like vertical bricks. He was looking with no particular direction, perhaps for Hemingway, or maybe Faulkner. There were several of each, but he didn't know what he wanted when she patted him on the shoulder and said softly, just above a whisper, "I found these two for you. I think you'll like them."

He looked at the two paperbacks, a thin one titled *Platte River* by someone named Bass, and another, *The Monkey Wrench Gang* by Abbey. He had heard of Abbey. He flipped through them and read their back covers; both caught his interest and mood. He had made the decision and had begun trying new things, so he kept these with him. Kate had also recommended them, and he, without realizing it, trusted her to make him whole, maybe mold him into something new and different. She did know him and had picked these books well. The one had a beautiful, magical sadness, or maybe poignancy, to its stories, set mostly outdoors along rivers, and the other a mad joy in the destruction of artificial, untrue constructs that unfairly altered the natural. She smiled at him, happy with her choices.

They went downstairs to the bookstore's coffee shop. She ordered a French press, and he ordered a chai. There was time before they were to meet her friends for dinner, so they sat back on the bench next to each other, looking outwards to the rest of the bookstore, and read their books. He picked up *Platte River* and began reading. Both books became important to him.

After dinner, they came back to one of the friends' houses to spend the night before driving back to Eugene. They sat on the couch with logs burning in the fireplace, putting off a fresh scent of cedar and pine with the smoke that escaped the flue. At first, while the flickering orange light of the fire remained enough, they read. Through the quiet, a tension began to build, an anticipation. He could feel it in his chest and an almost nervousness in his stomach. With a final pop and hiss, the last log collapsed and fell apart, and the last flame died, leaving only glowing yellow-orange embers. They each put their books down, and Kate took his hand, pulling him close to her. They leaned their heads together, nuzzling hair and neck, then kissing lightly then more strongly, straining and pushing together. Her lips were warm and soft; her hair smelled of lavender and pine smoke. Her fingers were in his hair and at the back of his neck, and then under his shirt. His hands reached up under her shirt to her warm, soft skin, tickling and stroking lightly along her spine, making her shiver, then on her chest, squeezing and holding. She leaned back on the cushions, pulling him down on her and between her legs. Clothed, they moved and rubbed against each other. She was panting, and he was too. They moved together more vigorously, continuously, and he realized, with surprise, that she had put him inside her and that he had been there. It had been a long time.

<hr />

Kate wanted him to see the Head of the Metolius, and she described the clear spring emerging, being born from the rocks and earth of the Cascades, in ways he had never heard a river described before. At first, holding hands and then with Kate wrapping herself around his right arm and nestled on his wool-sweater-covered shoulder, they drove up the road winding through the Cascades alongside the swift-flowing McKenzie and past the red pie restaurant. They drove up into the heights and into the forest veiled and hidden here and there by low-settling clouds and mists that hung beneath the green needles and leaves of the almost black, wet-barked trees. She pointed out the Metolius through the trees as they climbed up the mountains. It was warm and soft in the car, made even more so by the cool damp of the mists and occasional rains that fell upon their car as they drove through.

He couldn't see any signs and didn't need to as she knew the way, occasionally looking up to gently say, "Turn here," and he did. She sat up and looked at him, smiled, and said in a soft, sleepy voice as she brushed his hair with her thin fingers, "We're here. You can pull over wherever you want." He parked the car and came around to her side. She had already gotten out and closed the door. He wrapped his arms around her lithe, willowy body, as hers did around his. He brushed a smooth brown strand from her eyes and across her nose, tucking it behind her ear, and they kissed. He felt the warmth of her body on his hands and through her woolen sweater; her fingers playing along the back of his neck, and he felt her breasts in his hand and against his chest.

"Come, follow me," she said, holding and warming his right hand with both of hers. She pulled him up the gentle slope through the wet, brilliant fresh green of the grass that fleetingly called to his mind the vibrant greens of the grass and leaves that glowed after the early spring rains back home. He could hear the trickling and chirping of the Metolius ahead, here, so close to its source, a thin-but-deep brook that he could jump across. She looked back, smiling, and laughed, saying, "C'mon, were nearly there," and she pulled at his hand, laughing again, a beautiful happiness that lay over the misting rain sounds on the trees and the warbling little stream. He stepped quickly through the grass to walk next to her along the stream dropping over small, rounded stones, moving along the soft banks overhung with thin-bladed grass that bent down into the water and waved with its running.

She stopped and squeezed his hand and looked down into a small, clear pool of water with grass growing in its sandy and rocky bottom. "Here it is," she almost whispered and pulled him close, putting her arm around him, and he did the same. They stood on the bank, looking at the water so clear that it was almost not there, only visible when the surface condensed and was stretched to flow out and down a narrowness between two rocks at the end of the pool to become the brook that, farther down, became the river. They stood there quietly, holding each other in the green grass and moss under the trees with gray clouds blowing, drifting, and flowing like a river above them.

He let go of Kate to touch the water. He bent down on his knees to lean over the edge and dipped his hands in the water. The icy clarity of the water was bracing, making him gasp, and it shook his heart from its rhythm. But he kept his hands in the water, letting the cold current flow over them and through his fingers, stirring, brushing the hair on his wrists and arms. The water and its clear iciness on his skin cleansed him and took away, burned away his troubles and their pain. He scooped water into his hands and splashed it on his face and over his eyes, awakening him and clearing his sight. He ran his wet hands through his hair, and some of the still-cold water dripped inside his sweater and down his chest. He felt newly awakened and a thrilling stirred him. And he found, to his surprise, that his heart was lighter, happier.

Kate knelt down and put her arms around him, pulling him closely tight to her. With her lips just beside his ear, she said, "It's wonderful, hmmm?"

"Yes, wonderful. The cold is shocking ... it's hard to describe, Kate," he said, turning around to her.

"I know. There's something special about this place and its waters. I wanted you to come to it.'

"Thank you."

Kate stood and pulled him up. "OK, let's find a place for you to fish." She lightly, almost skipping, pulled him back to the car.

They got in, and she directed him back the way they came, following the stream as it grew, flowing farther from the spring. They took a narrow side road, where the paths of the road and river departed and were hidden from one another. The road led through a wall of trees and bushes to a virtually flat area where there were parking spaces and the river flowed through. They parked and got out to go to the river. Here it was wider, reminding him of the small streams he fished back in Minnesota or just across the border in Wisconsin, but still shallow and crystalline though pock-marked by the rain that had begun to fall. They could see the many different-colored rocks that were the stream's bed.

At the edge, they leaned down together, and Kate said, "Let's see if there are any caddis flies here."

So, he reached into the cool water, which was not as cold as at the spring but was still bracing and refreshing, and pulled a rock up and through the surface. Kate giggled in joy at the many caddis fly husks that were latched onto its surface, some empty, their flies having already emerged, but others were full, the larvae still there, their pinchers grasping the rims of their husks.

"I love these little caddis flies," Kate said. "I'm building a clay sculpture of a husk in the studio. I want you to see it. I think you would like it a lot."

He looked over to her, at her brown eyes and her smile. "I would love to see it," he said, his own eyes opened to the possibilities of her art, things he couldn't have conceived of before.

He tied on a caddis fly and cast it out into the stream, watching it ride the current to his left before lifting it out to cast it upstream again. He aimed for a spot upstream that would bring it down alongside a rock close to the other side. Kate stood behind him, watching the rhythm of his casting, hoping he caught a fish. After a few casts, the rain came down harder and colder, making bigger splashes in the running water. Laughing, he and Kate rushed back to the car, fumbling with the wet handles to get inside. He tossed his gear quickly into the front and climbed into the back seat with her.

She leaned against him, and he wrapped his arms around her warmth and the peaty smell of her wool sweater. With his fingers, he combed her hair, dark brown in its wetness, and tucked it behind her ear. They kissed, their hands under their sweaters and jeans. Her skin was warm and smooth, her muscles taught, her fingers played along the base of his spine, causing a tingling ripple to spread through his body. The rain thrummed the cocoon of their car, and the windows fogged up.

He softly leaned away, smiling, and laughed, "It's like we're back in high school."

She smiled back with a glint in her eye. "Are you done with fishing?"

"Yeah, for today," he said, and he leaned back in.

⌇

After cleaning up the dinner dishes, he sat back down at the table so Uncle Johnny could show him how to rig the salmon hooks for egg sacks with chartreuse yarn. The hooks were a shiny silver and huge, compared to the tiny hooks he used for his dry flies when fishing the Kinnickinnic or even for the nymph patterns. They sat and talked about salmon fishing and the monstrous Chinook, and he felt a beckoning to become part of this life. He wrapped the shank of the hooks with thick filament, securing the yarn and creating a loop that would cinch down to hold the egg sacks, and then attached the filament to a braided metal leader. The work was good, and the methodical repetitive motions were pleasing; he learned and remembered the knots, was doing them without thinking as he listened to Uncle Johnny.

Later, when the hooks and leaders were finished and wrapped up in the inner fleece of the leather fly wallet, Kate led him into the cool night outside the house. The yard, as he thought of it, gave the only gap overhead in the thick canopy of the forest in which the house sat. The sky was a deep bluish-black, the night completely black, as the stars shone clear with a silver-blue light, as did the Milky Way river, flowing across the open window through the trees. There was no moon, but the stars were so bright that the yard, and everything in it, including Kate, glowed silver.

She took him across the yard to the path through the trees. Under the thick, tall canopy, the glowing vanished into darker shadows, and he could only follow her lithe movements. The path led to the sauna that Uncle Johnny had built, a wooden room with benches and a wood-burning stove, set upon a deck beside a small, trickling, bubbling brook that flowed down the hillside to the right. Set into the floor of the deck was a round, wooden basin, almost like a hot tub but constructed like a bourbon barrel. Johnny had diverted some of the stream's fresh, cold flow so that it filled the basin. The water was icy, colder and even more exhilarating in the night air than the Head of the Metolius.

Kate lit the fire in the stove and closed the wooden door to let the heat build up. She took off her clothes, free and unbothered here in the woods. He did so as well, not used to this lack of inhibition, but he was beginning to shed the formality of his life before. The cold air prickled their skin. He found it enlivening; she smiled at him and pulled him by hand into the sauna, where the glowing old stove had heated and lit the inside. He sat next to Kate, their legs and hips touching, quickly sweat-slick and shining. The heat, like the cold outside, gradually took his breath, so he breathed deeper and tried to slow down his breathing and his heartbeat, to relax, to calm as the room, already hot, became dry and stifling. The kettle on the black top of the stove began to steam. Kate lay back on the bench, stretching out her long, lean, doe-like body, eyes closed. He watched her and her slow breathing, sweat beading on her thighs, her flat stomach, her taught breasts, and her cheeks and forehead, pooling on her stomach and in the depression between her breasts, her wet skin glowing and flashing in the yellow-orange light from the fire in the black stove. Sweat ran through his hair and down his chest, and he felt as if the heat was drawing his strength at the same time that he wanted her, her beauty, her free abandon, and her unrestrained spirit.

She propped herself up on her elbows and said, with a smirk on her face, "Are you looking at me?"

"I sure am. Admiring is really closer to the truth." He smiled back.

She sat up and leaned her forehead onto his, both of them breathing heavily, panting in the heat and sweat. He pulled her closer and kissed her. Her skin was hot and pouring salty wet, her hair damp as if she had been swimming in a river, as he ran his hands over her. He was wet too and pulled her closer to him.

She looked at him, panting, and said, "Now? Here?"

"Yes," he panted back and took a deep breath of as much of the hot, moist air as he could.

She leaned back onto the bench, pulling him down onto her wet, smooth body.

They fell apart, flushed red, wetter than before, and exhausted. They smiled at each other and said nothing, lying next to each other on the bench, hot skin touching. He felt as if all his energy had been spent, a good, pleasant weakness, but one that was shocking in that he had never felt this before. She stroked her fingers through his hair, her fingernails gently scratching and tingling his scalp. He played his fingertips lightly along her smooth stomach and into her hair. Her stomach fluttered at his touch, and she giggled out "Oooh, that tickles!" He kept stroking gently around her navel and below, enjoying the leaps of her flat stomach.

Laughing and eyes glinting, she sat up, pulling him up next to her. "Let's take a jump into the cold tub. I am drained, need that to revive." She stood up slowly and pulled him up with her. "C'mon, up you go." He wobbled as he stood and stumbled into her, his legs weak and shaky. She steadied him and looked at him with a playful, wry smile. "Exertions drained you?" she asked.

"Oh my God, yes," he gasped and smiled as she pulled him by the hand through the door.

The cold night air on his hot sweaty skin was refreshing and began to bring him out of his exhaustion as he passed through the door onto the deck. The moonlight and starlight made the edges of everything glow blueish silver, reminding him of the nighttime phosphorescence on the sea. Some of the silver-blue light made it through the canopy and lit and outlined her body as she walked across the deck boards to the cold tub. She moved beautifully.

She stepped out over the water, seeming to float in the cool air before dropping straight down into the black water, its unrippled surface untouched by the glowing night light until her body slipped through and below the surface, creating soft, slow undulations without splashing that caught and flickered the light.

She came back up slowly, her hair streaked back on her neck. She took a shuddering deep breath and beckoned to him. "It feels great. You'll love it. Come in with me."

He came to the edge and hesitated, knowing the basin's water, holding a branch of the living water flowing below down the slope, would be cold.

"C'mon, don't be scared!"

He walked in and dropped to the bottom, bending his knees to be totally submerged. The cold, icy water hurt, like when he stepped into Lake Superior in sandals to fish the mouth of the Baptism, and it shocked him. He felt his heart flutter, as if skipping beats, reeling from the iciness. He came back through the surface, gasping, and Kate floated over and grabbed the back of his head, bringing his mouth to hers and kissed him, her lips warm on his, and she rubbed his arms and legs under the water, bringing some warmth and life back into them. He caught his breath, and his heart slowed to a regular beat, and he was refreshed, a vigor brought back into his body by Kate and the fresh cold of the mountain stream. He was alive.

She held onto him and they kissed, surrounded by the captured icy run-off. She climbed out of the wooden tub and stretched, reaching her arms above her head. The light illuminated her body again. God, how he enjoyed watching her. She bent down, smiling, and helped him out. He stood on the deck in the light and enjoyed the new warmth and the fresh life in his body.

"Come on," she whispered, and they went back into the glowing orange heat of the sauna.

<hr />

He was sore and still mostly asleep from last night with Kate at the sauna as he rode with Uncle Johnny in the dark predawn through an even darker tunnel of trees to the river, where they would put in to fish the chinook salmon run. Last night, as they had rigged hooks to drift egg sacks before he and Kate had gone off to the sauna, Uncle Johnny had described the fishing.

"You'll cast out to your right and feel for the rhythm of the hook bouncing along the bottom, a shelf of rock. When the rhythm stops, you know that a salmon has taken it. They hold in the hole below the shelf before continuing their run up. They don't strike the egg sack; they just engulf it. That's when you set your hook."

He thought about what Uncle Johnny had said but wanted more advice because he had only fished for trout before.

"Johnny, I was thinking about what you said last night. What advice do you have after setting the hook?"

"When it's kicking your ass, let it kick your ass, but when it's not kicking your ass, kick its ass."

"OK." That wasn't the type of advice that he was looking for, but he thought he got the idea. He also thought, in his still-waking-up head, it was pretty funny to think of kicking the ass of an ass-less fish.

It was still dark when he and Uncle Johnny got to the river. He got out of the cab, and Johnny turned the pickup around and backed the trailer with the McKenzie River boat down to the water. Brother-in-law John showed up and helped him unhitch the boat and guide it into the water. Brother-in-law John loaded his gear into the boat and then held it while he and Johnny brought their gear down to the boat and climbed in. Johnny took the oars, muscling them across the swift-flowing stream to the opposite bank to his spot between two overhanging trees where he wanted to tie up. Johnny dropped the anchor and set a small kerosene lantern-like heater in the bottom of the boat. While John and Johnny sat at the stern and prow, waiting for dawn to come, he sat in a tight ball as close as he could get to the lantern's warmth, tired and sore but with pleasant memories of the night before.

A boat of Johnny's friends rowed across from the put-in and moored next to them just upstream to their right. The cloudy sky was becoming lighter, now a faint steel blue. It was a dawn that was slowly growing, sneaking quietly upon them, as cloudy mornings usually do. He glanced up from his ball of warmth at the sky and felt the water moving beneath the boat, no slapping of the sides, simply a gentle flowing movement as the boat road the current in place. Uncle Johnny and brother-in-law John were quiet in their seats, both staring out into the river, watching for and imagining salmon beneath the water.

He was floating in and out of dreams of Kate and salmon when Johnny told them to get their rods ready and that it was time to fish. It still seemed pretty dark, and he could only make out faint outlines of Johnny's friends in the boat next to theirs; he could hear their rough voices as they got ready to begin fishing too.

He was still sleepy, tight from the bottom of the boat, and sore, and his first cast landed in the friend's boat.

"Sorry about that," he loudly whispered across to them.

"It's no problem at all," one of them said back, tossing the hook back in the water.

The line came back to him, and he reeled in to check that the egg sack was still looped onto the top and back. It was, and he cast it back out, this time sending it to where he wanted it to go, where Johnny had said to put it. Just like Johnny said, he could feel the hook at the end of the weighted line bouncing downstream on the shelf-like bottom until it came to a point straight out from him, where the bouncing and the line both stopped.

Huh, he thought to himself. He jerked the rod straight up, again thinking to himself, still sleepy and sore, *Might as well try to set the hook just in case a fish is there.*

Nothing moved, not the line, not the hook. It was just a dead weight. But it didn't feel like a snag; it was different, so he jerked harder and the taught line moved away from him from the direction of the pull. *My God, there's a fish there.*

The salmon came up from the hole, breaking the surface with its dark and silver-gray back, rolling over and around through the top of the stream, sending up foaming splashes. The other fishermen near them on the river reeled in their lines to allow the fight to go on without tangling.

"Let it kick your ass," Johnny said, almost shouting, his voice shaking with tension and excitement. He was laughing, too, through his grizzled mountain-man beard.

He let the fish have some line but made it work for what it took from his reel. The fish was strong, not in a jerking way, but simply a constant weight that dragged the line out of his reel and down into and through the running current. He tried to muscle it back to him, but the weight went only where it wanted to.

"Let it kick your ass," Johnny said. "Let it tire."

He did not want to lose this fish, and a shivering thrill from the excitement and anticipation of bringing the fish to the boat ran through him. He tried not to get too excited that he lost control and lost the fish. It was pulling again through the dark water, and it rolled again to the surface, trying to escape the pulling thing in its mouth.

It was running downstream, taking most of his line with it. Johnny untied the boat to chase it, guiding the boat out into the stream to buy some distance for him as he continued to fight the pulling heaviness. He regained line into reel, the river water spraying him as he wound it back in quickly.

The chase gained him time and line, and the fish was now tired. Johnny brought the boat back upstream, with help from John, to their spot between the trees. Johnny had to ask a boat that had taken their place to move.

Now began the struggle to bring the fish into the boat. He was still hesitant, not wanting to lose this big fish, his biggest ever, so he tugged his rod and the line, reeling slowly in, and repeated, pausing between repeats. The fish seemed to come in slowly, hesitating when it could. But he was too slow, and the fish began to regain some strength.

"Kick its ass, kick its ass. You're not kicking its ass!" Johnny shouted at him.

Even the quiet, shy-like brother-in-law, John, joined in "Kick its ass. C'mon, kick its ass!"

He began kicking its ass, reeling in fast and strong, bringing the fish closer to their boat. The fish was strong, too, and fought to stay away, back to the deep trough below the shelf, anywhere away from the pull at its mouth.

It was a powerful fish, different in a bigger way than the trout he was used to catching in Minnesota and across the St. Croix in Wisconsin. There sure was some life still in this fish, dying on its way upstream to its home bed to spawn. He muscled it to the side of their McKenzie River boat as it tired and thrashed and drummed against the boat's side with its tail and thick body, as Uncle Johnny dipped the net into the brown water.

Uncle Johnny heaved the fish on board and unhooked the line. The fish's jaw was strong and hard. As he did so, the fish, sensing freedom, death, and yearning, straining for its watery home, its journey, heaved out of the net, thrashing and thumping the bottom, its eye looking up at the sky and the three men.

"Get the priest, get the priest! Where's the priest?" Uncle Johnny shouted.

Brother-in-law John was shouting too, "Where's the priest? Where's the priest?" There was something funny, especially to a Catholic, about calling the club a priest.

He found it in the bow, a small wooden club about a third the size of a bowling pin, grabbed it up with his wet fish-slimed right hand, shouted, "I've got it," in the excited chaos of frenzied, "Where's the priests'" and "Get the priests," clomping the bottom of the boat, trying to avoid the fish. He knelt and smacked the fish on the head, a wet thwack. One of the Johns shouted, "Harder," and quick, harder blows were repeated until the fish's life had ended.

It was done, a thing that he hadn't really thought he'd get a chance at, much less get done. The fish lay still in the boat. He sat on the middle bench, unwinding the twists in his line, like braids, and looked at the long, thick fish, colored brown like the water. He let the excitement lessen and caught his breath after the long fight to bring it in. He was stunned by its size and was surprised, happy, and now calmed that he had brought it in. Later that afternoon, he and brother-in-law John filleted their fish on a board in Uncle Johnny's backyard. He was tired. He could tell from the almost tan color of his fish's flesh that it had been in the river a long time. They put it in the smoker.

That night, after dinner, he and Kate walked through the black woods to the sauna and tub, where they undressed and lit the stove. The cold air revived him, and then the quickly hot air in the sauna relaxed and soothed his sweat-loosened muscles. Kate's lean, beautiful body shone in the orange light from the stove, the light flickering and glowing along her sweaty arms, legs, and taught stomach as she lay upon the bench.

He woke up first with the light from the rising sun shining down through the east-facing window just above the long side of the bed back in Eugene. Kate lay quietly in his arms. He propped himself up on the pillows, trying not to wake her, to enjoy the peace of the moment and reflect on the streams and waters and Kate and whether he'd been saved. He was leaving this afternoon, and he didn't want to. Here, there was no pain and a life that he wanted, and he feared what he would return to.

They showered together, another new experience for him. They used a homemade soap that smelled of mountain sage, and he brushed his teeth with her natural toothpaste. She smiled at and with him, and they dried each other off with the heavy cotton towels. He splashed his face with bay rum. While he dressed and made sure he had packed his clothes and fishing gear, she warmed up some brioche buns she had made and prepared a carafe of French press coffee. The warm morning smells drifted up to the bedroom, comforting him and making him feel at home, and he wished that this was his home.

They stood outside by his car in the cold drizzle, holding onto each other, with Kate's head resting on his shoulder. And Kate, who had smiled and laughed throughout his visit, was now weeping.

"I don't want you to go," she said, her tears mixing with the drizzle on her beautiful face.

"I don't want to leave," he choked.

"Please stay."

"I will be back."

They stood, holding each other for a long while as the drizzle picked up and became a heavier, colder rain. They kissed long and heavy, and he crushed her into his chest and stomach, and she pulled him close too.

He got into the car, already thinking about when he would come back and how to make this place his home. It was a cold drive up to Portland, but he was happy now and felt that he had been healed, cleansed.

CPSIA information can be obtained
at www.ICGtesting.com
Printed in the USA
LVHW101916200223
739947LV00002B/253